TWINFLUENCE

GRACE COSTELLO

Addison & Gray Press

Paperback ISBN: 978-1-950093-24-3

Ebook ISBN: 978-1-950093-22-9

For the true friends.
May we have many. May we be one.

Chapter One

#TheTwinSwap

In movies, identical twins are always getting into crazy hijinks. There's an inevitable scene where they switch places and someone finds out because twin A has a mole just above her right eye or twin B says something out of character. Luckily for Sophie, I'm a lot better at being my sister than anybody in any movie. The truth is, if you get the character right, nobody notices the mole. Or in our case, the fact that I have a tattoo of a monarch butterfly just above my ankle and Sophie is terrified of needles.

I can't really slam the movies because without them I wouldn't know about all the pitfalls to watch out for. Thanks to my Olsen twin education, I know to keep wardrobe changes to a minimum, only speak when spoken to, and never ever date a boy while wearing your sister's identity.

It used to be fun for both of us.

When we were kids and wanted to fool someone in the neighborhood or drive a waitress crazy on vacation, it was always good for a laugh. It was useful too, like in high school when I talked Sophie into taking my SATs and sitting through Dad's cringe-worthy one-on-one birds and the bees talk.

Being a twin was the ultimate out clause, but somewhere along the line our relationship began to suffer. I think the real breaking point was college. We both knew we wanted to be teachers. I was the theatre princess, and she studied economics and math. We went to the same Colorado university, lived in the same dorms, and helped push one another right up to the finish line. There was just one problem. When it came time to get our teaching license there was a test.

It's not like I am dumb or anything. I got great grades in high school, and college was no different. The problem was testing. I got major anxiety any time they put one of those scantron fill in the bubble forms in front of me. Sophie and I had been through enough testing meltdowns together to know that the Praxis test was going to be a disaster.

The way I saw it, there was an easy solution. Sophie could take the test as me one week and as her the following week. I tried explaining how that would actually give her an awesome advantage, but she wasn't into it. I told her I understood when she said she couldn't risk getting caught and losing her own chance at becoming a teacher, but things changed between us. Our trajectories changed.

She started a year of student teaching, and I started spending a lot of time online. Before I knew it, we were watching each other's lives over social media instead of participating in them. Sophie moved over the border to Oklahoma to start her dream job as a high school econ teacher, and I went *viral.*

I always dreamed that my social commentary on things of great importance, such as Zac Efron's hair style or Jon Snow's minor foray into incest, would grant me a rabid following, but it didn't happen that way. Nope, I went viral because Nico's Pizzeria delivered me a green pepper and olive pizza that bore a striking resemblance to Oprah Winfrey.

Now, I, Dani Sparks, am a rep for the Live Love Laugh box, the Babe Book Club box, and a half dozen other sponsors who send free products and a monthly paycheck in exchange for posting pictures of myself digging their products. I was always the girl giving awesome recommendations, so why not get paid for it?

Not everyone understood it though. Last year at Christmas, when I tried explaining to our grandmother for the umpteenth time what an influencer was, Grandma Jane smiled gently, patted my hand, and said, "You know, I used to sell tupperware."

I brushed off the comment with a smile, but it bothered me. If I'd become a teacher or an actress like I'd hoped, no one would compare the way I made my living to schlepping garlic presses at the tupperware parties grandma forced all her "too nice to say no" friends into attending.

So, why was I thinking about all of this today? Because for once in our lives, it was Sophie, the boring, responsible twin, who needed a favor.

Last night, as I was digging through the latest Babe Book Club box to practice my totally authentic surprise reaction to each item, my phone lit up with Sophie's picture. She didn't call much anymore, and when she did it was usually to update me on some lame family happenings back in the big CO. *Reunion's at Aunt Becky's house this year!* That sort of thing.

I thought about letting it go straight to voicemail, but I missed her and I wanted things between us to be better. I picked up the phone, kicked my feet up on the coffee table, and sank into the couch.

"Oh hey there gorgeous, are you taking good care of my face?" Sophie and I were identical, from the cowlick on the right side of our forehead to the slope of our nose. If Sophie wasn't a terrible dresser with a bad bob, I'm not sure *I* could tell us apart.

"Minor zit outbreak last week," replied Sophie. "Aren't we supposed to be outgrowing that?"

"I could recommend a product," I joked. Okay, half-joked because I did have my skin care routine down to a science.

"Sure, but wouldn't it be twice as effective if you recommended it to me online while standing in front of your impossibly well-lit bathroom mirror and talking about how this video is all about helping your twinnie out?"

"It's hard work, but someone has to do it." Outside my apartment window, I watched the tops of palm trees sway. "What's up Sophie? You don't call just to chat."

She sighed over the other end of the line. "You remember my friend Nova?"

How could I not remember Nova? Nova was Sophie's college roommate and thus the first person to infringe on our sacred twin time. She was also really bad at life and constantly in need of a rescue.

"Do I want to know what she's gotten herself into this time?"

Sophie groaned. "It may provide comic relief?"

I eyed the bag of gourmet popcorn in the Babe Book Club box in front of me, itching to tear it open. A Nova story would be a lot better with snacks, but I knew better. If so much as one kernel was missing from that unboxing video, it wouldn't take more than a hot second for my sponsor to blow up my phone with thinly veiled threats to cut me off.

"Let's hear it," I replied, settling for a box of half-eaten Milk Duds on the coffee table. It was my treat for a particularly grueling leg-day this morning with my trainer. I expected to hear that Nova had maxed out her credit cards or totaled her car for the fourth time. I did not expect to hear that Nova had flown to Mexico for a discount on a tummy tuck and was now being told she couldn't actually have the procedure if she didn't provide her own support person.

Of course she would call Sophie for help, and of course Sophie would feel obligated to say yes.

"How can she not have known that in advance?" Only Nova scheduled a surgery without reading the fine print.

"Just a week," said Sophie. "She swore. One week and I can get back to work. Ordinarily, this would be a hard no."

I stifled a laugh. Sophie had only given one hard no in her life, and the two of us were still working our way around the fallout of that one.

"But she's my best friend, other than you of course."

I rolled my eyes and shoved a Milk Dud in my mouth to keep me from saying something stupid.

"And it's not like she just wanted cosmetic surgery. It's for her Halloween wedding next month. She met the guy online, and she wants to look her best when they meet in person for the first time."

"Halloween wedding?" I almost choked on my Milk Dud. I didn't know whether to be more shocked by the questionable theme choice for her wedding or the fact that the woman was getting married to a man she'd never met in person.

Classic Nova.

"Yeah, she's got this whole costume party thing planned out…" Her voice trailed off, and I could tell she was worried about her wacky friend. Who wouldn't be?

"So you're going to Mexico," I deadpanned.

"Well, maybe, hopefully."

There was a big fat but hanging in this conversation, and I was getting tired of waiting for it. "What's the hang up?"

There was a long pause before Sophie answered. "I kinda can't miss work. The new principal has it out for me, and no one takes vacation the first week of school."

That's when it clicked. She wasn't calling to tell me a funny story about Nova. She was calling because she needed me.

"What do you say? One last twin swap?"

Chapter Two

#WereNotInCaliforniaAnymore

"At least I didn't have to cut my hair," I muttered to myself as I ascended the crumbling steps of Halo High School in the middle of nowhere Oklahoma.

Earlier, I swore on my Louis Vuitton handbag that if I had to chop off my luscious blonde locks and adopt Sophie's ugly utilitarian bob as my own, I would jump on the first flight home. Luckily hair extensions were a common enough thing, and even though I didn't *actually* have them, extensions were my story and I was sticking to it.

I peered around at the pathetic scenery, at the rolling fields on one side of the red-brick school and the little run-down neighborhood on the other side, and half expected a house to fall out of the sky and land on my head. Because yeah, I was being a witch with a capital *B*, and this was Oklahoma. Or, wait, is that Kansas? Either way, I was on Sophie's stomping grounds now, and for some crazy reason, she liked teaching here, so I couldn't be the one to screw it up.

Not this time.

Halo was no place like home. It was pretty much the opposite of Dana Point, California. Located in between L.A. and San Diego, Dana Point was magical and cool, and even though my apartment was way smaller than Sophie's house, I wouldn't have traded it for the world. Dana Point was the kind of place with dog spas, vegan eateries, and picturesque beaches. But it turned out I would temporarily trade Dana Point for Sophie. Anything to repair our relationship. I really, really missed her.

My twin and I have been trading places on and off our whole lives until three years ago when I went too far and asked too much. In my defense, she'd been taking tests for me *forever* so how was I to know she'd adamantly refuse this last and most important one? In the end, we both got our degrees, but only one of us became a teacher. I can see now that she was right and it wasn't really fair to ask her to do that for me, but at the time, I'd been so angry that I let us drift apart. She followed her teaching career, and I followed my theatre degree to L.A. I never made it as an actress, but I worked hard on my Instagram account to the point of having half a million followers and counting. So what if I got my start by spotting the visage of Oprah in between cheese swirls and green peppers? Oprah changed a lot of lives!

And despite what you might have heard, Instagram Influencer is a *real job*. I had the paychecks to prove it. Plus the cute apartment three blocks from the beach. The silver Lexus. The product parties and beautiful friends and designer wardrobe. Almost the life of an actress.

Almost.

Way better than teaching high school theatre anyway.

With a heavy sigh, I pulled open the metal door, the handle already hot from the September morning sun, and stepped inside the high school. I was met with a blast of air conditioning and a million memories. It wasn't the Colorado high school I graduated from eight years ago, but try telling that to my brain. It looked the same—long wide hallways, blue lockers everywhere, and cream colored linoleum floors. It even smelled the same—chemical cleaners, cheap perfume and cologne, a hint of mildew, and an undercurrent of body odor.

I shook the mind trip away and strode forward. Room 217. That was my target.

My high heels clacked against the floor, making me feel extra official, and I arrived at the classroom in no time. It was surreal, walking into Sophie's place of employment, pretending to be her just like old times. It was also surreal pretending to be a teacher, but I squashed that thought down immediately.

The room looked just like how I imagined Sophie would want it to look—organized. She had glossy posters with inspirational quotes pinned to the walls, all the desks lined up in neat rows, and a spotless whiteboard on the far wall. Outside the windows, the student parking lot remained mostly empty.

It was her third year teaching here, but apparently, she couldn't take a week of PTO without notice and especially so early in the school year. I suggested she call in sick but she laughed and said she couldn't call in from Mexico. My heart clenched a little at that. She was flying off to Mexico to help her friend get a tummy tuck for crying out loud. A tummy tuck! When was the last time she flew anywhere to see me?

Anyway, here I was, Dani Sparks to save the day. It would only be a week pretending to be Soph. Shouldn't be too hard, right? It wasn't like she taught calculus. She taught life skills to the senior class and economics to the freshmen and sophomores.

I snorted a little at the idea of Life Skills and slid into her desk, rummaging through her drawers to get myself acquainted.

Economics might be a little tricky. Life Skills? No problemo.

A grin stretched across my lips when drawer number three revealed that though time and circumstances may have changed, our culinary twinness had not. I popped a Milk Dud in my mouth before continuing to scavenge.

Apparently, the class covered how to file taxes, build a good credit score, change a car tire, how to budget, meal plan, and so on. Easy peasy. They could have called it "Adulting 101." I'd just turned twenty-six. I had the whole adult thing down. I'd almost paid off my student loans and had my own apartment and car. I only kept friends that were actually friends, took care of my body, and practiced safe sex when it happened. I mean, really, what more is there to know?

"There you are! You're here." A lady with wiry grey streaked hair and massive glasses came flitting into the room, her arms stretched wide. I jumped up from the seat just as she pulled me in for the tightest hug of my life. "Dani, I'm so happy to finally meet you." She gushed into my ear, a little too loudly, before stepping back and surveying me up and down. "Oops, sorry, I should call you Sophie." She winks. "Actually, Ms. Sparks. I know. But wow, this is so exciting, isn't?"

I smiled. "You must be Ms. Thompson. Sophie told me about you."

She gave me a little bow. "At your service! And call me Jeanine, please." She let out a small whoop. I grimaced. It was way too early for that nonsense. "I can't believe Sophie has a twin and she didn't tell me."

"That makes two of us."

She frowned. "Right. Well, I'm sworn to secrecy! Your little switch-a-roo is safe with me. Us girls have got to stick together."

I'd hardly call her a "girl," the woman had to be in her 50s, but I appreciated the support all the same.

"Now," she continued, taking my hand in hers and tugging me out the door. "If we don't hurry, we're going to be late for the staff meeting."

"Sophie never mentioned a staff meeting." She had mentioned it being the first day of class. She'd been prepping for weeks. She'd mentioned the layout of the school, the kids to watch out for, the schedule, and her expectations of me. Spoiler alert, they were high. Not that I was surprised.

Jeanine nodded vigorously. I didn't think I'd ever met someone her age with so much energy. "Every Monday morning, seven-thirty AM on the dot. Principal Beck doesn't tolerate tardiness, you know. Well, actually, Sophie knows." She giggled, the sound like a high-pitched chirping bird. "The two are *frenemies*." She air quoted when saying that word, no doubt feeling hip with the kids. But I shouldn't be so harsh. I was actually starting to like her. She was a good ally, and if anything else, she'd be entertaining. "Foster Beck used to teach eleventh grade history. He never got along with Sophie, but they had to be friendly because the old principal made a big deal of everyone being chummy. Well, Mr. Frazier retired, and Beck is basically in the superintendent's pocket so he got the job. It was all very dramatic." She wiggled her eyebrows. "Now that Foster is the boss, let's just say he has no problem pushing Sophie's buttons."

I released a laugh. "It sounds to me like they need to jump each other's bones and get it over with."

Jeanine blanched, cheeks flaming. "Oh, never! They *hate* each other. Plus, principals can't date teachers. It's unprofessional. Neither would risk it. Foster and Sophie are too alike in that way. You'll see."

And when we entered the staff meeting, all eyes turning to face us, I did see.

Principal Foster Beck was many things. *Hot*—tall and broad shouldered, with dark closely-cropped, curly black hair, tan skin, and cobalt blue eyes. Oh yeah, definitely good looking. *Professional*—perfectly pressed white shirt and maroon tie, with a strong stance that commanded the room. *Young*—probably in his late 20s or early 30s, and also probably on a mission to prove himself. I mean, Jeanine had said he was in the superintendent's pocket. The guy was most likely a tool.

But there was one thing Principal Beck was clearly *not*, and that was happy to see me.

He glared and then barked out, "You're late, Ms. Sparks." But did he even look at Ms. Thompson? No. His eyes were pinned on me like two little laser beams bent on destruction. *What on earth did Sophie do to this guy?*

His eyes narrowed. "You changed your hair."

"Umm, yeah. They're called hair extensions."

I swallowed hard, smiled coolly, and settled into the closest seat. My palms were sweating, my ears were burning, and my throat felt like someone had tied it in a knot.

If there was anyone capable of figuring out my secret, it was Foster Beck.

Chapter Three

#InfluencerIsARealJob

Fortunately for me, Foster Beck loved the sound of his own voice. He got over examining me real quick and launched directly into boring everyone in the room with the year's staff expectations. I was in full daydream mode by bullet point three on the oversized whiteboard behind him. He wrote "stay within the school budget" and underlined it for extra emphasis.

Two things I should not be thinking during my first official staff meeting portraying the role of Sophie Sparks:

1. None of the other teachers look like people I want to hang out with and
2. Principal Beck is actually the missing baby

of Paul Walker and Paul Rudd, the two greatest Paul's to ever live.

"Sophie?" he asked, staring down at me with pursed lips, his hands planted firmly on the waistband of his nicely fitted dress pants. What was it about nice strong hands that made a girl's stomach flip? Well, that and—

Jeanine jabbed me in the ribs with an elbow, and I jerked my head up to his face where they belonged.

"Hmm?" I asked, a guilty smile stretching across my lips.

Principal Beck sighed dramatically. "Any ideas for the fall play?"

This was my first real test. What would my sister say? Probably nothing, but then again she wouldn't have been caught daydreaming about the origin of her boss either.

"We should have one?" I tried.

There were snickering noises emitting from the room around me, so perhaps everyone here in Oklahoma did not have the same enthusiasm for theatre as they did back in California.

"Well, Sophie I'm glad you feel that way," declared Principal Beck. "Because we are going to have one, and you're going to be the director."

I nodded affirmatively and tried to disregard the oddly gleeful expression on his face. What he was saying didn't sound like a punishment, but the way he said it certainly did. Well, it probably would be for

Sophie. She wasn't blessed with the thespian gene like Yours Truly.

Beck continued to gaze at me ruefully. "It's already been decided that you'll put on *Oklahoma!* because that show is always a cash cow."

"Right." My voice trailed off, trying to imagine a world in which *Oklahoma!* was a cash cow.

This felt like one of those moments where you know a bad thing is happening, but you're not entirely sure *why* it's bad yet? Even Jeanine was frowning, and up until a second ago, I wasn't sure her face was capable of relaxing that far. I mean, *Oklahoma!* wasn't my favorite musical, but I was sure Sophie would be able to sort it out when she got back.

"Better her than me," someone coughed-shouted from the back of the room. I whipped around, but by the time I could cast an icy glare their way, everyone was back to being boring.

I wanted to know why theatre was the kiss of death here at Halo High, but I didn't dare ask any follow up questions just yet. It had been a long time since Sophie and I did a swap, but I still remembered the rules. The less you speak the less likely you are to screw up.

So, instead of getting the scoop on the theatre program, which apparently did not include a drama teacher, I spent the rest of the staff meeting taking in my surroundings.

The teachers' lounge was sad. There was just no other way to describe it. The cabinets were lined with Easy Mac, Cup of Noodles, and a completely irrational amount of herbal tea. If I were a betting woman, I'd bet at least half of this stuff was expired. These were the food and beverage choices of depressing people, and it hurt my heart to think that Sophie was among them.

Case in point, across from me sat the math teacher, aptly named Mrs. Drabney. She was clutching a pink purse against her lap. At first I thought, *Kate Spade, a friendly bag in unfamiliar territory*, and then I looked closer and realized that instead of a little gold spade near the handle, there was a metal clover. It was a knock off, and I felt betrayed.

I took a deep breath and reminded myself that this was a swap. A week max. I'd done a week in New Jersey. I could do a week in Oklahoma. When things got tough, all I had to do was scroll through my Instagram and remind myself that palm trees and brand name clothing were waiting for me back home in sunny California.

"That's a wrap, folks," Beck announced. "We're in for a great year. Now, go forth and shape the minds of our youth."

A few teachers snickered, and the room broke out into conversation.

I peeked a look at the clock. 8:00 AM. Only twenty-five minutes until I was to teach my first ever class of high schoolers. I mean, I had once been a high schooler, so it wasn't like I was completely unfamiliar with the process. I just wasn't sure exactly what was required of me role model wise. Like was I going to be Whoopi Goldberg in *Sister Act 2* or more of a solemn stand and deliver type? My money was on Whoopi because she had better outfits and also got to balance the fun task of lying about her identity.

"I guess it's time we throw you to the wolves." Principal Beck sidled up next me, his blue eyes gleaming with mischief.

I froze. Had he already guessed I wasn't Sophie?

"You know," he went on, "the play. Directing." He sighed heavily. "You'd better not mess this up, Sparks. The school board wants to cut the funding as it is. And nobody ever wants to direct the play, so this time it's on you."

This time it's on me? This dude really had it out for Sophie.

I released a scoff that sounded like a disgruntled hyena and met him with a sarcastic tone. "It's a musical actually."

I was ready to put him in his place with my theatre knowledge, but Principal Beck had already moved into the morning coffee line.

I rolled my eyes. "You can count on me, boss." I murmured, fully aware that I was talking to no one and making Sophie look just a touch crazy.

A good twin always pays attention to her sister's interests. Unless those interests are economics. I'm sorry, but there was nothing more boring to me than numbers. Unless those numbers had something to do with shopping or my growing bank account balance, then I could be enticed. But hey, it was time to buck up and do what needed to be done. I was in it to twin it!

I chuckled at my lame pun as I slipped back into Sophie's classroom, finding the worksheets she'd printed out for today's classes. She'd even provided a written script of exactly what she wanted me to say and possible Q and As the students might ask. The girl was Type A to the max, which was lucky for me, seeing as how I was Type Q and rarely rolled out of bed before eleven most days.

She had everything laid out for the whole week. I scanned through it quickly, but honestly there was nothing of note. I could handle this, no problem. I still had fifteen minutes until class, and since no students had arrived, I pulled out my phone to check my Instagram account. It was my job after all. It had to be done.

A DM waited for me. Truthfully, I had enough followers that a DM always waited for me, but I still clicked over anyway, expecting it to be a regular response to a sexy picture I'd posted of me running on the beach.

Nope.

Hi Dani! I just wanted to let you know that your Live Love Laugh box should've arrived yesterday. Check your mailbox! We need you to post your unboxing video tomorrow. Oh, and please use the same hashtags as always. I'm transferring the funds for the sponsored ads right now, and we'll transfer your payment once everything is done. Have a great day!

. . .

It was from Annie Spencer, the social media liaison with my biggest sponsor and basically the reason I'd made it as an influencer in the first place. She'd been the first person to take a chance on me.

"Oh, no, no, no!" They weren't supposed to send the box for another two weeks. Why'd they send it early? And now they needed me to post my unboxing tomorrow? No. Freaking. Way.

My pulse jumped, my heart careened inside my rib cage, and tears sprang to my eyes. What was I going to do?

I had to meet their deadline with exactness to get paid. All the influencers revealed the items in the box on the same day to avoid spoilers, and then we promoted our videos using Instagram's advertising, all paid for by the company. When it was done, we got our payday. The amount in payment depended on the size of my following, the engagement on the post, and the number of people who clicked on the ad's link.

I'd been working with them for over two years now. And I'm not talking about a few hundred bucks and some free stuff here and there. I'm talking thousands of dollars per unboxing—my rent and living expenses for the next month depended on this one box, which was apparently waiting for me in Dana Point.

I was pacing the length of the empty classroom without even realizing it. A bead of sweat dropped down my temple, and I brushed it away. I still had ten minutes before class. No students had arrived. I stumbled into the corner of the room, faced away from the door, and called Sophie.

"What's wrong?"

"I need your help!" I squealed.

"Did you find the lesson plan? Is something missing?" I could hear her Type A anxiety gearing up with each word.

"No, it's not that. It's my Live Love Laugh box."

She paused. "Your what?"

"You're on your layover in L.A. right now?" I pressed on.

"Yeah, we just landed. Why?"

"When does your next flight leave?"

"Forty-five minutes." She sounded breathless. "I'm walking to the gate."

"No!" I yelled. "No! Okay, umm, I'll pay for you to get another flight out of L.A. later today or first thing tomorrow morning, but I need you right now."

"What are you talking about? You need to focus on teaching my classes, and I need to get on this flight to go help Nova."

"Nova is your friend. I'm your blood. Your twin. I need you more!"

She scoffed, years of tension rising between us like a tidal wave. "How did I know you'd make it about that?"

"Just listen, please. I need you to rent a car, go to my apartment, get my Live Love Laugh box, film the unboxing video, and send it to me."

"Wait, what? Slow down."

I took a deep breath, willing the tears from spilling over, and explained everything to her in as much detail as I could. She needed to understand!

"Please," I begged. "I'll pay for everything, but I can't lose this sponsor. This is my livelihood. I'm helping you with your career. I need you to help me with mine."

She paused, and I held my breath. "Okay, I'll do this for you under one condition."

"Anything."

"You never ask for a twin swap again."

My entire body relaxed. "Agreed. Also, I think it is only fair that I point out *you* asked for this one."

"Dani," she warned.

"Okay, okay. I'm sorry. Yes, done deal. No more swapping."

I gave her the final details, and we hung up. I wiped away the tears, inhaled a steadying breath, and turned around to a room full of gawking teenagers.

My heart about dropped into my butt.

"Umm, are you okay, Ms. Sparks?" An innocent looking young girl with two perfect french braids down her back asked. Her eyes welled up with concern. Aw, how kind and cute she was. Too bad I had done a lousy job of studying Soph's notes and didn't have a clue as to her name. But hey, it was the first day for everyone, a brand new year, so I figured I could fudge it.

The bell rang as if to announce my failure to be prepared.

"Screw that!" another kid interrupted. "If she can be on her phone, I can be on mine, too."

The boy slammed his backpack down to the ground with so much force I yelped and stumbled back. Did these kids not have any respect for their personal property?

"Tyler!" a man's voice bellowed into the classroom, and Principal Beck appeared. "What's going on here?"

The kid pointed at me, a look of outrage plastered to his sour face. "She was on her phone!"

"Pick up your things." He directed his demand to Tyler. "Let's start the school year out right, shall we?" The boy rolled his eyes but did as he was told. "Maybe I'll sit in on this class today," Principal Beck continued, striding into my classroom like he owned the place. How dare he? Okay, technically it wasn't *my* classroom, and he *was* the principal, but have a little faith.

"Ms. Sparks," his eyes flashed to where I still gripped my phone, "whenever you're ready."

Chapter Four

#TeenagersAreTheSpawnOfSatan

Economics, I wrote the word on the whiteboard with a pink dry erase marker, and tossed a heart above the i for dramatic emphasis.

"Welcome to tenth grade economics," I declared, smiling brightly at the class. "Raise your hand if you invested in essential oils last year? I know I did!"

Twenty-four sets of eyes stared at me with blank expressions before someone in the back snorted with laughter. Humor wasn't my intention, but I'd take it.

"Ahem," coughed Principal Beck. "I'm sure you are aware that no one in this classroom is old enough to manage a stock market portfolio."

"Of course," I lied, smiling through grit teeth. "Just a little joke to kick things off." I bugged my eyes out at him as if to say, shut your trap and let me talk.

And anyway, I wasn't talking about the stock market, I was talking about the two-hundred-dollar kit of oils I had stashed under my bathroom sink back home. Nature's medicine.

"Anyway," I went on. "I'm Ms. Sparks, your teacher and guide to all things economics." I waved hello, but nobody waved back.

I could practically hear the stream of unfavorable thoughts coursing through Beck's brain as I turned on my heels and dug around on Sophie's desk for the stack of syllabi she'd left me and the day's lesson plan.

"This is your road map." I slowly worked my way through the rows of students and placed a syllabus face up on each desk. "Follow these instructions, and you literally cannot fail."

Principal Beck raised a skeptical eyebrow, but I wasn't letting him get to me. I was teaching tenth graders, not astronauts. It wasn't like this was going to be hard.

The girl with two braids raised her hand. "Last year, there was an assignment where students got to write their own business plans, and then the student with the best plan got an automatic A on the final." She looked down at the paper on her desk and frowned. "But I don't see that on here."

That sounded like a fun assignment. A lot more fun than the three-page essay on the effects of globalization that Sophie had actually assigned.

"Add it in," I answered, looking for an open spot on the syllabus. "You can put it after the unit on supply and demand."

"Add it in?" questioned the boy who'd begun the classroom by throwing a tantrum, "As in, add an additional assignment to this already lame syllabus. I'll pass, thanks."

Principal Beck scowled.

I hadn't actually considered the fact that not everyone was going to be as enthusiastic about extra work as the girl sitting front and center of the classroom, but I couldn't very well back down now, not when Principal Beck was sitting at the back of the room, hungry for me to slip up and give him further motive to dislike Sophie.

There was obviously something deeply personal about his negativity toward my sister, and when we talked next, I was going to make her spill the beans, but for now I would continue to muddle my way through her syllabus, starting with putting Tyler in his place.

"Not optional, Tyler, but thanks for your input," I stated then firmly ignored all other protests from the classroom.

Forty-eight painful minutes later economics was officially over, and I could escape the watchful eye of the world's hottest but meanest principal. The rest of the morning's classes went better than the first, with a general buzz of excitement and distractedness at this being the first day of school. When we broke for lunch, I didn't want to spend a second more of my day in the sad teachers' lounge, so I grabbed the lunch tote Sophie had left me from the inside drawer of my desk and found an empty table out in the courtyard to spend my free period.

Right away, I realized it was a weird choice. Not a single other teacher was eating outside. Instead, I was surrounded by rowdy students, all of whom were probably thinking I had lost my mind or was trying too hard to connect with them. Little did they know, I didn't want to connect with them at all.

I unzipped the purple insulated tote and smiled. Peanut butter and honey with bananas, a bag of baby carrots, and a Diet Peach Snapple. Sophie still knew how to properly fuel her sister.

I felt bad, but three years of living apart and the emotional rift between us had left me slightly rustier when it came to remembering how to be Sophie. I wasn't exactly killing this swap. I had only been my sister for a couple of hours, and already I had mucked up her syllabus, ticked off her rival, and volunteered her to direct a pretty lousy musical. Okay, I hadn't exactly volunteered her on that last one, but I hadn't put up a fight either.

A little ping from my phone reminded me that I wasn't the only one currently on swap duty. It was lunchtime. I could probably be on my phone now, so I decided to risk it. A text from Sophie displayed across my screen. *"I did the thing, and honestly I have no idea how you swindled people into paying you to open mail, but I want you to know I'm proud of you and also I stole the leggings. They belong to my butt now. Talk to you in Mexico. You owe me $300."*

I hit play on the video attachment and held my breath.

Nothing happened.

My data connection sucked out here, which explained the buffering. I shoveled in a few more bites, threw the remaining lunch back in the tote, and hustled toward the building where I could get decent WiFi. Still staring at my phone, I didn't notice the boys tossing a football until one of them plowed right into me. Everything flew from my grip. I squealed as I fell, catching the ground with my left hand, pain slicing through my wrist like a hot poker.

"Ouch," I groaned, sitting up and holding the sprained wrist to my chest.

The kid was huge, probably twice my size. No wonder! He shot out a half-hearted "sorry" and jumped back up, throwing the ball to his friend as if he hadn't just tackled me.

"You have got to be kidding me," I muttered to myself, gathering my things and stumbling into the school. Did any of the students bother to help me? No. They just stared. Some of them laughed.

Why does Sophie like it here? As far as I was concerned, I'd dodged a bullet when I'd failed to take the Praxis test.

"I saw that!" Ms. Thompson came running out of nowhere, looking as frazzled as I felt. "You poor thing. You have to watch out for those football players. They think they run this place."

"So, not much has changed since I went to school." I sighed.

She frowned at that. "You know, I've been teaching journalism for thirty years. I consider myself a feminist, but you're right, not a whole lot has changed." Her voice took on a passionate tone, her eyes lighting up. "Maybe that's why you're here. To infuse Halo, Oklahoma with some fresh ideas."

I just stared at her. Activism wasn't really my thing.

"Come on." She directed me toward the front office. "We'll have Nurse Greene take a look at that wrist for you. Alison's great."

I held up the phone. Thankfully the screen was still intact. "But I need to check something first."

She waved my protest away. "It can wait."

I shrugged and followed her to the nurse's office. I really wanted to check the video in case I needed to have Sophie retake anything. She was on her way back to Mexico already! I hoped she took the whole box with her and not just the leggings, just in case I needed her to take some photos or another video. I sent a silent prayer to the Twin Gods that Sophie managed to pull this off because Ms. Thompson was right. My wrist was killing me. What if it was broken?

"What happened here, Sophie?" Ms. Greene smiled brightly when we entered her office. She was a pretty young woman with bright amber eyes and shiny auburn hair. Jeanine explained everything with enthusiasm, her voice raised and hands flying every which way, before leaving me and the nurse to it.

"I think it's a bad sprain," I complained between deep breaths.

"It's a football school. No doubt about that. Gotta watch out for those boys. Go Spartans!" Sadly, she wasn't joking. Her school spirit was real.

"Let me guess, you were a cheerleader?" I winced

through the question as she gently twisted my wrist to and fro.

"Is it that obvious?" She giggled. "I'm a proud graduate of Halo High, but what am I saying? You already know that."

I nodded vigorously. Sure I did.

"My freezer is broken." She nodded toward the mini-fridge in the far corner. "I've got all the ice packs in the faculty lounge. I'll be right back." She dashed out, leaving me to stare at the boring white walls. Maybe now I could finally get to my phone.

"You've had quite the first day back." Beck leaned against the doorframe, and I nearly jumped out of my skin.

"Geez, knock much?" I muttered.

He twisted his lips as if deciding he didn't hear me. "Here, let me take a look at that."

Before I could stop him, he towered over where I sat slouched on the exam table. His calloused fingers were surprisingly soft and gentle as they inspected my bruised wrist. I closed my eyes, trying not to wince at the pain. Beck was close, too close, close enough for me to note that he smelled nothing like the antiseptic of the sterile room. No, he was all spicy citrus and freshly showered man and had me counting back the months since I'd last seen any action in the bedroom.

Let's just say it'd been too long.

He let go, stepped back, and my eyes popped open.

"Which player was it? I'll have a word."

I shrugged. "I don't know."

His eyebrows drew together and I immediately realized my mistake. What kind of teacher doesn't remember her students in a school the size of Halo?

"A freshman?" he asked.

I nodded, my cheeks flaming. "Must have been." I clucked my tongue. "Need to get control over them new kids, Foster."

He blinked at me. Shoot, was I not supposed to call him Foster? Sophie probably didn't, and I'd just made a mistake. He stared as if trying to figure me out, and my cheeks flared.

The bell rang. Saved by the bell! I jumped up. "Time to go."

Nurse Greene skipped back into the room, holding an ice pack like it was the Holy Grail. "Let's wrap that and ice it."

"Sounds good."

"Hi, Foster." She smiled coyly at Beck, her cheeks turning pink. "It's always good to see you."

"Hi, Alison." He smiled back.

So, I guess *some* people were on a first name basis. Foster Beck left as quickly as he'd arrived, sending me one last lingering look on his way out that made my stomach flip, and all I could wonder was how mad at me Sophie would be if I hooked up with her boss before the week was out. Too bad I already knew the answer to that one.

Chapter Five

#ThisIsWhyWeCantHaveNiceThings

By the time I got home from school, my entire body felt like I'd been ran over by a truck. Considering a burly football player had bulldozed me to the ground, it made sense. My wrist was crazy sore, my hair no longer fell in beachy curls but was a frizzy mess thanks to the humidity, and my ill-advised choice of high heels had resulted in several blisters. This whole teaching thing wasn't for the faint of heart.

Sophie's house was a little, white, one story with a picket fence and a massive weeping willow in the front yard. It was cute—the kind of place that would cost a fortune in Dana Point but that a single school teacher could afford here in rural Oklahoma. I pulled her sedan under the carport and let myself in. Being older, the place didn't have the best A/C, so I peeled off my dress clothes, took a cold shower, and dressed in cotton pajama shorts and a tank. No bra, naturally.

It. Had. Been. A. Day.

I needed HGTV, a glass of wine, and carbs. But first, I had to watch the unboxing video.

I never did get it to play at the school. Turned out the WiFi there just wasn't strong enough for video, and my cell phone network liked cities—big ones. So, I'd refocused on doing a kick-ass job of teaching life skills. I'd actually liked the senior class way better than the know-it-all sophomores and the freshman babies. The seniors had been nicer, participating in the "getting to know you" activity without complaints, before going over the syllabus and expectations for the year.

Only four more days to go. I could do this.

I plugged in my phone next to Sophie's bed and plopped down on the bright white comforter. Her signature lilac scent wafted around me, and I smiled to myself. This switch-a-roo was going to work in my favor. I was going to bring our duo back together and regain Sophie's friendship.

I opened the video, hoping for the best, preparing for the worst, but what I found was beyond anything I'd ever imagined.

"Oh my God!" I squealed and sat up.

Was that even Sophie? What was she thinking? Her short hair was pulled back into a ratty baseball cap that cast dark shadows over her face. I could hardly see her at all. She sat centered on my tan couch, the blinds open which lit her from behind and made her even harder to make out. The box sat in her lap, and she smiled at the camera. It was, without a doubt, the fakest smile I'd ever seen.

"Hello, followers," she said, addressing my audience in a way I would never ever do myself, "and welcome to another unboxing of," her eyes flashed down to the bright pink box in her lap, "the Live Love Laugh box. Which is, umm, the best subscription box *ever!*"

"Laying it on a little thick there, aren't you, Soph?" I grumbled.

Okay, I wouldn't let myself panic. This—whatever it was—was workable. I'd just have to put my editing skills to the test and mess with the exposure, shadows, brightness, and contrast. No big deal. I rolled my eyes. So long as she didn't say something totally asinine, we'd be in business. When I did these unboxing videos, I always opened the box before filming so I could plan out exactly what I would say about each item. Sophie clearly hadn't done as much. She hadn't even removed the seal. Instead she scratched at it with her fingernails, but the thing didn't budge.

"Hmm…" She lifted it to her mouth and tore it open with her teeth.

Seriously? *Her teeth?* I was going to have to cut that part out.

"Let's see what we have here, shall we?" Her fake enthusiasm was about as obvious as a kid pretending to like vegetables. She pulled out the first item. "Wow, isn't this a nice candle?" She put it to her nose. "Mmm, and it smells so good, too. Like soap."

I snorted. Nobody liked soap-smelling candles.

Couldn't she have at least said it smelled like fresh laundry?

The next item appeared in her hand, a black mug with a neon yellow daisy printed across the front. It was adorable, and she held it up to the camera for a better look. Good girl. That's the way. "Oh, I actually love this," she gushed. "I wish I could bring it in my suitcase!"

Okay, that was workable. People would definitely comment asking where I was going, and that would give the video a little more interaction. Engagement was part of the paycheck, so maybe it wouldn't be a total flop.

The rest of the video continued on in the same manner. Sophie commented on items, mostly with fake enthusiasm, but a few earned a genuine smile. Unfortunately, the bad lighting was what really killed it. This was going to need a ton of editing to be remotely appropriate for tomorrow's post.

But what other choice did I have?

I could lie and tell Annie the package had been stolen. Or I could tell her the truth, that I was out of town and needed to skip this month's job. But no, I needed the paycheck. So, I resolved to edit the crap out of the video and turn lemons into lemonade. Maybe lemonade was stretching it. How about, I'd turn lemons into shinier, prettier lemons.

I groaned. HGTV would have to wait.

. . .

The next morning arrived too quickly. I'd been up late fixing the video and scheduling everything to go live online while I'd be teaching. And then, I'd crashed. By the time the blaring alarm roused me, I was already a half hour late getting up. I hurried to get ready—no beachy curls today—and rushed off to Halo High. I swept into room 217 seconds before the bell rang. Not exactly impressive, but I'd made it, and that was what mattered.

Day one hadn't been the best, so I was determined to make day two better. If I could turn Sophie's disaster of an unboxing video into something decent, then quite frankly, I could handle four more days of teaching teenagers.

I fastened a confident smile to my face, straightened my pencil skirt, and strode to the front of the room. "Please open your textbooks to page thirty-two. Today, we're going to be comparing the Tulip Mania of the Dutch Golden Age to the Housing Bubble of the 2000s, and of course, the crippling economic recessions that followed both events."

A flurry of turning pages sounded as the kids took my direction. Maybe the sophomores weren't so bad afterall. From the doorway, I caught Ms. Thompson watching. She nodded encouragingly before stepping into her classroom.

That's right, kids, I thought to myself. *I'm about to blow your minds with economics.*

Sophie would be proud.

Principal Beck, on the other hand, was not.

I didn't even realize he was in here until our eyes

met across the room. He pushed off the empty desk he'd been sitting in at the back and strode over to me, a look of disappointment etched across his handsome face. "I just wanted to make sure your wrist was feeling better." His voice was low. His words? Not at all what I'd been expecting. Excitement sprang to life in my stomach.

"Umm, yeah, thanks." I lifted up my wrist where I still wore the brace. "I think by tomorrow I'll be able to return this to the nurse."

"Glad to hear it."

I smiled brightly. He'd come to check on me? That was actually pretty cute. Sophie was an idiot for letting this guy get away. He was the total package. And *maybe* he didn't actually have it out for Sophie. *Maybe* he was crushing on her.

"Oh, and Ms. Sparks," he added, his voice going stern. "Teachers are required to be here by eight AM on Tuesdays. Don't be late again."

My cheeks flamed. *Okay, maybe not.*

Chapter Six

#TheFinalCountdown

In forty hours and forty-one minutes I would get to shed my Sophie skin. Don't get me wrong, I missed my sister. I just didn't miss *being* her. We differed in many ways, most of them involving fashion. Perfect example, an hour ago, I spotted her gym card in a drawer and decided I'd grab a swimsuit and head over for a swim. Only, when I actually located her swimwear, there wasn't a single bikini in sight, and almost all of her suits had a skirt attached. Swim skirts were for women over the age of forty or girls currently going through puberty. They were not for super hot chicks in their mid twenties. I loved her, but I could not be her.

That explained why I was currently in yoga pants and a sports bra, running on one of her gym's treadmills instead of swimming laps in the sparkling pool outside. Halo didn't have a lot going for it, but at least the gym reminded me of home. I'd missed five days of workouts for Sophie's shenanigans and resolved not to miss another. I eyed the weight equipment on the other side of the warehouse-style space and vowed to put in a grueling leg-day tomorrow.

I came to Halo to help Sophie keep her job, and although my performance was a little on the average side, I did feel like I'd earned back some lost sister credibility.

Come to think of it, I actually had a few aces in my back pocket thanks to her awful video performance. Even Talia, my self-proclaimed California bestie, had texted to ask if I was intentionally trying to sabotage my career via baseball cap and bad lighting.

If Sophie got extra agitated about being forced to direct *Oklahoma!* I could just remind her that I lost approximately four hundred and fifty followers based on her bad hair day alone.

Also, maybe I didn't have to tell her I forgot to feed her cat two nights in a row and he destroyed one of her couch cushions in protest. In my defense, the cat was always hiding from me. Half the time, I forgot he was even there.

My phone buzzed, interrupting my exercise playlist, and I smiled at Sophie's picture lighting up the screen. I paused the machine and answered, my breaths slowing to catch up to my elevated heartbeat.

"I was just thinking of you." I leaned the phone up against my ear and took a long drink from my water bottle.

"Were you thinking really awesome *I love my sister* thoughts?" Something about the tone in her voice warned me I would not be thinking them by the end of this conversation.

"Hmm," I said, eyeing a hot guy from across the room who'd just taken off his shirt, revealing a gorgeous six-pack. What? Gyms were a known breeding ground. Sue me. "That's part of what I was thinking," I went on, "but I was gonna lead with this town is full of hillbillies and why didn't you tell me that your big fat jerk of a boss bears a striking resemblance to the man of my dreams?"

Sophie groaned. "You really have to not think that way."

"Eh, it's one week. Let me think away. I need something to fill the evenings. You don't even have a Roku. What kind of monster invites her sister to stay at her place for a full week and doesn't provide a streaming service? I've been casting mine from my phone which makes it harder to watch tv and scroll."

There was a loud crash on the other end of the line and a mumbling in Spanish that I couldn't quite make out but definitely understood to be hostile.

"Is everything all right over there?"

"Um…" There was a long pause and the sound of my sister borderline hyperventilating through the phone.

"Sophie?"

"Everything is not all right. Everything is bad. Everything is awful. I am screwed."

"Whoa, whoa, whoa, slow down and explain."

"Remember how Nova neglected to read the fine print on this whole out of country medical extravaganza?"

"I recall." I wouldn't describe myself as one hundred percent jealous of Nova, but it did irritate me that the person my sister was closest to these days was other-level dumb. Like if she needed a dumb person in her life, she could take the girl who couldn't pass a test. No reason to go recruiting outside the family.

"Well, her surgery doesn't have a three-day recovery time. It has a three-week recovery time, and neither she nor I are allowed to leave the hotel grounds until her waiting period is up."

My mouth formed a little O shape. One week in Halo was less than fun. Three weeks give or take a few days? Was that even manageable?

"Sophie, I don't know." It was Friday evening, and by this time Sunday, I was supposed to be done with this whole charade, not to mention this podunk town.

I heard her swallow on the other end, and I knew her eyes were welling up with tears without having to see her face to face.

"I know it's asking a lot, but she's already had the surgery. She's in a lot of pain, it didn't go so well, and I can't just leave her like this."

A very selfish part of me thought back to three years ago when I'd stood in front of Sophie begging her to take the Praxis test for me. She wasn't helping me cheat because I didn't know the material. She was just helping me get over the hump of the testing atmosphere—just like all the other times. My tears hadn't changed her mind then, so it hurt that she was willing to risk her job to help Nova now.

"How long exactly would I have to do it?"

Sophie sniffled. "Just three more weeks, maybe a little longer if there are any more complications."

I took a deep breath of the conditioned air, ignoring the stinky undertones of testosterone and sweat, and attempted to calm myself. So much for California sun and product parties.

"I guess I could stay a little longer."

"Really?" squeaked Sophie. "Like really, really?"

I sighed and smiled against my will. "Like really, really, but I have some requests."

"Anything!"

"Take some sexy pictures on the beach and by the pool pretending to be me. Put your hair up in a sun hat."

"I don't know."

"Yes." I pressed. "I need them for my account. Nobody else knows I'm in Oklahoma except for my close friend Tabitha, and I'd like to keep it that way. You mentioned your suitcase in the unboxing video, and I'm rolling with the idea that you slash me is on vacation."

"I guess." Her voice trailed off.

"No guess, just yes. *And* you have to send me frequent emails reminding me what the heck is supposed to happen in high school economics class."

"No problem." She perked right up. "And I'll send you some tips for life skills too."

"No need," I replied. "I've been going off book with that one the whole time, and it's been going fine."

There was a long silence on the other end. I could just picture her trying not to reach through the phone to strangle me.

"Anything else?" she asked, the gratitude leaving her voice a little sooner than I would have liked.

"Yeah, what's the deal with Foster? Why does he hate you? He's very hot, and it seems to be a tremendous waste."

"Don't even think about it."

"I could lay the groundwork for you."

"Dani!"

"Enemies to lovers. It's this whole thing."

There was another big clatter behind her, and something that sounded like a cat fighting a chihuahua.

Sophie squealed. "I have to go."

"What the heck is happening over there?"

"No time to talk. Don't bang my boss!" she cried then hit end call before I had a chance to ask how firm that last command was.

I turned the levels back up on the machine, this time running to a full-out sprint. My tennis shoes pounded the belt below me as if I was being chased by my bad decisions. I had an inkling once the endorphins faded, I'd realize continuing the twin-swap was one of them.

Chapter Seven

#OklahomaWhereTheWindComesRollin

Monday morning felt like a betrayal. I was supposed to be having a Dana Point Monday, not a Halo Monday. Dani of Dana Point had a nice ring to it. Dani of Halo? Not so much. I should be in bed, scrolling through my phone right now, my biggest responsibility being to make a messy bun and latte look enviable.

Instead, I was standing in Sophie's bathroom with a curling iron in one hand and lip gloss in the other. Getting up at six AM wasn't growing on me, and it wasn't getting any easier either. Instead of feeling like a professional, I felt like a student again—overly tired, and absolutely positive that the principal had it out for me.

Today was not going to be great. I had some Cliffs-Notes from Sophie, but they were nothing like the full lesson plans she'd drafted for our originally-scheduled swap. I could wing it, but it was going to be a lackluster performance compared to week one.

My bigger concern was the musical. When I accepted the position of director, I was accepting on behalf of Sophie. I had zero intention of getting anywhere near a production of *Oklahoma!*. Now, I was actually going to have to see the thing through.

There was so much wrong with this, starting with the fact that I didn't know anything about Halo's theatre department.

After a morning of so-so classes, I drug my lunch into Jeanine's classroom on a mission to get a little intel. She wasn't much help.

"Theatre department?" She laughed. "We don't have a theatre department. We have an old auditorium we use for band and choir, and occasionally, plays happen there."

"Okay, but who usually directs the plays? Someone obviously did it before me. Where are they and how come they got to quit?" I popped a Sun Chip into my mouth while I awaited her answer.

Jeanine took a long drink from her mug of herbal tea. "Sophie really didn't give you a lot to work with did she?"

"She's been busy."

"Mmhmm." I didn't like the way she mmhmm'd me. No one needed to remind me that Sophie and I had years worth of recon to do, certainly not her nearly geriatric work bestie.

"Look," I pleaded in a hushed whisper, not that any

of the others in here were paying us any attention, but just in case, "point me to the last teacher stuck with the task, and maybe I can get some pointers."

Jeanine opened her mouth to answer me and then quickly changed her mind. A huge cheesy smile stretched across her lips as she waved enthusiastically at the janitor. Was it my imagination or was Janitor Fred trying to look sexy with that mop?

I looked from Jeanine to Fred and back to Jeanine again. Was this how old people flirted? Was I witnessing an interoffice affair? I had a lot of questions, but they would have to wait because there was next to no time before my next class, and Jeanine still hadn't told me who the old director was.

"*Ahem.*" I coughed.

Jeanine tore her eyes from Fred's swishing behind and pointed across the hall to the break room where Principal Beck waited for the communal coffee pot to finish brewing. He wore a sweater vest over his crisp blue button down today, and I'd had to force myself to look away.

I was not proud of how attractive I found this particular ensemble. I blamed the rolled-up sleeves. Did men know how hot it is when they exposed their forearms? If they did and they did it anyway, I am filing a formal complaint. It is very hard to teach high school economics and life skills when your boss kept walking by the classroom window all hot and flexing his forearms. A fundamental life skill had to be knowing how to stop drooling over your boss, right?

"That doesn't make any sense. In the staff meeting,

he acted like nobody would want the job. Why would he quit and then assign it to me of all people?"

Jeanine sighed, her features arranging into a sympathetic pout. "No time for extracurriculars now that he stopped teaching history to pursue school administration. You may have noticed principals are extremely busy." Truth be told I hadn't noticed, but then again I didn't realize I would be here long enough to need to know that sort of thing.

"So?"

"So, he got the big paycheck, but he had to give up most of the time he had with the students to get it."

My eyes drifted back to where Principal Beck sipped his coffee and scrolled through his phone with a frown. Something told me he was reading a work email and not checking his socials. That's assuming the man had any social media. I'd tried to stalk his accounts last night and couldn't find anything.

"Did he like directing?" I asked. I would understand if he did. No, I hadn't turned out to be a big Hollywood actress, but that hadn't soured me on theatre. I still loved to take in a good show, and a tiny part of me was thrilled by the idea that I was going to be in charge of one. Even if it was the only musical Hugh Jackman couldn't make bearable.

Jeanine smiled. "Oh, honey, he loved it. And the kids loved him. You're going to have big boots to fill."

"Just for a couple of weeks," I reminded. "Then, Sophie can swoop in and get everyone over the finish line. She's good at that."

"That's a shame," said Jeanine with a wink. "I feel like it's your turn to finish strong."

I didn't know what to say.

The bell rang before I had a chance to outline the long list of things I had not 'finished strong' prior to my visit to Halo. No harm, no foul. I now had three weeks to demonstrate to Jeanine that her hopeful enthusiasm was unwarranted.

Not wanting to be late, I swooped my bag off Jeanine's desk and hustled out of the classroom.

In true romcom fashion, I pushed through the door without looking where I was going and ran face first into a rock solid chest. One that just so happened to be covered with a sweater vest.

Principal Beck startled and took a step back. "I guess I'm lucky you didn't remember the name of that freshman last week," he said.

I was primed and ready to explain that getting clobbered by a laughing, unapologetic jock and bumping into someone because you didn't want to be late to perform your job were hardly comparable when a warning cough from Jeanine reminded me to keep my mouth shut.

Maybe, just maybe, he was acting like a big chum bucket because he was overworked like Jeanine implied. There had, after all, been that one mildly redeeming moment when he stopped by the nurses office and eyed my wrist. He can claim he was there to find out which student needed a talking to, but I was pretty sure there was a moment there where he was actually worried I was hurt.

"My bad." My voice came out sort of breathy, and I mentally kicked myself to get it together.

He looked up at the clock above our heads. "You'd better get to class."

"Yes, Principal Beck," I replied, doing my best Halo High student impression as I pushed past him to where Sophie's students waited. He tried to remain neutral, but I caught a glimpse of a smile twitching at the corner of his perfect lips before I closed the door to the classroom.

A jolt of anticipation raced through me. I told myself it was because I only had three more hours to kill—okay, teach—before it was time to start *Oklahoma!* tryouts, and not because of the man I was forbidden to date. Sophie never said anything specifically against harmless flirting. This time, it was my lips that twitched into a smile.

I leaned back in the hard, squeaky auditorium chair and willed my face to remain professional. Teenagers littered the seats in front of me, nervous anticipation hanging in the stale air. Most of these kids were doing a better job at keeping their nonverbals to themselves than I was, so it was a good thing the only light in here was a spotlight facing away from me.

On stage, an all-American young man belted his way through *Oh, What a Beautiful Morning* so poorly that I was surprised my ears weren't bleeding. I hid my face behind my curtain of hair and made a note not to cast him in a named role. In his defense, everyone auditioning had to sing, even if they planned to lip sync in the chorus later. So, actually, he had guts getting up there with a singing voice made of gravel and nails on a chalkboard.

He finished, offering a beautifully flamboyant bow, and smiled wide. "Thank you. Again, my name is Benjamin Bailey, and I'm auditioning for the role of Curly."

I blinked, and the auditorium hushed. I realized everyone was waiting on me when I'd been busy processing the fact that Benjamin Bailey was serious about landing the lead role. I cleared my throat. "Um—thank you." Still crickets. "Next."

Ben looked the part of the good ol' boy farmer Curly, there was no arguing that. But what about his singing voice? I couldn't cast him. No. Way.

A freshman girl with braces and pigtails climbed up on stage, and so started the process all over again.

I'd been to enough auditions to know how these things worked. The hopefuls had received a script and a few bars of music on Friday so they could prep in advance for auditions Monday after school. Everyone who auditioned was promised a spot in the production, even if that meant we had a chorus twice the size needed. As the director, I had final say in everything—*that* part I didn't mind. The part I did mind was finding out our weekend of performances was scheduled in only one month's time.

It was too soon. No way we could pull it off.

We always had at least twice that long to prepare when I was a theatre geek. A month was doable, but it meant rehearsals every single day after school. As if I didn't need another reason to get back to Dana Point, now my free time would be eaten up with a musical I hated. Sophie owed me big time! But, lucky for her, I knew what I was doing. I'd work my booty off to have this thing in ship-shape by the time she came home and took the glory.

At least Mrs. Sanchez, Halo's choir teacher, was required to lend her talents. Though, she didn't seem thrilled about the constant rehearsals either. The woman reminded me of the typical hispanic grand-mother. She was currently pounding at the piano a little too forcefully if you asked me. I could barely hear the pigtail girl. At the rate things were going, we'd be lucky to find a single student with a decent singing voice. We'd been at it for over an hour, three quarters of the way through the auditions, and so far, none of these kids had voice talent. Whose idea was it to put on a musical, again? Oh, that's right, Sophie's enemy. I was questioning the validity of that feud before, but I'm certainly not questioning it any more.

Chapter Eight

#HelpNotWanted

"Speak of the devil," I mumbled under my breath when Beck slid into the seat next to me.

"How's it going?" he whispered, eyes facing forward to take in the room. I had to force myself to ignore the undertones of citrus cologne wafting off his body this close. He was warm, and part of me wanted to lean into him. "Has Ben auditioned yet? The kid is an amazing actor. He played Hamlet last year and had the audience in tears."

I snorted. "You obviously haven't heard the boy sing."

"We haven't had a musical in a while." His voice trailed off, concern creasing the tanned skin between his eyebrows. It was hard not to stare at him, but I forced myself to turn back to the stage. Another senior girl was in the middle of her singing audition. She wasn't any better than the rest. I cringed at a high note and crossed her name off the list for possible Laurey candidates.

"And you decided *Oklahoma!* fit the bill? These songs are …"

"Iconic? Cheesy? Yeah, the school board voted on it. You know budget is the big thing this year."

"Yeah, yeah, yeah."

Another girl climbed on stage. She was a little too tall for what I had in mind, and a little too frumpy looking, but I could work with tall and frumpy. I was the queen of makeovers. Inwardly, I prayed she would be a good fit for the female lead. If she had even an iota of a pretty voice, I could cast her. She did have that dazed cornflower 'prance about the daisies' look to her. I could translate that into a farm girl deciding between rival beaus, no problem.

She introduced herself as Kayla, the music started, and she began. Relief washed over me at the very first note. The girl could sing. I did a little happy dance in my seat and wrote her name down on my notebook, drawing little stars all around it. I didn't even mind when Beck raised an eyebrow at my doodles. This was awesome; I had my girl! Now, I just needed to find a good Curly. The antagonist, Jud Fry, and side characters like Aunt Eller and the others didn't need to have amazing voices to pull this off, but Curly and Laurey did.

Maybe someone else would appear on that stage and blow me away like Kayla did.

Or maybe not.

The auditions ended without fanfare, and without a clear contender for Curly.

"Good job, everyone," I announced. Now, it was my turn to stand on the stage. "I'll have the cast list posted as soon as possible on the outside of the auditorium doors. Please let me know if you have any friends who would like to join the tech crew, we still need a few more helping hands." I nodded toward the group of three kids keeping to themselves already dressed in black. They must take their job seriously. Or maybe they always dressed this way? Goths for the modern age. "We'll be having rehearsals everyday from three to four-thirty if we're going to pull this off."

They cheered, and my heart swelled. This wasn't so bad.

Truth be told, it was exactly what I wanted and went to college to do. Thinking about what could have been stung. But life had taken me in another direction, a direction I enjoyed and was good at, a direction with money and free stuff and loads of fun parties, so I'd just have to appreciate this opportunity while I had it and do the best job I could.

The kids dispersed, and Beck joined me on stage. It was painted black but the paint was peeling in several places, the dusty curtains appeared to be about a million years old, and apparently half the stage lights didn't work anymore, but I didn't mind so much. It was *mine*.

"I have another stage hand for you." Beck called out, "Tyler!"

I swallowed hard.

"Please, no." I groaned between my teeth, but the man pretended not to hear.

Tyler must've been hiding out in the shadows off stage, and I hadn't even noticed him. Little twerp! Tyler was my least favorite student. Tall and lanky, curly brass hair, giant adam's apple—the fifteen-year-old sophomore hadn't quite grown into his body. Or matured. He was always giving me hell in economics class, always tardy, and was always making asinine comments.

And now, he was here. My problem in the morning. My problem after school.

"Tyler has agreed to crew the musical in exchange for some detention he needs to make up. Isn't that right, Tyler?"

Tyler shrugged. "Whatever."

I couldn't help it. I glared at Beck. Did this guy have it out for Sophie or what?

"Good luck," Beck added. "Oh, and if I were you, I'd give Ben a fighting chance to play Curly. He really is a good actor…"

I had a feeling he wanted to say more. "And?"

His lip twisted. "And his dad is a friend of mine. He's on the school board."

"There it is." I rolled my eyes. "Maybe you'd better go. You're so busy and all. Don't you have a meeting to get to?"

He didn't take the bait. "In fact, I do. I'll see myself out."

He jumped off the stage in a display of athletic

prowess and jogged out the back of the room, leaving me and the spawn of satan alone.

"You're going to have to lift heavy pieces of scenery and stay out of the way." I narrowed my eyes on the kid. "Do you think you can do that?"

"Whatever," he said again.

"Whatever you can or whatever you can't? Because you can either be a team player here or you can go to regular detention with the rest of the delinquents."

"Whatever I can," he snapped.

Then, he too jumped off the stage and walked toward the exit. I studied the back of his head, annoyed with him for being *him* and annoyed with me for not being better with the troubled kids. He found his backpack in the last row, slung it over his shoulder, and began to quietly sing—almost as if he didn't realize he was even doing it.

Just a few lines.

Not on purpose.

"I've got a beautiful feeling, everything's going my way…"

But they were pure honey, pure perfection, and I about fainted right then and there on the spot.

"Wait," I called out, my voice bordering on shrill. "You can sing?"

He laughed bitterly. "Church choir since I can remember." He turned around, his face flaming red. "You better not tell anyone that!"

"I won't."

"Good," he called back. "I'll crew your stupid play."

"You'll do whatever job I need you to do in our *musical*."

He glared at me from across the room, long and hard, the line of his lips angry, the brown of his eyes challenging, but I gave it right back. Two could play at this game, buddy. He pointed at me. "Don't even think about it, Sparks! I won't embarrass myself."

"It wouldn't be embarrassing."

"No."

"We need you."

His reply to that was the finger.

"Excuse you!"

But he was already gone.

I taped the cast list up on the auditorium doors first thing the next morning. Top of the list, next to Curly McLain in big bold lettering, was Tyler Conrad. I knew there would be some backlash when I walked into the auditorium and saw all the hopefuls waiting for me. They crowded the cast list the second I stepped away. I did not know Benjamin Bailey would shriek like a banshee and demand to see the principal.

"Tyler? Tyler!" he howled. "Who even is that?"

"I think he's a sophomore," someone called out.

Ben yanked the list off of the wall.

"What? But he didn't even audition. This is blatant favoritism." Ben's dramatic outrage was the kind specially reserved for thespians. Apparently, Ben hadn't seen Tyler terrorizing my economics class because if he had, he would know that Tyler was a far cry from my favorite.

Standing across the room with his arms crossed over his chest was none other than Tyler himself. He snorted and stood a little taller. I hadn't expected Tyler to be here early, and something about that made me think the kid was going to accept the job.

"Ah, Benny," he cooed, sauntering over to where Ben and his angry fist full of paper stood fuming. "What did Shakespeare say again? There are no small parts, only small…" His voice trailed off as he looked *down* at the older boy. Everyone hushed. "Actors." He grinned, reminding me of the Grinch. "You'll be great in whatever role you were cast in. Here, give me a looksie."

Tyler pried the paper from Ben's fist with little effort, and I watched in horror as the smirk on his face stretched to an infinite degree. He ran one finger down the long list, making a big show of how far down he had to go before spotting Ben's name.

"Ah, here you are, chorus. Ooh! Looks like you scored the farmer and the cow party scene! That will be fun." He was so smug I almost regretted casting him. Almost… but then I remembered Ben on stage belting out *"Oh, What a Beautiful Morning"* with all the musical talent of Arnold Swartzeneggar on a heavy dose of tranquilizers.

Kayla, who I had pulled the trigger and decided to cast as Laurey, took a baby step toward Ben and placed a cautious hand on his shoulder. I probably should have intervened, but honestly the whole thing was riveting, like Netflix but with no swearing.

"The chorus isn't so bad. You'll get to play a whole bunch of characters, and you'll be in most of the scenes." I couldn't help but notice that Kayla was dropping serious crush hints. Yesterday, at auditions, she was all frump. Today, she was rocking hoop earrings and a pretty decent attempt at eye makeup.

The girl obviously didn't get have gay-dar. Poor thing.

Ben shrugged her off. "Easy for you to say. You're the lead."

Kayla attempted to grin and bear it, but she looked a little bit like she was fighting off a stroke, and the whole scene was starting to head into train wreck territory.

They were far too old for the light-flip method of getting kids to settle down, but this group clearly needed a reset, and I hadn't prepared any inspirational words to manage the fallout of casting Tyler as Curly, so I accessed my inner kindergarten teacher and furiously flashed the house lights on and off until everyone was silent.

I opened my mouth to attempt a poignant explanation of my casting choice but was interrupted by the sound of the double doors screeching open as Principal Beck attempted to slide into the entryway unnoticed.

Ben's eyes went wide, and his nostrils flared. He was totally going to tattle on me.

"We need to talk about *her* casting," growled Ben with

a pointed glare in my direction. Principal Beck looked expectantly from Ben to me. Suddenly, my great idea to cast Tyler felt like a liability. How exactly was I going to explain to him that I'd ignored all protocol and picked the one kid who had absolutely no desire to participate?

Tyler handed the crumpled cast list to Principal Beck, slung his backpack over one shoulder, and worked his way out of the arts wing. He hadn't said he would play Curly, but he hadn't said he wouldn't either. Maybe ticking Benjamin Bailey off was just enough motive to get him to do what I needed.

Principal Beck read through the list, a worried expression creased his eyebrows, and his shoulders slumped in defeat. *Really dude?* I wanted to scream. *You're gonna show your cards like that? Right here with all the students watching? How about a show of confidence? Fake it already!*

"We can talk after class, Ben. For now, you need to head to first period. All of you," he added.

I watched as my newly formed cast gathered their things and scattered through the double doors and out toward their various classrooms.

"This is an interesting cast," said Beck, looking more closely at the list now that the kids weren't around to judge. "Are you sure about Tyler?"

I was one hundred percent sure about Tyler's *voice.* There was a good chance he wouldn't show up for rehearsal let alone actually carry his weight as the lead of the production. I couldn't say that though. Principal Beck had no faith in Sophie, and admitting I was gambling with the play wasn't going to beef up her credibility with the boss man.

"He's got a great voice. And Curly's a bit of a rebel. He can channel that, right?"

Beck smiled, but it didn't reach his eyes. "I hope so, otherwise Benjamin Bailey has just lost his last shot to play the lead in a high school play to a sophomore who was supposed to be working off a detention debt."

I swallowed hard. I hadn't thought about the fact that Ben was a senior and there wouldn't be other high school plays for him.

"I was trying to pick the right voice for the role. Ben just doesn't have it," I tried, hoping Beck understood that I was determined to make the play the best it could possibly be, and not just trying to be contrary.

He sighed. "I hope you're right because there's no time to recast."

"About that." I narrowed my eyes. "Why does the production have to be in a month? We *need* two. Can't we schedule it for later? There's so much work we have to do to get this ready in time."

He frowned, those piercing blue eyes shifting away. "There's just a lot we need to do in here this year. Anyway, we better get going." He turned and hurried out the door.

Why did I get the feeling Principal Beck was hiding something?

Chapter Nine

\#ImTheAdultHerePeople

No matter how many YouTube tutorials I watched on how to change a tire, nothing could have prepared me for the real thing. How was it my fault roadside assistance wasn't an option? I'd always had it. Either that or a boyfriend I could call on for help.

Today, I didn't have either of those things.

I did have a wrench, a jack, lug nuts, a spare tire, and a class of teens staring at me like I was a helpless moron. They weren't wrong.

"And now for the part where we remove the tire from the vehicle."

They stood in an arc around my car, the September sun pressing down on us. I channeled confidence as I kneeled beside the tire and stared at all the little silver hexagons, but who was I kidding? If I managed to get the tire off, it would be a miracle. Replacing it with a new one was never going to happen. I needed to pause, assess the situation, and go in a completely different direction.

I dropped the wrench beside my knee and stood to face the class. "You know what? On second thought, this isn't a real life skill. They pay people to do this for you. Most of you have roadside assistance on your phone for less than five bucks a month, and if you don't, let me teach you a hot tip, a *real* life skill if you will. All you have to do is call police dispatch, and a really nice cop will come do this for you."

Jaws hung open in front of me.

"So, we aren't going to learn to change a tire?" asked Sariah. The girl normally sat in the back of my class with what I could guess were her band geek friends, but it took until this very moment for me to take notice of her. She looked mildly disappointed, her face scrunched up all judgy-like, and it saddened me. Come on, Sariah, live a little!

"Nope. This is your senior year. We can't waste time. Forget the syllabus. I'm going to show you every-thing you need to know to actually survive." I scoured my brain for a good first lesson. "For example, how many of you enjoyed calculus?"

One lone boy in the back of the group shyly raised his hand. I had a moment of clarity where I realized my mouth was getting away with itself and Sophie was going to kill me when she got home, but that moment was quickly squashed by the twenty-four pairs of eyes staring at me. These kids deserved a little truth talk.

"Guess what?" I pressed on, pretending not to see the one math-lover's raised hand. "You will never use it. *Never.*"

"Well, I mean, like if you become an engineer," tried the boy.

"Never," I corrected. "Math is a real thing but only some parts of it."

No sooner had the words popped out of my mouth than I spotted Principal Beck standing at the back of the crowd of kids, his car keys hanging in his hand. He mouthed the word, *"what?"* but I chose to ignore him. I was feeling this lesson, and I wasn't going to let his doom and gloom bring me down.

"Here is the kind of math you need to know. If you buy one latte every day from Irish Gal's, you'll get a free one every fifth day. You might think that's a great deal, but it's not the best deal. The best deal is if you get an Irish Gal's points card and let your points pile up all month long. Then, instead of one small latte every week, you score enough points for three large beverages, no limitations on extra shots."

Beck shook his head in disbelief and parted the crowd, taking over the tire change operation. "Let me show you guys," he muttered, then jumped into an explanation as he expertly removed my tire and placed the spare.

I didn't mind watching his pretty little booty hunched over the car, not one bit.

"And now, we'll take it off the same way and put the real tire back on," he continued. "Watch carefully."

I turned back to the class. "Any other questions about adult life?"

Bored expressions disappeared as they forgot all about Beck and the tire. For once, the class was eating this up. Instead of sitting there with blank stares, scrolling on the phones they had hidden in their laps, they were actually listening to what I had to say. Life skills for the win!

"What about Chipotle?" asked Carter. He didn't talk too much in class ordinarily, but he was one of the few kids to have turned in all of his assignments so far, and he was constantly offering to help pass out papers, so I liked him well enough.

"What about it?"

"Do you have hacks for that?"

I smirked. Was he joking? Did I have hacks for Chipotle? Every California girl knew their way around a takeout menu.

"You like a nice burrito?" I asked, raising one perfectly plucked eyebrow.

Carter nodded affirmatively.

"What if I told you that if you order the burrito bowl and then request two tortillas on the side, you have all the fixings for *two* burritos for the price of one?"

Carter furiously scribbled in his notebook.

"In and Out," shrieked Sariah, and so it continued, each student probing for tips on their favorite takeout.

For the first time since I started filling in for Sophie, I actually felt good at teaching her classes. I mean yeah, it wasn't rocket science, but this was life skills, and no one could argue that they weren't learning completely relevant tools to enhance their future.

"All right, I think that's enough for today," Beck cut in, standing with a little grease on his brow and a scowl on his handsome face. "You guys can go back inside."

I winked at him. "Thanks for your help, Principal Beck. I think this went well."

He blinked rapidly.

The bell rang, and the kids ran back inside to gather their things. Beck walked away briskly. I had to keep myself from staring at his backside as he went. I returned to my classroom, fishing out an apple from my bag, and prepared myself to go to rehearsals.

Jeanine caught me in the hallway. "You did the change a tire demonstration today? How did that go?"

"Great." I hid my smile behind a massive bite of the apple.

"I overheard your students going on and on about how cool Ms. Sparks is when they came back to pick up their things and how she 'like totally understands what's happening in the real world.'"

No matter how hard Jeanine tried, her attempts to sound cool reminded me of fifth grade D.A.R.E. If you don't remember that acronym, your school district clearly wasn't into saving you from the perils of cigarettes, alcohol, and heaven forbid, the use of marijuana! Drug Abuse Resistance Education was basically forty minutes a day with an officer trying to use hip new lingo to connect with kids. Jeanine was like that, only she saved it all for conversations with me. But I don't know, I kind of loved her for it. I could see why she and Sophie had become so close.

"I have to get to rehearsal. Walk with me?"

She nodded and led the way.

"I offered them some real world advice, and they liked it," I boasted, proud of myself for my quick thinking. "Beats learning to change a tire."

Jeanine sipped the herbal tea from her ever present mug. "Mmhmm, so you didn't change the tire?"

"Well, Beck showed up and did that part while I taught them some more important skills"

She chuckled. "And that curriculum switch had nothing to do with you not knowing how to change a tire then?"

"Well, there was that too," I admitted, and my cheeks warmed. "But I feel like it was a good pivot."

"I'm not sure everyone thought it was a good pivot," whispered Jeanine, raising her chin toward where Principal Beck pounded down the hallway, eyes narrowed in our direction.

I grimaced and grabbed a hold of Jeanine's wrist as she tried to escape. Surely he wouldn't yell at me in front of another teacher. That would be unprofessional, right?

"What on earth did I just witness?" he hissed the second he got within earshot.

Jeanine tugged, attempting to break free of my grasp, but I was locked on her like a bargain hunter on Black Friday.

"That was life skills. Alternate edition."

Principal Beck squinted. "You're not serious?"

"I am." I released Jeanine and shuffled into the auditorium, refusing to act like a puppy with her tail between her legs.

He followed me inside, voice low. "Sophie, you know better. You can't just change the curriculum every time you get a good idea."

"So, you're saying it was a good idea…"

Beck's expression softened. "I like that you're looking for ways to connect with the kids, but you can't keep swapping assignments on the syllabus. Stick to your approved curriculum, make *that* stuff fun."

I had to physically restrain myself from rolling my eyes. *Make that stuff fun?* Sophie's curriculum included real party items like learn to write a check and file your taxes manually, both of which I considered completely irrelevant for today's young adult.

"Got it," I replied, biting the inside corner of my cheek to keep from saying anything stupid.

He let out a long-suffering sigh, like I was nothing but a thorn in his side. My heart sank a little. What happened to the flirty Foster Beck of last week? I liked him more than Principal "The Superintendent Owns Me" Beck.

"I have to get going, but I wanted to introduce you to someone first," he said.

Benjamin Bailey came bounding down the aisle, appearing much more chipper about things than he had this morning. He smiled, his eyes alive with triumph. They weren't going to demand I make him the lead, were they?

"Trick question?" I countered. "I already know

Ben." I smiled at the twerp. "Nice to see you again, Ben."

Beck cut in. "I'd like to introduce you to your new stage manager."

I looked back and forth between the two of them, wondering if this was some kind of joke. "You're not here to spy on me for Principal Beck, are you?" I teased, but deep down I was actually quite serious.

But when neither answered, I realized that's exactly what this was—a setup. Ben didn't get his way, and Beck didn't get to direct the show, so the two of them had cracked a plan to keep me in line. Inside, I was seething mad, but outwardly, I smiled bright as sunshine. "Welcome to the team, Ben."

"I'm excited." He was lying through his teeth.

"Me too." But then again, so was I.

If they thought Ben was a good actor, they didn't know Dani Sparks.

Chapter Ten

#HeavenHelpUs

"Being the stage manager means you can't actually be in the show." I eyed Benjamin wearily. "Are you okay with that?"

"I'm great with that," he supplied. "This is much better for my college apps."

"Atta boy. That's the spirit." Beck patted him on the back and took off, hurrying away to whatever millionth meeting he had to attend for the day.

I turned to the students littered across the auditorium. The seats were dated, some of them broken, and the whole place smelled like dust bunnies. But they didn't seem to care. Actually, quite the opposite. They were thrilled to be here. And crazily enough, so was I. I cleared my throat and attempted to speak over them, but they were way too loud. They talked as if having the most deafening voice was a competition and the prize was popularity—only among themselves, of course. Plus, there were over forty of them. How was I supposed to compete with that?

Benjamin smirked at me. "These are high school theatre geeks."

"And?"

"And they all want to be the center of attention, which means you need to yell."

But he didn't wait for me to take his advice.

"Listen up, everyone," he bellowed, his voice commanding. The cast fell to silence and turned to us. "I'm your stage manager." Most of the kids cheered at this, but a few rolled their eyes, Tyler included. "Which means you get to listen to me." It took every ounce of self control for me not to join the highschoolers and roll my eyes at that one. "After, Ms. Sparks, of course. She's first in command, so show the woman some respect and shut your pieholes."

Good save, kid.

"Thanks, Ben." I smiled at the group. "We will start at three-ten on the dot everyday. You come prepared to work. We don't have a lot of time to get this musical ready. We're going to have fun, but we're not going to goof off. Absolutely no talking amongst yourselves unless we're on a five-minute break, you got that?"

They nodded in unison and relief flooded through me. I had to remember these kids weren't like most of the ones I had in class because they actually *wanted* to be here. They'd auditioned, hadn't they? Well, everyone except for Tyler. But by the way Tyler was eyeing up the senior girl he'd get to stage kiss, not to mention his pride in besting Ben, I had a feeling the kid had had a change of heart.

"*Oklahoma!* isn't exactly the most inspiring musical in the world," I continued, and a few students snicked, "but it's popular, and it's going to fill the house." I swept my hands out for dramatic emphasis, and their eyes lit up. "We're going to squeeze every ounce of talent from each one of you. To do that, we must respect our time, respect each other, respect our theatre, and respect ourselves. If we can manage that, I know we will put on the best show Halo High has ever seen."

They cheered again, louder, excited, and fueled by optimism. I stood a little taller—I was feeling it, too.

I caught Mrs. Sanchez's eye from across the top of the piano. She winked and nodded once as if to say "we got this." Seeing her attitude do a one-eighty made me smile even bigger.

"Everyone in?"

"Yes!" they yelled back.

"Then, let's get started."

What kicked off with passion quickly deflated into a wrinkly old balloon. These kids were clearly not part of the award-winning choir I'd overheard Mrs. Sanchez boasting about in the staff room last week. Quite the opposite.

"Okay, okay, okay," I cried when I absolutely could

not listen to *Many a New Day* for a second longer. "We have a problem."

Benjamin looked up from the overly precarious clipboard he had permanently fused to his hand and nodded in agreement. I was pretty sure he had no idea what I objected to, but I was beginning to like the kid now that he backed up everything I said and demanded the rest of the cast do so as well. The number was made up of Kayla as Laurey and the rest of the female ensemble. The problem was, it didn't sound like Kayla plus chorus; it sounded like Kayla plus six cats fighting in the dead of night.

"I know you all want to make your presence in the scene known, but there is something to be said for subtle background contribution."

The girls stared at me with blank faces.

"Let Kayla be the lead and blend in," barked Ben. "You're condiments, not the burger, people."

I raised an eyebrow in deep appreciation. The kid was a terrible singer, but it was very possible that stage managing was exactly what he should have been doing all along.

This time, when Kayla hit the chorus, the ensemble joined in, but with a modicum of reservation.

"Better," I called out then flipped open my phone to see what scene was on the docket for the next half hour of rehearsal. It was the first scene to rely on Tyler, so I made a quick scan of the room to make sure he had bothered to stick around. He was sitting in the back with headphones on, his usual pissed off scowl had returned, but he was still here, so I was giving him brownie points for that.

Ten minutes later, and a few poignant notes from Mrs. Sanchez, and Kayla was done. "That was good, ladies," I said. "Practice at home tonight. And Kayla?"

She smiled at me nervously.

"Your voice is beautiful."

"Thank you," she mumbled, barely raising her eyes to meet mine.

It was my intention to compliment the shy out of her and replace it with confidence, but it was proving to be harder than I thought. Every time I gave her direction, she apologized as if she was doing something wrong. The result was my saying everything in a sugar sweet voice that even I found revolting.

"But keep working at it and make sure to memorize your lines. Two weeks and you need to be off book, okay?"

"Sorry, no problem."

I opened my mouth to explain that "sorry" was not necessary, but Benjamin tapped my shoulder with the pencil he kept tucked behind his ears at all times and whispered, "Let it go."

How quickly he had gone from my number one problem to an actual asset? Amazing!

With a smirk that was only partially condescending he turned and hollered toward the back of the auditorium.

"Tyler, you're up!"

His headphones must have been turned up full-blast because the kid didn't react in the slightest. In his defense, I'd told the students if they weren't on, they could do whatever they wanted as long as they stayed quiet. Most had opted to work on homework—the sensible choice—but of course, a few were glued to their phones. Not that I was judging, I'd done the same thing, and it had turned into a lucrative career.

Benjamin, it seemed, didn't see it the same way. He marched over to Tyler, waving his hands around like a lunatic. I was probably going to ask him to tone it down, but it was the first rehearsal, and he'd been helpful up until this point.

"Hello! Are you here to work, or are you here to slow us all down?"

Tyler pulled his headphones off. "What?"

"Get your butt on stage. It's time to show us all why you are so special."

He said the word "special" like it was a taunt, and Tyler stiffened. This could've gone one of two ways. Option A—Tyler could have thrown a fit and quit the show right here, opting for detention instead. Option B—Tyler could have stepped up and dazzled everyone with his singing prowess. I was gunning for option B.

What I didn't expect was Option Punch Ben's Lights Out.

It happened so fast I almost couldn't believe it. Tyler jumped from his seat, backpack, phone, and headphones flying. He sucker-punched Ben square in the face, and then before I could even react, the two were rolling across the aisle, pummeling each other. Girls screamed and boys hollered as the two went at it, grunting and cussing, neither letting up.

"Break it up!" Mrs. Sanchez yelled, rushing forward.

I took that as my queue to join her. Some of the older guys jumped in as well, two of them ripping Tyler off Ben and two more holding Ben back from further retaliation. They were both bleeding and bruised, scowling and hurling insults.

"You think you're better than everyone else but you're not," Tyler hissed.

"Why are you even here? Nobody wants you here," Ben growled.

Cats and dogs, these two.

"Cut it out!" I screamed, coming between the boys. I glared at them both. I was an equal opportunity glarer. "We do not have time for this behavior. It cannot happen."

"Tell that to him." Ben scoffed. "He hit me first."

"You provoked him."

Ben stilled and looked away. He knew I was right. Maybe Tyler was in remedial classes, I didn't know, but something about the way Ben had said "special" in that nasty way had cut Tyler to the core.

I turned on Tyler and pointed. "And you shouldn't have hit him. We don't resort to violence here, you got that?"

His jaw tensed, brassy hair hanging low over one bruised eye. He had nothing to say.

"Listen up," I lowered my voice. "Tyler has a great voice. That's why he got cast as Curly." I looked pointedly at Ben. "And yes, Ben, you are a fantastic actor, but you need voice training before you're going to get cast as the lead in any musical. Get over it. You want to be a professional? Then, act like one."

A knowing expression crossed his face as he straightened. "Fine. It won't happen again." The guys holding him back let him go, and he shook out his shoulders.

I turned back on Tyler. "And you, if you so much as lay a finger on anyone in this cast, you'll be back in detention so fast your head will spin."

He smirked. "What about Kayla? I read the script. There's a kiss. So, can I lay a hand on her?"

Kayla shrieked. "Eww, you jerk! I don't want to kiss you." She was next to Ben now, hanging onto his arm like he was her knight in shining armor. When was the girl going to get the hint that Ben played for the other team? Sigh… wasn't my place.

Tyler waggled his eyebrows at Kayla and blew her a kiss. "Oh, but I think you do."

"Not helping the situation," I ground out. "Boys, get yourselves cleaned up." I turned back to the group. "Everyone, take five. When you come back, you had better leave the drama at the door."

They dispersed in a frenzy of conversation, and I sank into one of the chairs. My heart was still racing, and I had to sit on my hands to keep them from shaking. Who knew directing a musical could be so intense?

"Are you going to report that?" Mrs. Sanchez joined me.

I hesitated. "I don't want to."

"Well, you kind of have to." She sighed. "That's the policy."

"Right. Of course." But I wasn't going to. If I reported them, I might lose my stage manager and my lead. We couldn't afford it. At this point, I had to hope that everyone got over themselves and focused on the performance. Best case scenario, nobody brought the fight up again.

We could all be mature about this. Was hoping teenagers would let it go too much to ask? I let out a groan. Who was I kidding? The news of this fight would be all over the school by tomorrow morning. I just prayed it didn't make its way back to Principal Beck.

Chapter Eleven

#ToBangOrNotToBang

Please sir, sexy swimsuit pics.
If Sophie didn't get that I was doing my best Oliver Twist impression in that text, then she really didn't deserve to call herself my sister.

I watched as the little dots danced across my phone. How long did it take for Sophie to send a simple, "Sure, babe, no problem?" I was literally playing her nine hours a day, every day, all I needed her to do was take some pictures every couple of days and text them to me. I was trying not to get irritated, but it felt like I was living on her back burner, whereas she was my number one priority.

Come on, Soph, text me back. The sound of the first period bell startled me, and my eyes snapped up from my phone to the entrance of the school. Just seconds ago, it had been crowded with students, now it was eerily silent.

Poop on a stick! I cried inwardly. I was late for the third time since I'd started subbing in for Sophie. Frantic, I shoved my phone into my purse and attempted to hustle into the school unnoticed. A feat that would have been easier if I wasn't wearing three inch heels and a pencil skirt. Why was it that my need to set a good fashion example always seemed to cause me problems?

"Good morning, Ms. Sparks," grumbled a voice from behind me. I didn't have to turn around to know that it belonged to Tyler. After all, arriving five minutes late to first period was kind of his trademark, but I turned anyway because it had been a good fourteen hours since the fight broke out in rehearsal, and I needed to know if his face was going to tell on me.

He wore a gray hoodie hanging loose over his shaggy hair; if he kept his head down and didn't make too much eye contact, maybe no one would notice the little shadow across his cheekbone. The claw marks raking down his neck on the other hand were going to be a little harder to miss.

Damn, Benny-Boy was savage.

I took a steadying breath. Tyler wasn't going to want to draw attention to the fact that Benjamin had landed any punches. He might not say anything that would give Principal Beck pause, and maybe, just maybe, Benjamin would be vain enough to have thrown a pack of frozen vegetables on his eye last night. Heck, the kid might have access to a little concealer.

There was a chance this could go unreported.

I ducked my head low as I passed Principal Beck's office and entered my first period economics class with Tyler in tow.

"Decision making and cost benefit analysis," I started, placing my purse on my desk and spinning to face the class. "Or as I like to call it, *should I have done that or not so much?*"

The class chuckled, and I relaxed. Of all the lessons that Sophie had prepped for me, this one actually held my interest. How many failures could I have avoided in life if I'd simply done a cost benefit analysis before every major decision? College was a prime example. Seeing as how I was not a teacher, might I have been better off to not spend sixty grand in pursuit of a degree? That was probably not the best example to use with the class of college hopefuls sitting in front of me, so instead, I broke it down in a way they could understand: bangs vs no bangs.

"Bangs seem like a good decision. After all, there are a lot of perks to cute *fringe* as the British call it. Could someone please give me an example of a perk of having bangs?"

I could tell that Tyler was shaking his head with disapproval at the back of the classroom because his own shaggy blonde bangs flipped back and forth from beneath his hoodie, but he stayed quiet, true to my earlier assumption.

After a moment of silence, a hand went up. "Jessica?" Jessica was a mousy type, brown hair, brown eyes, nondescript glasses and, you guessed it, bangs.

"Good for an extra long forehead," she squeaked out.

"Excellent, also covering acne, even if that acne is a result of said hair choice. But bangs have their own drawbacks too, like the fact that you have to go to the salon more often and they get in the way of facial masks."

Jessica nodded, bottom lip protruding.

Sariah popped up her hand, speaking before I had a chance to call on her. "Yeah, and my cousin has like really thin hair, and she did bangs, and they like didn't look right. So be careful if you have thin hair is all I'm saying."

I nodded sagely. "That's right. They don't look good on everyone."

The boys of the class were staring at me with mixed expressions of shock and boredom. But hey, this kind of lesson may come in handy for them one day, too.

"So, before you get bangs you have to ask yourself, does the cost of constant upkeep and inability to thoroughly clean your pores outweigh the benefits of looking cute and saving cash on cover up? The answer might be different for each person, or for the purpose of this class, each business."

The next part of the lesson was to ask each student to put a tough decision on the whiteboard along with some of the pros and cons of deciding one way versus the other. We didn't get that far, however, because a crackling noise from the intercom warned us all that an announcement was coming.

"Ms. Sparks to the Principal's office, please."

I felt my cheeks turn ten shades of red, a burning sensation that only worsened when a sheepish Jeanine stepped inside the classroom and let me know she had been instructed to watch my class while I *visited* with Principal Beck.

"Ooooh," chorused the class as I trudged down the aisle of desks. If I wasn't already on thin ice, I would have told them all their response was completely immature and also predictable, but I wasn't feeling very feisty, especially not when I saw Benjamin Bailey exiting Beck's office with one eye completely swollen shut.

The snake held up his hands in surrender. "Hey, I didn't say anything. He already knew." He shrugged as if to say "don't blame me" and then scampered off.

The front desk ladies shot me pitying looks, and my heart fell.

"Fan-freaking-tastic," I muttered to myself as I squared my shoulders and entered Beck's office. It was tidy and smelled like whatever cleaning solution the school used intermixed with undertones of his spicy citrus cologne. The walls were painted an inviting sage color with framed pictures of his degrees, an old rendering of the school before it was built, and a cast party pic from last year's production of *Hamlet*. I couldn't stop myself, I paused for a second and examined the image. It was like looking at two different people, the man in front of me and the man in that picture. There he stood in the center of a group of kids, some that I recognized, some that must have graduated last year. His smile was bigger, more genuine and he was dressed down too. I squinted, was that a *Star Wars* T-shirt?

"Have a seat."

I tore my eyes from the photo and reminded myself that I was not here to see the fun looking guy in that photo.

Principal Beck stood at the back of the office, staring out the large window. The blinds were pulled all the way up, letting streams of sunlight in. His view overlooked the courtyard area where a lot of the students liked to take lunch—where I liked to take it, too. At least his window didn't face the faculty parking lot, which meant less chance of him seeing me arrive late. He turned and motioned for me to sit in one of the two plump chairs on the other side of his desk.

"Listen," I started, "I can explain."

He frowned and sat down too. His desk was mostly clear, but he took the pile of papers that looked like balance sheets and some blue prints, and stuffed them into a drawer. "Ms. Sparks, we have a problem."

My throat went dry.

His eyes met mine; they were so blue they matched the sky outside. They also whirled with torment, disappointment, and confusion.

"You've changed," he went on. "I don't know what happened to you over the summer, but you're different. In some ways, it's good." His eyes softened. "You're more relaxed, and you connect well with the kids."

"Thank you."

"And your appearance has obviously changed. I think every male has noticed that," he went on and then stopped himself, cheeks flushing pink. I didn't know the man could blush. He was so tan, not to mention stoic and put together.

I smiled.

He closed his eyes for a second as if to regroup. "But in other ways, the changes aren't good. You've been late three times by my estimation, and we're only on the eighth day of school."

Well, crap.

"You veer away from the approved curriculums nearly every day to suit your moods."

"Um—"

"And now, you've let a fight go unreported."

Is this the part where I lie and insist that I was going to report Tyler and Beck? It would be so easy. I could fib, and then I could grovel. This was Sophie's job we were talking about here. I would be gone in a few weeks, but what about her? The whole reason why I'd agreed to the twin swap in the first place was because I wanted Sophie back in my life, not the other way around. The last thing I needed was Sophie to come home and be mad at me.

"I'm sorry," I gushed. "I will do better. This is just all so new for me."

His eyes narrowed. "New? This is your fourth year."

My heart skittered. "No, I mean directing is new." Good save, Dani. "I'm just a little overwhelmed I think. And scatterbrained. I'll do better. I promise."

He nodded once, but I could tell he was skeptical. "I was really hoping you'd report the fight. I shouldn't have found out about it through the gossip mill. I've already talked it over with Ben and will be talking to Tyler next. Tyler was already on thin ice... "

"Ben provoked him," I cut in. He didn't like that, so I backpedaled. "But you're right. Violence is never the answer."

"And why didn't you report it immediately?"

I had no answer for him so I offered the truth. "We handled it during rehearsal. It won't happen again."

"I hope you're right."

"I am."

He let out a long-suffering breath. "I hate to do this, Ms. Sparks, I really do, but we have certain standards to uphold at Halo, and I can't be seen as giving preferential treatment to any one staff member."

What was he talking about? According to Jeneane it was the opposite. Everyone knew that Sophie and Foster Beck had beef.

He retrieved a crisp piece of paper from his desk and slid it to me. My eyes ran over it, taking in the listed bullet points where he'd written in my infractions in his perfect pointy scroll and at the bottom, the signatures of not only himself but of Superintendent Tom Wainwright. There was a space left for a teacher to sign it, too—me.

"You'll need to sign that." He sighed heavily.

But my eyes were stuck on the big bold lettering at the top, disbelieving.

"I'm afraid you've been placed on administrative probation."

Chapter Twelve

#FailureForBreakfast

It took every ounce of channeling my inner Lady Gaga, Michelle Obama, and Lizzo not to cry right then and there. But I sucked it up, signed Beck's paper, finished life skills, and made it through day two of rehearsals without giving in to the emotions. The same thing couldn't be said when I finally made it back to Sophie's house. The second I walked in the door, I burst into tears.

I was such a failure.

If I didn't get it together, I'd lose Sophie's job and probably my sister with it. I sank into her couch and pulled out the copy Beck had given me of the administrative probation notice. It talked about fostering professional growth and creating a safe learning environment—blah blah blah—and gave me an ultimatum.

In no uncertain terms could I make any more mistakes. In thirty days Ms. Sparks would have to meet again with Principal Beck, and again thirty days after that, and again thirty days after that.

Great. Sophie was going to kill me.

Speaking of the devil, or angel more like because apparently *I* was the devil these days, her name lit up my phone.

Don't laugh, was all she'd texted.

I clicked open the file of pictures she'd sent and burst out laughing. Nothing like some good comic relief to break up the pity party. The pics were professional but cheesy as hell, as if she'd hired the hotel photographer to take them. Rule number one of getting professional photos done: don't hire the hotel staff! First up was an image of her standing next to a palm tree, a colorful parrot perched on top of her head. Her eyes were wide, a look of sheer horror on her face. The parrot on the other hand? He'd done this a million times. He was over it.

It wasn't Instagram worthy, but I didn't even care. I'd be keeping this treasure forever.

I scrolled on through the file, taking in the rest of the photos. She'd braided her short hair back, so that was good. Sometimes she wore a sunhat. But couldn't she have at least put on a bikini? The woman was either wearing a sundress or a swimsuit with a skirt attached. We were twenty-six! Single! Hot! What was she doing? Clearly, my sister needed me to stage an intervention.

But she did have one thing right. Her opinion that

Foster Beck was a total jerk. I'd been glamoured by his good looks, spicy clean scent, and book-smart style. But now that he'd placed me on administrative probation, I saw the man for what he really was—a rule-following, butt-kissing, tool.

Now that I was on the same page as Sophie, I sighed in relief that I hadn't flirted with him. Okay, not very much, anyway. Flirting with him would mess up *her* life. And besides, I couldn't forget that Beck didn't know the real me even existed.

So, that was that.

I needed a way to get all this pent up energy out. Lately, I'd been crashing in front of the TV after work, too tired to drag my butt to the gym. I'd only been the one time since arriving. In Oklahoma, fitness wasn't as important as it was back in California, and especially in my chosen career as a social media influencer. Girls could rock whatever size they wanted online these days and gain followers as long as the confidence was there, but I'd built my brand on a certain aesthetic. Honestly, I worried what my sponsors would think if I didn't keep myself looking the same way.

It sucked, but it was life, and anyway, I liked to feel good in my own skin. Who didn't? Sophie may be too insecure to wear a bikini, but I wasn't that girl. And I wasn't the "lay around on the couch all evening" kind of girl either. I was the "workout everyday and drink a kale smoothie" kind of girl. Plus, the "hit up a fun party" at night girl. Not that there were any of those in Halo. In a few weeks, Oklahoma would be behind me, and I'd need to slip back into my old life as if nothing had changed. Keeping up on my fitness would help me accomplish that.

So, with California in mind, I forced out a groan and made myself go to the gym. I needed to lift, so I started there, powering through a total body workout with the guidance of my favorite fitness app. But all that iron wasn't enough to keep the anxiety at bay, so I followed it up with three miles on the treadmill. While I was on there, feet pounding the belt, music blaring through my headphones, I edited one of Soph's photos—a sunset beach closeup with the giant sun hat and a carefree smile—and posted it. I captioned it with the words: Mexico is good for the soul. I threw in a couple heart and palm tree emojis and added the appropriate hashtags. From there I went over to my DMs, hoping Annie from Live Love Laugh would have news of my payment.

There was nothing.

I turned down the level to three—a brisk walk—and reminded myself to breathe. This was probably just a fluke. They'd never been late before. But other sponsors had ghosted on me from time to time, so I knew how to handle it. I quickly typed out a polite but direct follow up.

Hey, Annie. I hope you're doing well. I just wanted to drop in and ask if there was anything else you needed from me on our latest collaboration. If not, do you still have my banking information? And as always, thank you for the opportunity to work with your wonderful company. I always love your boxes. You guys have the best products! XOXO -Dani

With that done, I strode over to the locker room and changed into my swimsuit, locking up my belongings and deciding on a quick dip in the pool and a soak in the hot tub. My workout had only slightly eased the negative emotions I had piled up inside of me. Water, the new black bikini I'd ordered in, and fresh air would do the trick.

The outdoor pool sparkled like blue and white diamonds. I took no time diving into one of the lanes. When the water surrounded me, shutting me off from the world, I had a brief moment of clarity. Everything was going to be okay. I would get through this trying experience and would come out on top. I just needed to keep going and do my best. Stick to the plan. The plan would work.

I swam laps for a while, relaxed in the hot tub for even longer, and then headed back toward the locker room just as the sun was sinking into the horizon. I closed my eyes for a minute, smiling against the cool breeze and breathing it deep into my lungs. I felt so much better. Truly, I was a new woman!

I nearly fell on my butt, my towel dropping away, when I ran right into something hard as rock.

Not something. Someone. A tall man in black swim trunks with a smooth tanned chest peered down at me, water dripping down his toned body.

"Sophie?" He frowned. "I didn't know you went here."

Of all people, why him?

"Uhh——hi, Foster." I stepped back. "I mean, Principal Beck." I had to force myself to meet his eyes and not oggle his sexy body, but then again, I was mad at him, wasn't I? Yes, I was. I hated him actually. So, I needed to act like it. I stepped back and retrieved my towel, pulling it extra tight over my bikini clad chest. I couldn't help but notice he was staring. Well, good. Maybe I could torture him with what he'd never have.

"Sophie, I wanted to say——"

"Sophie, is that you?" a chipper voice cut in. "Oh girl, it is!" Before I knew what was happening, I was being embraced by a busty twenty-something who I'd never laid eyes on in my life. But the woman clearly knew Sophie. She was a gorgeous African American chick with one of those stylish afros I could only dream about.

"Where were you on Saturday?" She pouted. "We missed you!"

Oh crap, I needed to think fast. "Oh yeah, I got busy with work stuff."

"Okay, but did you read it? Did you like it?" She grinned at me, her expression knowing. "Hot, right?"

"Um, yeah. Definitely." What was she talking about? If she said something that outed my true identity to Beck, I'd die.

"Okay, so I have to ask, are you team Hunter or team Blade?"

It was time to improvise. I was a trained actor,

wasn't I? "Definitely team Blade." I fanned myself. "So freaking hot."

"You dirty girl!" She squealed. "I didn't know you were into that bondage stuff." She raised a perfect eyebrow. "But you have to watch out for the quiet ones, that's what I always say."

"No, wait, no. What? That's not what I meant."

"Sure." She laughed. "No judgement here, babe. You do you."

This. Was. Not. Happening.

The woman took that moment to lock eyes on Beck, doing a quick double take. She immediately held out her hand to him. "Hi, are you Sophie's friend? I'm Aniyah. Soph and I are in a book club together." She winked, clearly pleased with herself and his sheepish expression. "An *erotic* book club."

I knew there was a reason I always hated improv class! If I could sink into the pool deck, I would. Foster's eyes flashed to mine—amused, intrigued, surprised, and a little embarrassed. His cheeks were pink again. I couldn't hold his gaze. I winced and looked down, staring at my chipping pedicure instead.

"Nice to meet you." He shook Aniyah's hand. "I'm Foster Beck. Sophie's boss."

I couldn't handle it anymore. I looked up. Her mouth had formed into a horrified O shape. "Nice to meet you, too." She dropped his hand and looked back at me, mouthed *I'm sorry*, and then took off with a quick, "I'll see you next month."

Sophie was in an erotic book club? Well, that explained some things. I guessed she had to get her pent up energy out somehow. If I wasn't so embarrassed right now, I would be laughing. I was pretty sure Foster was thinking the same.

"I better go home and work on my lesson plans, make sure they're written to the curriculum and not to suit my mood." I couldn't help myself. The quip came out all on its own. But something about the word "mood" had him blushing again. Okay, this guy was a jerk, but he was definitely crushing on me. Or Sophie? Me as Sophie? He also mumbled a quick goodbye and ran back to the pool so fast the teenage lifeguard whistled at him. "No running!"

I dropped the towel, flipped my hair and sashayed back inside, taking my sweet time.

At least Beck would be busy obsessing about the fact that Sophie was into erotic literature and not about the fact that I'd had no freaking idea who Aniyah was. That whole encounter could have ended in absolute disaster. What if Aniyah had said something that revealed me as Dani? I shuddered to imagine that conversation on the pool deck turning into an admission of guilt and everything that would've come with it. It had been a close call that left me more unsettled than ever.

But one thing was for sure. I needed to talk to Sophie, not only to discuss more of the ins and outs of her life here but to get the deets on these sexy Hunter and Blade characters.

Driving home, I let the window down to dry my hair in the crisp autumn air. Halo wasn't the town of my dreams, but there were nice things about it. Like the way the trees stretched out over the sidewalks, leaving splashes of red and yellow behind them, and how even though there was no traffic, people drove a little slower.

I pulled up to the crosswalk at the center of town and pressed down on the break waiting for the light to change. Halo didn't have a lot to offer in terms of recreation, but there was a pretty cute pizza shop with outdoor dining. I turned my head to the left, wondering if tonight was a good night to step inside and grab a pizza, only I was met with the totally bugged out, cheeks flaming red, gaze of Jeanine. She quickly jerked her hand out from under Janitor Fred's and clasped it in her lap.

Well, well, well, I was totally not imagining it when I spotted Jeanine lusting after his broom skills.

I leaned over the open car window and grinned like a cheshire cat. "Jeanine, Fred, so nice to see you two crazy kids out and about."

Fred gave an awkward wave, but Jeanine was still breathing out of her nose and motioning for me to call her as I hit the gas and headed home. This day had started pretty rough, but it ended with abs and potential blackmail material. Maybe I needed to hit the gym more often.

Chapter Thirteen

#OhTheDrama

Things were not perfect between Ben and Tyler, but true to his word Ben had actually approached the guy, and *gasp*, apologized. It was very awkward to witness, especially since I'm not sure that Tyler had ever been on the receiving end of an apology before. His response was garbled and sounded a little something like, "Okay, dude, it's fine," but it was hard to tell since he never once looked up at Ben during the conversation.

Kayla, however, had not forgiven Tyler for leaving the drama kid of her dreams with a black eye, and there was essentially no chemistry between them ever. We were a week out from rehearsing the kissing scene, and I was already dreading it.

On stage, Kayla sat in the center of three choir chairs we were using as a bench while Tyler forced his way through *Little Surrey With the Fringe on Top* in front of her. I fully intended to get a real set going by opening night, but until Principal Beck parted with the budget long enough for me to make plans, choir chairs and floor tape were going to have to do.

Tyler's singing was top notch, but I kept having to remind him that he couldn't block Kayla on stage, a concept that did not seem to click with him.

"It feels completely unnatural to sing to her while standing eight steps to the right and three steps forward. What kind of seduction occurs eight steps to the right?"

"Ew," cried Kayla with exaggerated disgust. "Don't say seduction ever again."

Tyler waggled his eyebrows up and down. "I won't *say* it again…"

These two were going to be the death of me. I had half a mind to park them in my classroom and force them to watch romantic comedies until they under-stood that enemies were supposed to be attracted to each other, but I had a feeling that was just the sort of thing Principal Beck and his "Probation List of Doom" prohibited me from doing.

"Enough." I stood from my seat in the front row of the auditorium and hopped up on the stage. "Look, I know it feels funny, but it doesn't look funny. The audi-ence wants to see Laurey's reaction to your serenade, and if you're turned with your back to the audience, singing directly to her, then they can't see her reaction or yours. Not to mention, it muffles your voice. You gotta work with the acoustics, which means you need to project toward the audience. Does that make sense?" I asked, feeling like I was explaining this for the hundredth time without a prayer of it sinking in.

I loved Tyler's voice, and he was starting to grow on me as a person, but there were definitely moments when I wondered if I had made a mistake by not casting Ben. The musical numbers would have sucked, but the performance would have been polished, and we wouldn't be going over basic blocking two weeks into the rehearsals.

Maybe what I said finally clicked, or maybe he was just tired of me saying it, but when we ran through the scene again he followed my directions and left the audience with a full access view of Kayla sitting on her bench and scowling at him.

I patted myself on the back. No really, I actually reached around and patted myself because I deserved it.

Now for part two of operation "I'm an awesome director."

Early on, I had come up with a strategy for getting Kayla to do what I wanted on stage. It was a simple one. I asked Ben to give her all of her directions and kept my mouth shut. To his credit, he took this job very seriously. What acting he did not get to do on stage, he channeled into his role as Kayla's personal acting coach. I think it helped that he ended every suggestion with a smoldering smile, but time was short, and it was working.

The second half of the scene went a lot better than the first, primarily because it involved Curly and

Laurey bickering and Tyler and Kayla were very good at that.

By the time we stopped for our mid-rehearsal break, I actually felt like there was one scene in the play I could consider performance ready. I made a quick run to the staff lounge for a diet soda fix and checked my DMs for something from Live Love Laugh. There was still no response, but the little *seen* notification at least let me know my message had been received. I expected to hear something soon, hopefully in the form of a direct deposit.

I popped the top on my soda and mentally prepared for the next forty-five minutes. It was time for another brutal ensemble number, and I was half tempted to subtly turn on the noise cancelling feature of my earbuds. Maybe I could suggest that to the audience before the play started.

Welcome to the Halo High production of award-winning musical Oklahoma! If there are more than three cast members on stage, please exercise caution and utilize earplugs. The exit of the ensemble will be your cue to once again tune in to the performance.

I crossed paths with Mrs. Sanchez in the hallway. "So what do you think? Are we going to be able to pull this thing off?"

The woman gave me a warm smile and pulled me to the side. "I was a little worried, but I've got to hand it to you, Ms. Sparks." She nodded enthusiastically, her head of natural salt and pepper curls bobbing. I was a full foot taller than her, and I was only 5'6". "I think we're going to make it. Of course, we're still a little rough around the edges, but we've got three more weeks to polish everything."

"My thoughts exactly." I bit my bottom lip, suddenly remembering that the real Sophie would be home in *two* weeks. What would happen then? Would she be able to seamlessly take over *Oklahoma!* during the last week of rehearsals? Unlikely.

I smiled even brighter at Mrs. Sanchez, realizing she might be making up the slack at the end of this thing. Hopefully she was paying close attention to everything, but I was pretty sure she was. The last few days she'd seemed just as invested as I was. "I'm so glad you're here to do this with me." I gave her a little hug, and to my surprise she hugged me back. "You're excellent with the kids, and none of us would be able to do this without you"

She blushed and stepped away. "I have to admit, I was a little reluctant at first."

I scoffed. "Ya think?"

"But in my defense, it was only because of what happened with the last musical." Her voice went low. "It nearly ruined my reputation."

"Oh, do tell!" I couldn't help myself, I was a sucker for good theatre gossip.

She looked around the empty hallway, as if to make sure nobody was listening in. I almost had to laugh, but I forced myself to keep a straight face.

"Five years ago, the drama department imploded," she whispered. "It was all over a performance of *The Pirates of Penzance.*"

"Gotta watch out for those pirates," I joked.

"*Pirates* was the last musical we had here. I used to help out with a musical every year. I've been teaching choir for over thirty years. I love musicals, but—" her voice trailed off.

"Out with it!"

"Well," she rushed on, "the drama teacher at the time, Mr. Leery, was dubbing in different voices over the musical numbers. That way he could have the best actors cast in the lead roles but the best voices backstage to do the songs."

"The horror!" This time, I was only half joking. It was actually pretty sad, but I guess, do whatcha gotta do? It wasn't a tactic I believed in, but I'd heard of it before.

"I didn't condone it, but I wasn't the director."

"Right."

"It wouldn't have been so bad if the singing voice he was using for the main character Frederic wasn't his own."

I gasped. "You're kidding!"

"Nope. And when the parents found out, they lost their minds. They said he was using the musical to give himself more opportunities than the kids. Things got out of hand after that because he refused to apologize. In fact, he boasted about it and said he was going to keep doing it. People were really upset. Someone went to the press, and there was even a protest!"

I had a hard time imagining the people of such a boring town protesting, but then again, the more I got to know them, the more I realized they were passionate about their little slice of the world. Maybe I had judged them too harshly upon arrival.

"So what happened?"

"The school board fired him and hasn't hired a new drama teacher since."

This juicy news explained a lot. The saddest part about the whole thing was that in the end, the kids were the ones who got hurt. Whether or not Mr. Leery should've done what he did wasn't really what bothered me most about the story. It was the fact that, after they fired him, the school board never bothered with a replacement. Every school deserved to have a theatre arts department, not just a crummy, run down auditorium with an occasional play directed by random staff members.

Speaking of which…

I pushed open the door to the auditorium and inhaled a familiar spicy citrus scent. The enemy was among us. It didn't take long to spot Principal Beck smiling and chatting with my big fat traitor of stage manager, stage right.

"*Ahem.*" I coughed, drawing the attention of the cast to the back of the auditorium. "Break's over. If you are in the Kansas City scene, you should be on stage and ready to go."

Bags of Doritos and other vending machine treasures crinkled as the cast scurried out of their chairs and up the staircase to the stage.

I waited, one foot tapping impatiently in brand new heels for Principal Beck to catch the hint and get off of my turf. When he didn't, and instead continued to stand there smiling and joking with the cast, his smokin hot swimsuit bod concealed under slacks and a white button down shirt, I decided to exercise my authority.

He may have been the principal, but I was the director of this production.

"Rehearsals are closed!" I called out, eyeing him coldly before gracefully lowering into my red velvet auditorium chair and crossing one leg over the other like a friggin' boss.

Chapter Fourteen

#WinnerTwinner

A nice girl wouldn't admit this, but it felt awfully good watching Foster Beck blush for the second time in two days and then exit the auditorium at my command. I definitely deserved some sort of tequila reward, which is why for the first time since I began filling in for Sophie, I accepted Nurse Alison's invite to join the staff at teachers vs. townies trivia night.

Okay, it wasn't really called that, but that was just a bad **PR** decision on the part of the bar. Wasted opportunity if you asked me.

"I'm so glad you came!" she squealed when I found her high-top table at the back of the crowded brew pub. It was my first Oklahoma bar experience, and I was trying to keep an open mind, but the mounted animal heads dispersed throughout the room were giving me a bit of a deliverance vibe.

I tucked my purse under my stool and placed my phone on the table while I awkwardly climbed onto the seat beside her. Bars always thought these extra tall tables looked cool, and I'm sure they served some purpose for the back of the house, but they were not fun to navigate in heels, and even less fun a few healthy pours in.

"Oh!" cried Alison, eying my phone. "You've got to turn that off and hide it."

"Wait, what?" Turn my phone off? That was crazy talk.

"You can't have phone's on during the game. To keep you from cheating."

"I'm not going to cheat."

"Those are the rules," barked a man three stools down with a baseball cap pulled tight over his eyes.

Fred, I mouthed, and he lifted his eyebrows at me across the table. Jeanine and I had only had one conversation regarding Fred since I caught the two of them canoodling over pizza. She made it very clear that their interoffice romance was top secret, which was probably why Fred got to be at trivia and Jeanine had to make up a lame excuse about her cat needing flea treatment.

Alison patted my arm. "It's just, we've won three weeks in a row. We kind of have a reputation to uphold."

I looked around the room and tried to imagine who within this bar one might desire to have a reputation with. There was literally one cute guy in the place, and he was serving the drinks, not consuming them.

"Please," whispered Alison.

With a very dramatic and authentic sigh, I held the shutdown button on my phone and watched as the bright light of my world fizzled to a black screen of sadness.

I flagged the hot server over. "I'll be needing a margarita please. Don't let my size fool you. Go big or go home."

He grinned exactly how I imagined Blade or Hunter might grin, before saying, "Yes, ma'am," and heading back behind the bar. Okay, I had to admit, the southern accent was a nice touch. He'd be getting a good tip from me, *yes, sir.*

"So, what's the deal?" I asked. "We answer a few questions over onion rings?"

Fred shook his head.

"There are three rounds," said Alison, ignoring his bad attitude. "We don't get to know the topics till the host comes out, but usually they are something pop culture, something sports related, and something random. Ten questions each, and we can all discuss the questions before we write and submit our answers."

"Don't you get enough of this at school?" I asked, smiling appreciatively as our server returned with my drink.

"There are no tests in the nurse's office, besides it will be fun. I promise. You had fun the time you came before, remember?"

I, of course, did not remember, but now that I knew

Sophie had spent a night out with Alison, I knew to curb my questions before I managed to make her think I'd recently had a traumatic brain injury.

"Of course, it's just been so long since I got out of the apartment—I mean house." I was mentally crossing my fingers that Sophie's last trivia adventure wasn't in the last couple of months.

"Too long," confirmed Alison.

I was beginning to be glad that both Sophie and I had agreed that this would be our last twin swap. There were too many close calls to pretend we were still able to slip in and out of one another's lives without other people noticing the differences. It also reminded me just how far my sister and I had grown apart and just how different our lives were now.

I thought about what Beck had said about how Sophie had changed, not just physically but in character. No one had ever noticed that before during a twin swap, and it had me shook almost as much as the pool deck erotic book club incident.

Round one, I was useless. The topic was kitchen conundrums, and those who know me know that adding grocery store rotisserie chicken to boxed pasta is about as gourmet as I get, but round two, I absolutely spanked. Even mysterious Fred was smiling and nodding when I cranked out four correct NBA All Stars answers in a row. It wasn't necessary for them to know that I had once ranked the entire NBA from hottest to very nottest.

When they announced that Team Hale No! would take home the trivia crown for the fourth week running, I felt a little bit invincible. Also a little bit drunk.

"I had no idea you knew so much about early 90's sitcoms," laughed Alison. We'd bailed on the rest of the group and snagged a spot at the bar where we could observe the room's best feature up close. Unfortunately, he spent a lot more time on the floor than behind the bar. How dare he do his job when we were hoping to objectify him and then leave a really average tip?

"My sister and I used to binge watch *Full House* and *Growing Pains* reruns," I explained. "Basically, the greatest moment of our young lives was when Kirk Cameron guest starred on Full House and two separate but equal worlds collided."

Alison smiled. "I didn't know you had a sister either."

Well criminy, alcohol foul number one! I did not have a good exit strategy for the sink hole I had just opened, so it was fortunate that Alison wasn't actually all that interested.

"I wish my sister liked the same things as me. The only thing we've ever had in common is my ex-husband."

"Ouch," I cried, pouring half of my margarita into her empty glass.

"She's the reason I have trust issues. If your own sister can't keep her paws off your partner, how can you trust anyone else will?"

I sighed deeply. Had I ever been cheated on? Absolutely, and I can still remember the gut wrenching feeling that your life is a joke that everyone is in on but you. Alison deserved better, and I felt it necessary to tell her right then and there. Dramatically.

"There is a thing called Girl Code," I declared, shaking my finger in the air like I was making an important speech and everyone in earshot had better tune in. "We're supposed to respect it. Don't let your sister and your douchey ex ruin trusting other women."

Alison clinked her glass against mine before tossing back half of what was left. Hunter/Blade had taken my request to go big or go home very seriously, and tequila was clearly assaulting her taste buds because she grimaced before setting the cup back down.

"Sophie, I have not had sexual relations in eighteen months."

I nearly spit my drink across the counter. "Two adult beverages and you're really letting it all out there."

Alison shrugged. "I may never get you out for drinks again. Might as well say how I feel."

"And you feel…"

"Lonely," answered Alison. I stilled; it wasn't what I thought she would say. "Lonely and bored."

"Maybe we could like… get you a man?" I tried. Actually, I quite liked the idea. Back in California, I hooked my friends up all the time. I was good at shoving people together in forced but highly productive ways. Just ask Luna and Alex, my former next door neighbors who now shared the flat above me. Or Carlos and Timmy, a freelance photographer and makeup artist who I booked for a shoot and the rest, as they say, was history.

"Really?" asked Alison brightly, her expression hopeful.

"Totally!" And I meant it. Next time I was at the gym, I was going to scan the room for potential Alison matches. Surely one of those protein drink guzzling hunks was also a closet trivia fanatic.

"Yay!" She shot back another drink and then leaned in close to whisper under her tequila-laced breath. "I'll date anyone as long as they look like Foster." She giggled, and her dark cloud of a mood shifted into loopy sunshine. "I have a major crush on him."

"Um—" My insides sort of twisted at this confession. I wasn't sure how to respond, so I said nothing.

"He's so hot and so, so, so nice. I bet he's great in bed. Generous, you know?" She waggled her eyebrows.

And here I thought I was drunk.

Smashing a finger against my lips, she shh'ed me. "Don't tell anyone. Okay, Sophieeeee? It's a secret."

I nodded enthusiastically. I was that person that loved to keep my friends' secrets. I took pride in each and every secret that was confided in me. I saw it as an honor and was great at keeping them locked away, even the ones I wish I'd never learned about in the first place.

"Don't worry," I promised.

She looped an arm around me and squeezed. "I'm so glad we're friends now." Her tone was lighter than it had been all night.

Were we friends though?

She didn't even know my real name. I had secrets

of my own. Suddenly, I felt guilty for being here. It was one thing to pretend to be Sophie while I was on the job, but maybe going out on the town as Sophie was taking it a step too far. I was drinking with her co-workers, learning secrets and forging bonds that my sister would know nothing about when she returned. I liked Alison. I liked all these people. They'd turned out to be just as cool as my friends back home. But they weren't *my* people. They were Sophie's. If I lost sight of that all-important fact, our twin-swap would surely end in disaster.

Chapter Fifteen

#DramaDoesntEndInHighSchool

"You officially made it to week three," I pep-talked myself in the little faculty bathroom mirror. "Only one more week to go. Actually, four more days. It's going to be okay. You're going to remember this time fondly and move on with your life." I stared into my hazel eyes for a long moment before attempting to shake away the onset of *feelings*. I washed my hands, ran my fingers through my wavy blonde hair, reapplied my coral lipstick, and strode out of the bathroom like I hadn't just had to tell myself how not to have a meltdown.

I thought I wanted Sophie back as soon as possible, but now that she was days from arriving, I was sad to be nearing the finish line. I couldn't think about that anymore or I would end up back in the damn bathroom.

I had to stay focused on doing what I was here to do without losing sight of my goal. Get in and get out, no making a splash, no getting attached. My real life was waiting, and it was a good one. Rewarding in different ways. Tons of people would kill to make it as an influencer. So, why was I suddenly so depressed to be leaving podunk Oklahoma?

The weekend had flown by in a blur of trying and failing not to warm up to Soph's cat, binge-watching Netflix, and taking naps instead of working on my online content like I'd promised myself to do. Before I knew it, I was in Monday's early morning staff meeting where I got assigned to yet another project without volunteering. This time, I'd be helping out with the homecoming court at Friday night's football game. I didn't complain though. It actually sounded kind of fun. I was definitely more into basketball than football, but watching girls have the night of their lives as their proud fathers drove them around the track in fancy cars? I lived for that sort of thing. And out of morbid curiosity, I was dying to see what Halo High considered formal wear. No mall existed nearby as far as I could tell. There was a very good chance of home sewn dresses and wrinkly internet fails.

In addition to enthusiastically joining the volunteer squad for homecoming, I'd been a model teacher lately. No bullet point on my stupid probation document went unaddressed. I'd been extra careful to follow the lesson plans; I did exactly as I was supposed to and taught directly to the standards. That being said, it was as tedious as watching nail polish dry on its own. Life skills especially. Who filed their own taxes manually these days anyway? Everyone I knew either had a CPA or TurboTax.

The musical though. It was melting my heart. We'd just finished our latest ninety-minute rehearsal, and I was feeling awfully warm and fuzzy about this place and those kids. It was so fun to see the way the kids lit up when the lines or the choreography or the acting clicked. Today's rehearsal had gone off without a hitch.

Well, almost.

Tyler was in economics this morning but didn't bother to show up for rehearsal. It was the second time he'd skipped out. Somehow, I knew he was testing me. Of course, I didn't like that he was bailing on rehearsals—anyone else would get cut without providing an adequate excuse—but I didn't want to push him too hard and have him drop out. It was all about picking battles with Tyler. I had gotten the impression he was the kind of kid who'd been dismissed by the adults in his life. If I did the same thing, the chip on his shoulder would get bigger and I'd prove his point. It wasn't gonna happen.

The school had cleared out by the time rehearsal was over, and I'd gone to the bathroom to have a little cry. Yes, I admit it. I lost it when I realized how much I was going to miss these theatre kids. It hit me like a ton of bricks during the final practice when they were all up there on the stage at the same time, singing and dancing their teenaged hearts out. Badly, yes, but passionately still. It was all that passion that kept triggering the water works.

Sheesh, when had I turned into such a baby?

Sniffling just a little, I walked past the front office and stopped short when raised voices sounded from inside. My heart picked up a beat, and even though I knew better than to eavesdrop, I couldn't help myself. I inched closer and cocked my ear toward the open door. I couldn't see who was in Beck's office without revealing myself, but it didn't really matter, I didn't recognize the voices anyway.

"Why is it all sports with you all the time?" an adult female shrilled. "Not everyone who goes to this school is an athlete!"

"Athletics are proven to bring in more scholarships and more revenue than the arts," a male replied, someone who wasn't Beck.

"That's not the point! Should everything come down to numbers? Some things can't be labeled and put into your neat little boxes, just like some kids can't be."

"Now, hold on," another male voice, also not Beck, jumped in. "Nobody is saying the arts aren't important."

"Then, prove it," the woman went on. "As PTA president, I have no qualms against going to the board of education about this."

"Be my guest, Carli Joe," the first male voice scoffed. "They value the booster club just as much as they value the PTA if not more."

The woman balked at that. "See? Mr. Vance just proved my point!"

I had to stifle a laugh when the woman threw on a Mr. Vance impression and bellowed, "If not more."

I was on Carli Joe's side here. The school didn't have a proper theatre department, the auditorium was an aging dinosaur, the arts classes were sorely funded, and there was a great pep band but a tiny orchestra. At least we had Mrs. Sanchez going for us. That lady was a boss.

"Beck," the second male voice chimed in, "handle this."

I heard the distinctive flap of expensive male dress shoes making their way toward the door, so I hopped backward a few paces and plastered a fake smile on my face.

A man pushed his way out the door. Not just any man. Superintendent Wainwright. I'd looked him up after receiving the administrative probation paper with his pretentiously messy signature at the bottom. He kind of reminded me of a potato, all bald and tan and round and grumpy. It was hard to forget the face of the potato man who wanted to crush your sister's professional dreams.

"Ms. Sparks, is it?" he questioned.

I nodded affirmatively.

"I'll admit, I wasn't surprised to see you and Foster at odds after you voted against him last spring."

"I—what?"

"But then again, tardiness and changing the curriculum are serious offenses."

My cheeks flamed, and before I could utter a coherent retort, the man strode out the front double doors as if anything I had to say in my defense was beneath him.

What exactly did he mean by "voted against him?" Seconds later, a stout man with bulging muscles and a beer gut followed out the door, calling after the superintendent like they were old friends. Judging by his singular focus on biceps, this guy was the booster club president. I'd seen enough *Friday Night Lights* to know that the booster club was basically a gang of student athletes' parents. All they cared about was making sure the football team reigned supreme, and based on the conversation I'd just overheard, anything that got in the way of sports, arts included, was on the chopping block.

"It's a real boys club here sometimes," grumbled the lady, who I could only assume was the PTA president, Carli Joe. Spotting me standing in the hallway, she smiled graciously, tugged at the bottom of her hot pink blazer, and made her way down the hall. I wanted to march right into Beck's office and demand he tell me why the superintendent, president of the PTA, and booster club bozo were arguing over an arts department that barely even existed.

But Superintendent Wainwright's comment still bounced around in my head. Did Beck have a genuine reason to hate me? No, not me, Sophie. I had to remember that I wasn't really *anyone* to Beck at all.

Chapter Sixteen

#MindYourOwnBeeswax

I couldn't stop thinking about what Sophie might have voted against. I had tried any manner of distractions, including but not limited to digging through her kindle and reading the first three chapters of *Hunter's Conquest: A Silver Fox Romance*.

Knowing that my sister found mountain men book smut engaging enough to participate in a monthly discussion should have more than entertained me for the evening, but by the time a rich socialite lost her way in the forest and stumbled upon a pleasure dungeon master with a heart of gold, I was already wondering how late was too late to call Sophie in Mexico.

We hadn't actually spoken on the phone since the conversation that ended in, "by the way, I need you to be me for a month and not a week." She didn't know that she was directing a musical, volunteering for homecoming, oh, and on probation. I was probably going to leave that part off when I gave her the update.

According to Google, it was only an hour behind where she was at so I dialed her number and crossed my fingers that she would answer.

"Ooh, look it's me!" cried Sophie, answering on the first ring and lifting a massive anvil from my chest.

"How goes the vacay?" I asked, hoping a little small talk would loosen her up for the big ask at the end.

"Well, yesterday, I changed Nova's bandage, and I have been on a diet ever since."

"You've been on a diet since yesterday?"

"Yeah, because it's better to be preventive than reactive."

"I see."

"Dani, they removed parts of her body and then sewed her back together like a doll." She was whispering, but apparently not quiet enough because the next sound I heard was a shriek followed by an "Ow!"

"I've been assaulted by a bedpan," she grumbled.

"Any non-medical related fun?"

"Tell her about the boy!" cried Nova in the background.

"Boy?" I asked. Sophie and I weren't super close these days, but my money was on the idea that her solo streak was longer than Alison's. A boy would be awfully big news.

"Eh, not important."

I was not settling for "not important," but if she wasn't ready to talk about whatever foreign romance she was having, I could coax it out of her later. Right now, I needed to know exactly what she did to Foster Beck to fuel his hatred.

"Hey, so I met the super today."

She made a gagging noise.

"I know, he's gross. He looks like a potato."

Sophie snort laughed on the other end of the line. "That is the best, most accurate description of his physical appearance."

"Thank you. I try. But the reason I bring it up is that when I met the potato-head, he said something weird."

"I'll bet."

"He said something about you voting against Principal Beck."

Sophie didn't have a snappy response. In fact, she'd gone silent. When a moment passed and she still wasn't piping up, I probed further.

"I thought that couldn't be true because why would you vote against your boss?" Silence. "And what did you vote against in the first place?"

Sophie sighed. "He wasn't my boss at the time. Look, I know Foster is bitter about it, but honestly I was doing what I thought was best for him and the students." This was starting to veer into controversial territory. How could Sophie know what was best for Foster?

"I'm going to need more details because for as long as I have been you, I've been getting a load of mixed signals. If he has good reason to dislike you, then I should probably be cutting him some slack."

Sophie growled. "I distinctly remember telling you not to bang my boss."

I rolled my eyes. "I was not talking about hooking up with Foster, I was talking about giving him a little leeway for being hurt by you."

"Ugh," groaned Sophie. "I don't like how you are calling him Foster. Please tell me you are not forging some relationship with my boss that I'm going to have to undo when I get home this weekend."

I was starting to get impatient, possibly because that was exactly what I wanted to do and possibly because, for better or worse, I already had.

"Sophie, I'm not screwing anything up. I taught boring taxes, I did a thing with a tire, I'm directing the most cheesy musical on the planet for cripes sake. You have nothing to worry about. Please just answer my question."

"Musical? I definitely did not ask you to direct a musical."

"Sophie," I begged.

"Fine. Our last principal left very suddenly. The job wasn't open very long, and the school board asked me to sit on the hiring panel. They wanted a staff representative, and Foster and I had worked together for a few years, so they thought I might have a good perspective on his ability to do the job."

"And you voted for him not to get the job?"

"Yeah, but not in a sinister way. It wasn't that I thought he was a bad fit for principal. It was more like I thought he would miss out on the things he enjoyed about working with kids. The principal spends all day in meetings. It's purely administrative. The biggest thrill he's going to get now is putting dud teachers on probation."

I gulped. Yeah, now was definitely not the time to tell her I'd managed to get her lumped in with the duds.

"He's really good with the kids and as a teacher he got to interact with them all the time. You probably don't get to see that, but I did, and I don't regret my vote."

The thing was I could totally see that. But I could also see why Foster would be furious that Sophie didn't think he could handle the promotion.

"They could've plucked any bossy, budget-minded person for principal. Losing Foster as the favorite history teacher meant losing someone who really connected with the students. I was supposed to be making the best decision for the school, and I think I did."

"I get it. I just kinda wish you two could have talked this thing out before you sent me in there to deal with the aftermath."

"I know," said Sophie, her voice softening. "I'm sorry for that. If I'd known we were going to have to swap, I would have tried to make it as smooth as possible for you. I swear."

Sophie's explanation wasn't going to make it any easier to deal with Foster, but at least I knew *why* he was upset with her. Maybe I didn't have to be so stingy about the closed rehearsal thing. Heck, maybe he would know how to handle Tyler. I certainly wasn't getting anywhere with the kid.

But how hard had I been trying, really? I could do better. No, not could, I *would* do better. Which is how I ended up finishing the conversation with Soph and logging into our school's computer system to look up Tyler's address. Google Maps placed it ten minutes away. I jumped up and gathered my supplies to leave. I could swing by and make sure he was okay to come to rehearsal tomorrow all in time to make it to the nine PM "Midnight Mamba" class at the gym. Why they counted nine as midnight around here was a mystery to me.

I peered up at the house—if you could even call it that—feeling a little bit stunned. I don't know where I expected a kid like Tyler to live, but it wasn't this gorgeous Persian mansion, complete with a dolphin fountain off the front. I didn't even know Halo had a neighborhood like this, but here I was, smack-dab in the middle of Oklahoma wealth. Apparently, it was as ostentatious as Dana Point wealth with everything out there on full display.

I rang the doorbell, and a smiley hispanic lady in a blue maid's uniform answered the door. "Can I help you, Miss?"

It suddenly hit me that perhaps this wasn't a good idea after all. Was this even allowed? Maybe I was screwing up. I swallowed and tried to relax my balled up fists. "Um, hi. I'm looking for Tyler?" It came out as a question, and I pressed on quickly. "I'm his teacher and director. I just wanted to check in with him."

"Right this way." She led me through the sparkling foyer to the formal sitting room off to the side. I settled on the edge of a plush, velvet white couch and looked around. Everything looked expensive and breakable. Nothing like the middle-class suburban home I'd grown up in.

"Mr. and Mrs. VanHill are traveling. Is Tyler causing trouble again? I could leave a message for them."

"No." I waved her away. "Everything is fine. I just wanted to speak to Tyler, thanks."

She nodded and shuffled off to retrieve him.

"What are you doing here?" he grumbled, sweeping into the room and plopping himself down on the chair opposite mine. "Is this about missing rehearsal? Because I had a good reason."

"And what reason was that?"

He went quiet.

"Tyler, I'm not mad," I went on. "I just want to know the truth."

"I'm not off book yet, okay? And I don't know if I'll be ready in time."

I frowned. "Then, that's even more reason to come to rehearsal."

He rolled his eyes, his face falling into his usual defiant mask.

"Do your parents know about the musical?"

He shrugged. "They wouldn't come anyway."

My heart twisted at that. What was the point of all

this wealth if they didn't care to come to see their son star in the high school musical? "I bet they would if you told them."

He just shrugged again. "You know, I heard them talking about sending me to military school? What kind of parents send their only kid to military school?" His mouth wobbled. "Whatever. Can't be worse than Halo."

I highly doubted that but knew when to keep my mouth shut. "What can I do to help you get off book faster?"

He worried his bottom lip between his teeth but didn't say anything.

"Maybe we can schedule a few lunch-time practices to go over lines? I'd even be willing to come in early."

"I'm not coming in early." He laughed, but at least his mood had shifted.

"Okay, good, because I hate early mornings, too."

"I noticed." He sighed. "Yeah, sure, I'll come to your classroom at lunch."

"You're going to be a great Curly." I promised. "In fact, you already are. You just have to believe in yourself as much as I believe in you."

His eyes watered, and he looked away, cheeks going pink. "Thanks."

"And maybe I can ask Kayla to come to some of our lunchtime practices?" I continued. "We still need to block out the kiss, you know."

He grinned from ear to ear and pointed at me. "That, I do know."

I laughed and said goodbye, making sure to stop the

maid on the way out when Tyler had gone back upstairs. "Actually, I do want to leave a message. Can you please tell them their son is the lead in the school musical next weekend? Friday is opening night. Seven PM. It would really mean a lot if they were there."

"Of course, Miss." She nodded. "And if they can't come, I'll make sure I can."

"That would be great," I replied and left for the gym, even though it was pretty sad that the maid was offering to be Tyler's stand-in parents.

But during the whole drive, all I could think about was how that actually wouldn't be great. Who would want their maid to show up to their school performance instead of their actual mom and dad? When I was a theatre kid, it meant the world to see my parents in the audience, smiling up at me and applauding and acting like I was the most talented human on the planet. Everyone deserved that. Tyler deserved that. I wondered how many more of my students were in similar positions. Rich or poor, broken home or not, so many of them had to be dealing with hard stuff. Doing something extra for Tyler, even as small as lunchtime rehearsals, felt like maybe I had a purpose for being in Halo after all. I just hoped I hadn't broken another school policy by showing up at his house uninvited like that. Last thing Sophie needed was a reason for Beck to enact his final retaliation against her. She'd never forgive me.

Chapter Seventeen

#MaybeIDontSuckAfterAll

I woke up the following morning feeling like there was a very good chance I was going to slay the day. A feeling that only got stronger when Tyler strolled into my class at noon, shoved the door shut behind him and said, "K, help me memorize this thing."

What this kid didn't know is that I had a lot of experience running lines with theatre boys. Usually, my objective was less about making the show better and more about making out afterwards, but nonetheless, many a young man found himself off book by the director's deadline thanks to my assistance.

"First thing you should know is that you are probably already closer than you think." I raised one eyebrow at him. "You would know that for sure if you hadn't skipped rehearsal."

Tyler shook his head and flipped through his script with an irritated little grimace. He was warming up to me. He just didn't know it. I snatched the book from his hand and flipped open to Curly's first scene.

"What I mean is, it is a lot harder to memorize lines when you're practicing alone. You second guess yourself, and the temptation to look at the page and confirm you're in the right place prevents you from digging deep and remembering the lines on your own. Here is what we are going to do. We will go through the scene, and if you forget your line, make it up."

Tyler frowned. "How is that going to help?"

"Look, you make it up, and we keep going. Then, at the end, we can see how much you really don't know and how much you are able to work through when you don't beat yourself up for forgetting a line."

At first, Tyler was hesitant. More than once I had to yank the script out of his reach, but by the end of lunch he had at least sixty percent of the scene memorized. Here was the shocking part: helping him was more rewarding than all of the times I made out with a theatre hunk in my youth. I wasn't positive that do-gooder teacher endorphins were a real thing, but it felt like they were.

What didn't feel quite as nice was the incredible sensation of hunger rolling through my belly and reminding me that I had completely forgotten to eat lunch.

Usually, I used my prep period to schedule Instagram posts and catch up on DMs, but I was never going to make it through life skills and rehearsal without some form of food, so I snuck into the cafeteria and begged Ms. Lula, the lunch lady, for a go at the salad bar before they wrapped it up for the day.

I don't traditionally moan with joy when biting into iceberg lettuce and bacon bits, but famine can change a woman.

"That good, eh?" A male voice chuckled.

I nearly choked on my shredded carrot. Of course Foster Beck had the same break period as me. Otherwise, how could he make sure I wasn't violating school norms and being even the tiniest bit interesting?

"I missed my lunch." I wiped the excess ranch from the corner of my mouth. "This was the only thing left that didn't give me horrible flashbacks to high school lunches past."

Foster smiled. "What a terrible thing to say on chicken patty day."

Was he flirting with me? Because that's what it felt like. He was hot and cold, this one. I mean obviously the words chicken patty were not a sexy pick up line, but he was leaning up against the staff room counter with his arms crossed in the "look at my bulging biceps through my businessman shirt" kind of way, and his smile was really more of a smirk. Like a cocky, hot guy smirk.

My brain immediately took a detour back to that night at the pool. Now, I couldn't unsee his dark hair dripping with water and his pectorals…

"Sophie?"

"Sorry," I answered. Was my entire body blushing, or did it just feel that way? "Did you say something?"

Foster grinned. He was definitely onto me, but I was not going to give him the pleasure of watching me squirm. A girl could lust. There were no rules against that.

"I was just asking how the play is going. Benjamin mentioned you'd been having some trouble getting Tyler to show up."

I straightened my spine. Benjamin, that little weasel. "You've got nothing to worry about. Tyler is back on track to being the perfect Curly."

"I hope so. This play is important…" Foster cut himself off, and I was pretty sure it had something to do with what I had overheard the other day outside his office. Suddenly, I felt compelled to assure him it would all be okay. That the show wouldn't just go on, but that it would be good, maybe even great.

And then, the bell rang. Probably talking to him was the only legitimate reason to be late for class, but I still didn't want to risk it. The last thing I wanted to do was have to tell Sophie she lost her job because I was heffing down cafeteria salad. I said a quick goodbye and went off to teach life skills. Today's fascinating topic? The cost benefit analysis of buying a car versus leasing one. Always a party, that class.

Walking into rehearsal, I was ready to continue my current streak of awesome. There was just one teensy issue. The piano bench where Mrs. Sanchez usually sat, polyester pants gliding along wood as her little glasses bobbed precariously on her nose, was vacant.

Dani Sparks was the late one. Mrs. Sanchez was not. Not once since rehearsals had started had she so much as been late returning from the bathroom.

"Has anyone seen Mrs. Sanchez?"

Benjamin glanced up at me from his perch on the end of the stage. A worried and overly dramatic expression crossed his face as he turned to the cast member beside him and said, "She doesn't know yet."

"Doesn't know what?" I asked, feeling all the good day vibes draining from my body.

Benjamin sighed and began his quick-paced scuttle up the aisle way to the back of the theatre where I stood waiting to discover what new and exciting obstacle this production had just been dealt.

"At approximately two-fifteen this afternoon, Mrs. Sanchez took her usual break. Though it has been ill advised by her doctor, Mrs. Sanchez often finds herself in want of a Snickers bar at that time." Benjamin paced in front of me, his hands tucked behind his back, his face serious. "The vending machine, however, was sold out, and she instead selected B34, the celery stick and ranch dipping sauce combo." Behind him Kayla nodded solemnly. Just how many times had Ben told this story today?

I held up one hand to halt the kid before he proceeded to tell me the rest of the details like a key witness on Perry Mason.

"Wrap it up, Ben. Where is our accompanist?"

"Puking," he shout-whispered. "Hopefully from food poisoning."

"Hopefully?" I cried. "What is hopeful about that?"

"Well," said Ben, matter of factly. "if it's the flu, she could be out for a week."

My heart dropped to a subterranean level. There was only a week left before opening night. We couldn't rehearse without a piano player, especially not with the full dress rehearsals next week.

"Food poisoning is two days tops," continued Ben. "Anymore than that and you're just milking it."

This could not be happening. I needed backup stat. I closed my eyes and took a deep breath. Ben was supposed to be the stage manager, now it was time for him to do his job.

"Ben, I need you to run the first half of rehearsal."

His eyes lit up in a way that could only be described as evil.

"Forget what is on the schedule. Run only the non-musical portions." I leaned in close and whispered, "And be nice! This isn't a Juilliard audition."

I was halfway out the auditorium door when I heard his loud and shrill voice proclaim, "Actors on stage. No dilly dallying. Enough time has been wasted already."

Lord help us all.

Ms. Thompson usually took her sweet time leaving the building. If I was lucky, I could still catch her. I didn't know a soul in Halo that wasn't on this staff, but she seemed like the type to have a few artsy contacts. I was judging this solely by the fact that she refused to use hair ties and, instead, wrapped her big curly mess into a french twist secured only by a pencil.

Sure enough, she was still digging through her email when I knocked on her open classroom door.

"Hey, girl, hey," she cried, causing me to wince. "How goes the musical?"

I perched on top of the nearest student desk. "Not the best."

Her chin wrinkled up in a concerned pout. "Well that's not good. How can I help?"

"You don't happen to be a secret pianist, do you?"

She giggled at the word pianist, and I resisted an urge to pick up the abandoned protractor from the desk beneath me and chuck it at her head.

"Be mature."

"Sorry," said Jeanine composing herself. "I do not possess that gift."

My face fell.

"But I know a guy who plays beautifully."

This was exactly why I had chosen to ask Jeanine. That and Alison left at two every day.

"Sweet, do you think you can call in a favor and get him to help. Like right now?"

Jeanine chewed on her bottom lip. "I can definitely get him to help, Dani, but there is a good chance you're not going to like it when you find out who it is."

I let out a primal growl that caused Jeanine to scoot back in her rolling chair.

"I'm sorry, but he's the only one I know, and besides, I think it would be a nice break for him, a chance to interact with the kids."

"Blah blah blah! Foster is great with the kids. Poor

Foster never gets to play with the children anymore. Whiny whiny boo boo."

"Do you want help or not?"

"Ugh, fine. Just ask him for me please."

Jeanine squeezed her eyes shut and pursed her lips together.

"He's right behind me, huh?"

She bobbed her head affirmatively, the little pencil eraser in her air laughing at me with each sway. I turned to find Foster Beck beet red and gawking from the doorway.

"So, you heard that whole little rant, did you?"

"I think so." He raised an eyebrow.

"Well, come on then." I jumped off the desk and marched out the door. I wasn't about to beg for his help. "The show must go on."

Chapter Eighteen

#StageKiss

As I reentered the auditorium with Foster Beck at my side, Ben was terrorizing the underclassmen.

"You see this X on the floor?" He strode across the stage, pointing like a mad man. "I didn't put it there because there's buried treasure under the plywood. Get to your mark or don't bother coming to rehearsal."

"Benjamin!" I yelled. "What did I say about being nice?"

He threw his hands up in frustration and huffed down the stairs to chug from his water bottle.

"Oh, wow," whispered Foster. "That's a lot."

I turned to look at him, my patience a thin thread already. "Yes, thank you for suggesting Ben be moved from the chorus to a position of *authority*."

Foster's mouth stretched into an uncomfortable grin. "Right then, I'll see myself to the piano."

"You do that."

I don't know what I thought would happen when Foster sat down at that piano and began running through his scales, but I did not expect to sink into a cushy red theatre chair and think to myself, *I wonder if he can play Ed Sheeran songs too, or perhaps a nice Backstreet Boy ballad.*

I watched for a moment as his hands ran up and down the keyboard. He cocked his head toward the piano, listening to be sure it was in tune before stretching his fingers and running through the introduction of the opening number. As if summoned, the cast began to assemble on stage.

In true director's fashion, I called out, "From the top!"

It wasn't food poisoning. Mrs. Sanchez called in sick for the rest of the week with the flu—poor thing. Luckily, it looked like nobody else in the cast and crew had caught it. I counted my lucky stars through Wednesday's and Thursday's rehearsals that everybody showed up on time, ready to work.

And Beck, too.

He had stepped into the choir director's role seamlessly. He played the piano like a champ and advised the kids on how to get their musical numbers into shape. Seeing him like this made it pretty clear that Sophie was right about Foster belonging with the kids not ruling over the administration. He was gifted at the piano, but he was even more gifted at motivating these kids to reach down inside themselves and pull out the parts that made them feel like less. I couldn't help but notice how Kayla sang with more confidence when he was the one cueing her in, and Tyler didn't just boom through the lyrics the way he did with Mrs Sanchez. He rehearsed like the room was full, and the energy left me reeling.

I knew that Foster had a million other things to do and places to be, yet he arrived without complaint and gave us his full attention. Was he doing this for the kids? For the school? For me? Sophie? I was starting to get confused. Also, we were nearing the end of Thursday's rehearsal, and I was staring—practically drooling—as Beck helped Tyler with a ballad.

Ben waved a hand in front of my face. "Hello, earth to Sophie."

"Ms. Sparks," I corrected him.

"Just testing you." He smirked wickedly. He was propped up in the chair next to mine, also watching Tyler and Beck do their thing up front. Farther on the stage, the rest of the cast was practicing some line dancing they'd need for a few of the numbers. "You were right, you know," Ben said. "I would've embarrassed myself as Curly."

"I wouldn't go that far."

"I would have."

"Okay, fine."

He continued to stare at Tyler, a flash of jealousy crossing his face when Tyler hit a particularly tough note as if it was nothing to him. "But that doesn't mean I have to like it," he continued. "Maybe if I'd had someone to help me like that," he waved between Beck and Tyler, "I could have been decent at least."

"I was a theatre kid, too. Did I ever tell you that?"

He side-eyed me.

"Don't look so shocked."

"Go on."

"Well, I was in your exact same shoes many times. I loved to act and was good at it, but try as I might, I wasn't a good singer." I shrugged. "You could invest in vocal training and pursue musicals, or you could let it go and focus on strengthening the talents you already have."

He rolled his eyes. "Oh, like you did? You're an economics teacher."

I wanted to confess my L.A. stories and rise to internet fame right then and there, but I held back. "Where are you applying for school?" I asked instead.

He shrugged. "Anywhere cheap or with good scholarships that also has a strong theatre department." He sighed, looking around at his peers. "Also, somewhere less…"

"Conservative?" I guessed.

He nodded once but didn't meet my eyes. It was fine. I suspected enough and wasn't going to push Benjamin to confess anything to me.

"You would fit right in in L.A.," I said encouragingly. "Stereotypes aside, it's a great place to be for talented actors such as yourself."

"Not New York City?"

I shrugged. "Well, if you want to get the vocal training and continue to pursue the stage, then absolutely go for New York. But the thing about L.A. is it's more welcoming to all different kinds of actors. Hollywood is brutal, don't get me wrong, but there's a ton of opportunity there. I knew so many people who gave up on Broadway to try film and television acting instead when I lived in L.A."

He tilted his head, frowning. "You lived in L.A.?"

Shit! Sophie never lived in L.A. She'd never even been. I'd moved there after college and then down to Dana Point shortly after making it as an influencer. "Um—" I stumbled over my words. "Not me, I mean my sister lives there and we talk all the time. And I visit. A lot. Every chance I get. Sometimes it feels like I practically live there, too."

What was wrong with me?

Skepticism flashed through his eyes as I continued to ramble. "Acting in general is a ruthless business. Lots of rejection. But the film industry is packed full of jobs. There's the actors, but that can be hard to break in, you know, but also there's directors, the casting people, art directors, props departments, the lighting and camera crews, tons of stylists, location managers, producers, sound—"

"Are you saying you don't think I can make it in acting?" His voice was steel, and he glared at me through long black lashes.

My stomach did a little twist of guilt. "No! Not at all."

His eyes narrowed even further as I backpedaled.

"I mean, yes, you can make it in acting. Absolutely! I'm just saying you're also good at managing people. You like to be in charge. Not everyone does. If you have a desire to work in the film industry, I'm sure you can build a great career in L.A."

"Got it," he snapped. "I'll consider L.A." His response was boiling hot as he jumped from the chair and stormed out of the auditorium, slamming the double doors behind him like only a true thespian could.

Everyone screeched to a halt. Even Beck stopped playing the piano.

"Carry on," I waved at the startled faces. "One more time through, and then we'll move on to the next number."

Beck looked back at me with concern. *Everything okay?* he mouthed.

I gave him a thumbs up and sank down into the uncomfortable chair. I was pretty sure I'd just screwed up that whole conversation—like big time stuck my foot in my mouth. My discussion on Monday night with Tyler had gone so well that I'd thought I was good at connecting with teenagers now. Ben just proved that clearly wasn't the case. Hopefully the kid didn't hate me. Hopefully, in trying to help, I hadn't said something to cause irrevocable damage. And I especially hoped he wouldn't question why Sophie had magically acquired insider knowledge into the Hollywood film scene. It was very likely Ben was on to me.

I dug my phone from my purse and shot Sophie a text. **Call me tonight. We need to talk.**

The cast finished up the musical number—the big party scene with the line dancing—and I clapped, jumping up from my seat to join them. "That was great, you guys! Now, just picture it in costume with all those old-fashioned skirts flying."

They smiled at one another, imagining it, too.

"Tomorrow, we're going to do costume fittings instead of rehearsals. We should be done with plenty of time for everyone to get ready for the homecoming game." The entire auditorium buzzed with excited energy. "And good luck to Kayla who's been nominated for homecoming court."

She blushed from ear to ear while everyone cheered her on. Earlier, there'd been a pep-rally for the football team, and she'd been announced as one of the nominees.

Everyone was excited, myself included. It had been eight years since I'd been to a high school football game. I'd love them when I was in school. I'd never missed a chance to cheer on our team while simultaneously ogling the guys on the field. I wasn't planning to check out teenagers now, of course, but there was a certain someone I wanted to see outside of a dress shirt and tie.

"Take a seat," I continued. "Tyler and Kayla, it's time to practice the proposal scene."

Yup, also known as the cheesiest kissing scene of all time. Everyone ohh'd and ahh'd while Tyler grinned suggestively and Kayla pouted like someone had just told her she needed to get a cavity filled.

"It's not so bad." Beck laughed, patting Kayla on the back. "It's only a stage kiss."

"Yeah, don't worry, sweetheart, we can make out somewhere more privately later," Tyler deadpanned with a wink.

"Okay, that's not helping," I chimed in.

The cast and crew settled into the squeaky auditorium seats while I blocked out Kayla and Tyler on the stage. By now, the lines were memorized, so we only needed to get the action of the scene down and put it all together. Beck stood off to the side, offering a helpful comment or two when needed.

"All right." I stood back. "Let's run it."

"I wanna see Curly awful bad. Got to see him," Kayla cried into the darkened stage. This was happening right after her character had a scary altercation with the antagonist, Jud, and now the poor girl wanted to run into the arms of the childhood friend who'd turned into the man of her dreams.

"Then, whyn't you turn around and look, you crazy woman?" Tyler stepped forward.

Kayla turned and jumped into his arms for a hug. She was a little stiff, but we could work on that. They continued the scene. Kayla babbled on about not knowing what to do, and Tyler finally cut in with a gruff, "Here, I'll show you."

And now for the kiss.

He jerked her against him, leaned in, and—

"Wait!" Kayla squirmed from him. "Isn't this supposed to be a stage kiss?" She looked back to Beck and widened her eyes desperately. "As in not a real kiss, right? Like, we just pretend."

"That's lame." Tyler scoffed. "Who would believe that?"

"It should be a real kiss," I announced decidedly. "But we need to work on your chemistry." I glared at Tyler. "Stop scaring her away." And then back to Kayla. "And be professional. It's not going to kill you to kiss your co-star."

Beck started to speak, but I held up my hand to cut him off. "But to compromise, we can do a bit of both."

"What do you mean?" Kayla questioned, her pink mouth returning to a pout.

"Well, he'll lean in and kiss you, mouths closed, while you're facing each other so the audience can see the beginning of the kiss. Then, he'll dip you backwards and away from the audience, so it looks like you're deepening the kiss."

"All right." Tyler grinned.

"Keyword is it *looks* like we're deepening the kiss." Kayla glared. "But we're actually not kissing anymore *at all*."

"Exactly." I nodded. "Why don't you give it a try?"

They did, and this time, Kayla held her hands up and away from him so when he leaned her back and let her go, she fell to her butt.

"Ouch!" Her face was bright red.

"Try it again," I coached. "Kayla, put your arms around his neck for crying out loud. You're about to get engaged. You love this man, remember?"

"Yeah, remember?" Tyler mocked.

"Not helping, Tyler," I growled. "You're supposed to be a *man* here, and a man wouldn't drop his girl on her butt. You need to dip her and then bring her back up before you let her go."

They tried it again, and while nobody fell, it wasn't much better than the first time. They were the textbook definition of awkward. There was no other way to define it. I'd hoped that awkwardness would translate into some kind of sexy "will they won't they" sizzle to the audience, but from looking at them now, they were rapt with amusement. Any minute and this kiss would have the crowd in stitches.

"Again!"

On the third try, Tyler swung Kayla back so fast that, this time, they both fell. Him on top of her. "Well, hello there, beautiful." He laughed as if he'd planned the whole thing.

"Get off me!" She pushed him away.

"Oh, for crying out loud," I huffed. "It's not that hard."

"It's not that easy either," Tyler replied, getting up and brushing himself off. He was beginning to redden as well. "Not when your partner kisses like a dead fish."

"What?" Kayla snarled. Her eyes were two round, horrified saucers.

I pointed to Beck. "Come here. Let's show them how to do the stupid dip."

By this point, Beck's expression was scrunched in as much frustration as my own. He strode over purposefully and pulled me into his arms. He didn't actually kiss me because that would be inappropriate, but he did press himself to me, turn my body to the side, and dip me backward.

Our eyes locked.

His were stormy blue but hooded with desire. I'd seen that look in men before. I knew exactly what it meant. When his gaze traveled down to my lips and back up again, my breath hitched. I leaned forward, wanting—no, needing—to kiss him. It was an intensity that crashed through my body like an ocean wave, cutting me off from everything and everyone else, pulling me under.

He leaned closer, too, as if eager to taste my lips. This was it. We were so close now, bodies aligned, mouths centimeters apart…

"Get a room!" someone called out.

Beck dragged us back to standing and stepped away so fast that I was hot all over and utterly speechless.

He wasn't. "Try it again, Tyler," he said sharply, "Just like that."

"But don't forget the kiss." I found a huskier version of my own voice.

Beck's gaze fired back to me again. "He won't."

Chapter Nineteen

#Homecoming

"Listen, Soph," I said through the line. "We've got to talk about L.A." On the other end, my sister must have been in the middle of a mariachi band or something because I could hardly hear her over the music and jeering.

"L.A.?" Her voice was slightly slurred.

"Wait, are you drunk?" I was a bit shocked. The woman never got drunk, not even in college. She was always the designated driver and wouldn't partake in anything that impaired her judgement.

She giggled. "Maybe a little."

I couldn't help it, I leaned back against her couch and full on belly-laughed. "Mexico isn't so bad now, is it?"

"Oh, Dani, it's wonderful!" Her voice was sweet as honey. "I met someone!"

"Ha! I knew it. Who is he? Spill."

The line went quiet for a minute as if she were holding her finger over the microphone while she talked to whoever this special someone was. A sexy deep voice murmured back to her. "Sorry." She returned to the line. "I can't really talk right now."

"But we need to talk," I rushed on. "Just give me two minutes, okay?"

"Okay, one sec." She didn't sound annoyed, more just busy. And drunk.

The line went quiet again, and moments, later she was back. "I'm in the bathroom now, but we're leaving any second. I won't have any cell phone service, so make it quick."

"Ooh la la," I gushed. "Going on a fancy holiday with your new boyfriend?"

"Dani! Just out with it. What's going on?"

"Okay, so a few things. Number one, if anyone asks, tell them you visit me in L.A. a lot and that's how you know about what it's like in the film industry there."

"But you don't even live in L.A. anymore."

"I live close enough. And number two, when you get back, you have to let me finish directing *Oklahoma!*. Next week is dress rehearsals, and then it's opening night on Friday, and you can't possibly take over without screwing up and giving our secret away."

"Agreed," she said simply. Relief washed through me. I was worried she'd put up a fight. "But I have a request of my own, too."

"Okay…"

"Well, Marco needs me for a few more days. I was wondering if I could change my flight from Sunday to Wednesday."

"Marco *needs* you, does he?" I teased. "Sexy."

I expected her to gasp or deny it, but she only sighed and said, "He is."

"Well, I'll be damned, is my sister in love?"

She went super quiet, and I decided not to push her on this.

"Okay, yes, fly back Wednesday. You can take over teaching classes for Thursday and Friday, but you'll need to leave the building right away so I can step in and take over the musical stuff. Got it?"

"Got it." Her voice was happier than I'd ever heard it. Where was the girl I knew who had planned her entire life out? That girl would never purposely postpone her return home and pass off her responsibilities to the less-than-perfect twin. AKA, me.

"I gotta go," she rushed out breathily. "He's waiting."

"Where are you going anyway?"

The line went dead.

Well, wherever she was and whatever she was doing, I was happy she was happy. This Marco character had better be one of the good ones, or I'd have to fly to Mexico myself and destroy him. When she got back she'd better be prepared to answer a million questions, and I didn't care how deep her blush got, I wanted to know each and every detail of this little sordid adventure. Sophie had gone to Mexico and fallen in love! I still couldn't believe it. I mean, it was quick. It had only been, what? Three weeks? That was super fast for someone as guarded as my sister. I hoped whatever happened it didn't end in heartbreak.

Putting it from my mind, I hunkered down for the night to work on the lesson plans for next week. I wanted to get ahead because I knew things were about to get crazy busy. I didn't mind it though. It was actually pretty cool to see how far I'd come in only three weeks in Halo.

Hours later, somewhere between grading a bazillion boring papers for economics and planning how I was going to explain mortgages to the seniors when I'd never so much as considered a mortgage myself—yet, here I was sitting in Sophie's mortgaged house—my phone rang. Yes, saved by the bell! Cheesy? I didn't care.

I picked it up to find an overdraft notification from my bank flashing at me. "What?" My heart dropped. I clicked it only to see that my account balance had gone into the negative by a few hundred dollars. "Well, that's not good," I groaned.

I moved money over from my meager savings account to cover the difference and popped over to my Instagram DMs to see if Annie from Live Love Laugh had good news for me. They'd never taken this long to issue a payment before. I'd sent another follow up a few days ago and was hoping for the green by now. Sure enough, there was a message. The first word alone made my heart sink even further.

• • •

Unfortunately, your numbers were quite low on the last unboxing, therefore your payment will be significantly less than with previous boxes. We'll issue that on Monday. In the meantime, please consider how you can improve your account. We'd love to keep working together in the future but, staying on brand is obviously very important to us here at Live Love Laugh. XO, Annie.

"XO, my ass!" I threw the phone down onto the couch and then immediately picked it back up. I needed to get some more good pictures up with catchier captions. I needed more clicks, more likes, and loads more comments. I couldn't afford to lose momentum in my real business—my real life—over a silly teaching gig that wasn't actually mine.

By Friday afternoon, I wasn't focused on the job whatsoever. My mind was entirely wrapped up in getting my analytics up. Gripping my phone in my hand like it was my life support, I scrolled through my Instagram account, making sure I'd replied to all the latest comments. I'd made a real effort to keep up on it since my wake-up call last night. No way was I going to let everything I'd worked so hard for slip away.

"Sophie? Everything okay?"

I popped my head up and smiled at Beck. I'd been waiting for him in his office and had gotten lost in my social media. *Whoops.*

"Yup!" I slid my phone into my purse, vowing to check it again as soon as possible, but maybe now wasn't the right time to be glued to my phone when I was supposed to be helping Sophie's boss.

His eyes traveled down the floral cotton dress I'd borrowed from Soph's closet. It was a little too youthful, a little too short at the bottom and too covered at the top, but the hungry look in Beck's eyes confirmed it was exactly the perfect choice for tonight.

"Remind me what my job is?" I asked, raising an eyebrow.

Beck straightened the bowtie at his neck and grinned down at me, the previous lust in his eyes clearing. Much to my dismay, he wasn't dressed down tonight, it was the opposite. Actually, maybe that wasn't such a bad thing…

"You have the very exciting job of drumming up the crowd for the big coronation moment."

I glanced out the window of his office and toward the football field. The game didn't start for another half an hour and already cars were bumper to bumper in the parking lot.

"Do I get to know the winner?" I asked, waggling my eyebrows hopefully.

"It is not our Laurey, if that's what you're asking," said Beck. "The artsy kids never win." He laughed, but was he really joking? I thought about the PTA president, Carli Joe, and her passionate claim that it was the kids who were different than got left behind at Halo.

"We could rig it," I offered.

Foster chewed the corner of his cheek, looking at me with interest. Was he actually considering swapping the actual winner for Kayla? How scandalous!

"I was joking," I cried, when he'd been thinking about it for a beat too long. "We can't steal that moment of glory from the rightful winner. Lord knows the Homecoming Queen never amounts to anything after high school."

That wasn't true considering Yours Truly had been queen, but I was playing a part here. Foster laughed along and grabbed the gold envelope off his desk. He tucked it in the inside breast pocket of his tan sports jacket and tilted his head to the side.

"You know, until this year I wouldn't have thought you were the Homecoming Queen type, but…"

I held back a grin.

"But what?" I asked flirtatiously. It was a dangerous question, but at the moment, I kinda wanted him to see Dani instead of Sophie.

The moment stretched between us, his chance to flirt back.

"Nothing," Foster said at last with a shake of his head. "Come on, we want to get a good seat for the game. Otherwise, by halftime, we'll be covered in popcorn and the spit of a hateful crowd."

"Dramatic," I whispered as we left his office and headed toward the football field.

Out of the corner of my eye I spotted Alison hopping out of her adorably sensible vehicle. She wasn't in scrubs like at work. Instead, she wore dark denim jeans that hugged every curve and a cute little leather jacket with a yellow scarf wrapped around her neck. She waved at us before disappearing into the stands and a wave of guilt reminded me that this guy beside me, the one I would be sitting next to for the whole game and had nearly kissed not twenty-four hours ago, was also the guy she had a big ol' thang for.

"You want popcorn?" I asked, putting a two foot gap between the two of us.

Foster shrugged but handed me five bucks before leaving to save our seats. I didn't actually want popcorn, but I needed to mentally unpack how I was going to get through the rest of the night without grabbing Principal Beck by his silly red suspenders and pulling him in for the uncensored version of that stage kiss.

A little hip check to the side shook me from my stupor. "Hey!" Alison beamed a flawless, autumnal-tinted smile in my direction. "I saw you walking with Foster. Are you two sitting together?"

My knee jerk reaction was to lie, but there wasn't much point in that. I had popcorn for two in my hand, and I wasn't going to walk back there and sit alone like a weirdo.

"Yeah, we are doing the coronation thing at halftime."

"Great!" said Alison, tucking her hands behind her back like a little girl and batting her eyelashes up at me. "I was wondering if maybe you could talk me up a bit while you have his attention."

Considering I had thought she would ask to join us, this request was a bit of a relief.

"I got you girl."

Alison squealed, and I watched her long auburn hair bounce up and down as she bopped back down the grass toward her seat. She was pretty and obviously intelligent, she killed at trivia, and they didn't turn dimwits into nurses, but was she Foster's type? It seemed like if she had been, she wouldn't need me to put a good word in for her.

I didn't really think the two of them dating would result in anything long term, but I was also keenly aware that the more I thought about Foster Beck, the more I thought about removing his clothing and letting the sparks fly where they willed. It was probably a good idea to take the energy out of him and I and channel it into something that wouldn't put me on my sister's hit list.

By now, the stands were as packed as Foster had suggested they would be. I had to turn sideways and apologize to ten people just to wiggle my way into the seat next to him. I shook the buttery popcorn and nudged it in his direction.

"Who's winning the sports?"

Foster reached into the tub and grabbed a handful of gloriously stale white puffs.

"So far, no one. Mr. Vance is going to be very disappointed."

"The booster club dude?"

Foster pointed to the sidelines where a handful of guys sat on the bench. I immediately recognized the one who'd pummeled me to the ground my first day on the job—number five. Thank goodness my wrist had healed up quickly.

"His pride and joy is number five. A real upset that he's been benched in the first quarter." He popped a few kernels into his mouth and stared out at the field with a tightlipped smile.

I couldn't help but smile, too. Served that kid right.

"You *look* upset," I said with mock concern.

What I lacked in sports knowledge I more than made up for in yelling things at the field. By the time the two of us were required to be on the track in front of the grandstand, I was parched from hooting and hollering for our boys in blue. Boys who were losing by a hefty margin, by the way.

It wasn't supposed to happen that way with a homecoming game, but hey, some teams sucked, and that was all there was to it.

"They're normally much better than this," Beck said, as if reading my thoughts. "We've won State a few times. But this year we're… lacking."

I snorted then chugged a wax cup full of gatorade from the cheerleaders station before grabbing the microphone. My insides were bubbling with laughter at the thought of Sophie flipping through this year's yearbook only to find a photo of "herself" leading the crowd through a rousing rendition of *We Will Rock You.*

Chapter Twenty

#AllAboutTheChase

It didn't take long to crown the homecoming court. Kayla got named Princess, and despite one loud call for the queen to be "your mom," the title went to the head cheerleader. Go figure. This was a typical all-American high school, was it not?

Before I knew it, the team was taking the field for the second half, and Alison was texting me non-stop: *So what did he say? Am I his type? Is he even single? Sophie!* I really couldn't put off my promise to find out what Beck thought of her any longer, so I eased into the subject with the grace and subtly of a rhino at the ballet.

"You know who is really hot?"

Beck choked on his Coke a little, and I had to pat him on the back until he regained his composure.

"Is it a real person or a character from your," he paused for a moment, "book club."

"Nurse Alison," I said, hoping to erase the thought of Hunter and Blaze from his mind.

No sooner had I said it than I realized that the flaming hot hue of his cheeks meant he had completely misinterpreted my statement.

"Not for me!" I cried. "For you. I just meant, have you noticed that Nurse Alison is really beautiful?"

Foster exhaled, and I was pretty sure I detected a tiny bit of relief.

"I try not to note the physical appearance of my co-workers. That would be incredibly unprofessional."

I nodded politely, but I distinctly remembered my probation meeting in which he pointed out the changes he had noticed that had nothing to do with my personality. Not to mention that first day of school staff meeting where he'd commented on how Sophie had changed her hair.

"So, you don't date staff members on principle or you aren't allowed to? There's a big difference."

Foster raised an eyebrow. "I'm not allowed to date faculty, though technically Alison isn't under my supervision. I suppose I could date her. Her or Marta," said Foster, looking thoughtful. "But only them."

I briefly envisioned Foster taking Marta, the school's crossing guard, on a date. She was a very attractive sixty-eight-year-old woman, but the image was still disturbing.

"So, what's holding you back? With Alison, I mean. Marta's taken."

I watched as Foster's eyes traveled across the bleachers to where Alison sat with three girls I didn't recognize. Her red hair shone brilliantly under the spotlights, and her whole face glowed as she laughed. She was pretty perfect for a man like Beck.

"She doesn't challenge me."

The reply was shocking. Sophie had challenged him *once*, and the guy spent all summer and the beginning of this school year on a mission to sabotage her. Was that hot to him? Was he into that sort of thing? My dirty mind raced back to Sophie's book club and the whole bondage thing, making my cheeks flame.

"And that's what you want in a girlfriend?" I asked. Guys were so typical, weren't they? Offer them a perfect girl, and they said they aren't interested. It was always about the chase. But then again, who was I to judge? I was the same way.

Foster let out a deep sigh. "Probably if I knew what I wanted in a girlfriend I wouldn't still be single, but yeah, I think I need the challenge. Otherwise, I get bored. Alison is pretty, and she's very kind, but I've never found myself wondering what she does after school."

I felt bad for Alison. She had this massive crush on him, which meant she thought about what he did after school and then some. Heck, she had already considered what he was like in the bedroom, and Foster didn't so much as wonder what TV shows she liked, let alone whether or not she had a boyfriend.

"So like, hypothetically, if you *did* want to date a staff member, would you lose your job over it?"

He pondered this for a bit. "I could, yes. I suppose if I declared the relationship to the school board before some big scandal came out, I might be fine."

"Hmm, interesting," I mused.

His eyes flashed to mine. "Why are you so interested?"

"Oh, no reason," I quickly backpedaled, but my face was burning because all I could think about was how hot it would be to have a secret, forbidden love affair for a while, and then just as we would be about to get caught, have the guy put his job on the line to "declare the relationship" to his bosses. I'd had boyfriends, of course. Even one serious relationship that had lasted for two years in college. But I'd never had a man go out on a limb like that for me. I'd never had someone risk anything for me. Or fight for me.

I could picture it now…

Wait. No, I couldn't! What was I thinking? No. Bad, Dani. Very bad. This whole conversation wasn't about me and Beck, it was about Alison and Beck. And besides, the guy thought I was Sophie, but my sister had a new man. And I was going home soon. We dropped the flirty conversation, and I could barely look at him the rest of the game without thinking about what he did after school. Not good.

By the fourth quarter, our team had managed the kind of miraculous turnaround only worthy of a cheesy sports movie. We were down by five with eighteen seconds on the clock. Our guys had the ball and were a mere fifteen yards from the end zone. This was it. The crowd roared, both sides screaming for victory. Energy pulsed with the pounding on the metal stands and the smell of warm bodies and stale popcorn. Bright spotlights contrasted the dark sky, lighting the bright green field and all the blue versus gold players. A whistle sounded. Everything stilled before igniting like spark to gasoline. The boys in blue passed the ball to our quarterback. He stepped back, raised his arm, threw it, and—

"Touchdown!"

Adrenaline shot through me like lightning. I screamed with the crowd, jumping up and down. Beck was right there with me, arms raised and deep voice whooping. We turned to each other and hugged. It felt right. And then, he pulled me in tighter, and it felt intimate. We broke away, eyes locked on each other in the madness. His hand snaked down my arm, cupping my hand. My stomach flopped, and I squeezed back.

Someone tapped on my shoulder. "Hey, guys," Alison yelled over the roaring crowd. "We won!"

I released Beck and hugged her, too. "Yes, that was amazing!"

"It was!" She squished past me to hug Beck. "I bet you're pretty proud of your boys, right, Foster?"

"They pulled it off." He beamed.

By this point, most of the crowd had abandoned the stands to storm onto the field, so the three of us had more space to breathe and less noise to yell over. It made me both happy and sad at the same time. I wanted to go back to that moment with Beck's hand in mine. Our secret touch in the middle of the roaring crowd had brought more excitement out in me than anything had in a long, long time.

Alison smiled up at Beck, her crush plain as day on her heart-shaped face. She was hanging off his arm, and I had to force myself not to grimace. Now, I was suddenly territorial, when an hour ago, I'd been trying to hook these two up? What was wrong with me? Beck wasn't mine. He never could be.

"You'll be chaperoning the dance tomorrow, right?" she asked.

"Always do." He stilled.

"Great. Me too. Save me a dance?"

"Sure."

Poor girl. She had no idea her feelings weren't being reciprocated. I didn't know how to tell her, but if she asked, I'd be honest because if the roles were reversed, I would want the same. In the meantime, this was my cue to leave. "I better get going. See y'all on Monday."

"Do you need a ride home?" Beck sounded hopeful. Hopeful and something I didn't dare visit right now.

"I have my car." I pointed to the packed parking lot. Already a line of red tail lights lit the way out.

"I need a ride," Alison jumped in. "If that's okay, Foster?"

He nodded once, but his eyes were still pinned on me. There was no denying it now—the man was interested. Crap. I waved goodbye and hurried off, both sad to leave and worried about how I was going to break the news to Sophie. "Oh hey, sis, welcome back. You know your new boss who you hate? Well, he's actually got it bad for you now. Have a great school year!"

I winced. Yeah, it was probably best to not to tell her at all.

Chapter Twenty-One

#DatingMyself

"Save me a dance," I grumbled, through massive bites of granola cereal. It was Saturday morning, and I had half a mind to spend the afternoon ravaging Sophie's closet for formal wear. If I crashed the homecoming Dance I could watch Alison and Beck accidentally fall in love via slow dance in person, rather than just on the constant loop in my head.

I hadn't slept much. I couldn't stop thinking about all the ways in which I had invited this trouble upon myself. Girls will pretend they can't see the first inklings of a guy going from just another person in the room to a guy whose eyes lift every time that *they* walk in, but we feel it immediately. It was the self doubt that made us pretend nothing was going on. I saw the signs. I knew that if I kept pushing, he would keep responding, and I did it anyway. Simply put, it felt amazing to watch someone fall for you.

The problem was, there were some people who weren't allowed to fall for you. Like the stupid time I flirted with the married guy at my first real job. I was forced to face the reality that just because a man wasn't supposed to act on his feelings, didn't mean he wouldn't. That first job had ended in me quitting and feeling like a total idiot. I couldn't very well quit Sophie's job for her, now could I?

I needed to get Foster Beck out of my head, so I decided to do the responsible thing: lust after another. I pulled out my phone and scrolled through the movie times. One of my favorite hot-guy actors was in a new heist movie that I fondly referred to as off-brand *Fast and the Furious*, and I was very into the idea of a matinee, just the two of us.

I assumed the noon showing on the Saturday of homecoming would be dead, so I didn't bother dressing to impress. Instead, I pulled on a pair of Sophie's jean capris with a soft, heather gray sweater and a Halo High baseball cap.

The parking lot was nearly empty, save for one very familiar vehicle. I stopped dead in my tracks, mouth agape. Was this real life? Foster stepped out of his car and offered an awkward wave across the lot. Even when I was trying, I couldn't avoid him. The man was everywhere! I raised a defeated hand and smiled back. One thing was certain, I could not be accused of attempting to seduce him at the theatre. My makeup-free face and sensible sneakers were evidence to the contrary.

Small towns meant small movie theaters. There were only two films showing today: the one I was seeing and *Thomas Jefferson, Werewolf Catcher*. I said a silent prayer that Beck was secretly into historical horrors, but wasn't the least bit shocked when he strode up to the ticket kiosk and requested, "One for *The Harley Hoax*."

I handed my credit card over to the teenage ticket taker and hoped that Foster would keep moving into the theatre, but he waited just outside the velvet rope, confirming everything I had been worried about earlier. I had been putting kindling in the fire pit since I got here, and he was about to strike a match and send it all up in flames. Trouble was, who'd end up burned?

"Can I see your ID?" asked the ticket taker, extracting me from my melodramatic internal dialogue.

"Seriously?" I asked. I had access to some pretty top of the line moisturizers, but nobody in their right mind would confuse me with someone too young to see an R-rated movie.

"It's for the beer," said the kid. "Sorry, but we ID everyone who looks under thirty-five."

I grinned, knowing full well that Foster had definitely overheard that comment and had definitely not been asked to pull out any identification. I still didn't know how old he was, early thirties? Beck smiled wolfishly, and my stomach did a little flippy thing. I handed the kid my driver's license and watched as he not so subtly glanced at the "do not serve anyone born after this year" sign that hung in the top corner of the window.

"Thanks, Danielle." He slipped the card back across the counter along with my ticket stub.

Every Mary Kate and Ashley Olsen twin movie had a moment like this. I made a frantic inventory of my brain for what you were supposed to do when someone calls you by your real name. Laugh it off? I couldn't do that here, the kid was literally reading off of my ID.

I now completely regretted turning and smirking at Beck after the ticket taker said "under thirty-five". I tucked my ID into my purse and tried to act normal as I walked toward Foster. "You ready for some car chases?"

"What was that all about?" His face had that little line between his eyebrows that happened when he was puzzling over something.

"I guess I just look younger than you," I tried, forcing a giggle.

"No, I mean, that kid called you Danielle."

I didn't want to say I was a good liar because that tended to go hand in hand with being a bad person, but I did have a hefty amount of experience fibbing my way out of uncomfortable situations. It only took me a beat before a plausible excuse popped to the surface.

"Oh! It's my middle name. I've got one of those sticker ID's from when you change addresses and you can barely read the Sophie at this point. I really need to get it replaced, but that would mean going to the DMV, and nobody has *that* kind of time."

I held my breath, thinking any second now Foster

would out me for the lie, like maybe they'd played some awful get to know you game at orientation and everybody already knew that Sophie's middle name was Ermenia—thanks for nothing grandma—but he didn't. He cocked his head to the side and opened his mouth like he was about to say something then snapped it shut again and stepped up to the snack counter.

"Jumbo popcorn with extra butter and two diet sodas, please."

"Oh, you didn't have to."

"I owe you from the game anyway," said Foster, justifying his very date-like action. He didn't, in fact, owe me for the game. He'd paid for that popcorn, too. I closed my eyes for a second and breathed in a slow sigh, catching both the scent of the extra-buttery popcorn and Beck's citrus-spice cologne.

I could have been like, *nope, I'm an independent woman, and I'll get my own*, but my bank account was looking woefully sad thanks to the Live Laugh Love debacle, and theatre snacks weren't in the budget.

When we entered the theatre, my breath caught. There wasn't a single other soul in here. We were sharing popcorn and matching sodas. Last night, we'd hugged and then deliberately held hands, our eyes locking on each other like we were the ones back in high school. I wasn't nearly a good enough actress to pretend this chemistry between us wasn't about to be a thing.

Beck cleared his throat and pointed to the back row. "What do you say? Sit in the back where the bad kids belong?"

I gripped my soda with an iron fist and marched to the back of the theatre. I wanted to respond with, *"Heck yes we're going to the back, and you better plan on coming to see this movie a second time because I'm about to spend the next hour and a half studying the inside of your mouth,"* but I restrained myself and instead pulled the cup holder into the slot between our two seats. It was a small barrier and would likely be breached by the time the previews finished, but it was my first line of defense, and I needed time to form a strategy.

Growing up, I always dreaded the sex scenes in movies if I wasn't by myself. It was especially mortifying with parents there. And if they weren't present, they'd magically walk in right when the characters were going at it. My mom would get all quiet, sometimes even cover my eyes, and my dad would demand I shut off my "slut show" or something equally offensive. But none of those adolescent experiences could have prepared me for watching a hot sex scene on a giant screen with Foster Beck at my side and nobody else in the dark theatre.

We were half way through the movie without any hand holding or accidental fingers brushing in the popcorn jug. I was just thinking that maybe the sexual tension between us could be ignored, that we could be professional adults about all this, when the leading man pushed his woman against the bedroom wall and stripped her to her lacy underwear.

"Damn," I whispered, my whole body going rigid.

Beck didn't say anything but I could tell he was watching me. I kept my eyes glued to the screen, hoping to appear cool as a friggin' cucumber. The scene ended in an explosion of *you know what* and flipped back to screeching car chases. But I was still burning up from head to toe, not because of the actors but because my mind had just put me and Beck in their shoes, actually their wall and bed, and I was pretty sure Beck's imagination was in the exact same place.

"Be right back!" I squealed, jumping up, popcorn flying everywhere as I made a break for it and ran out to the bathroom. I didn't actually need to go, but I definitely needed to splash cold water on my face. I looked at myself in the mirror, wiping away the water. "Don't go there, Dani. Don't do it." But I wanted to. So, so bad. "No, just don't."

Ugh! Stupid brain. Stupid conscious. Stupid twin-swap.

Turned out, I didn't need to worry because when I returned to the theatre, Beck was gone.

Chapter Twenty-Two

#DaniDontNeedNoMan

Beck never came back either. He never texted. Never called. Nothing. The man just up and disappeared without a word or any indication as to what was going on in his head. Whatever. I finished off the movie alone, telling myself I was happier to ogle Mr. Tatum in peace. But really, that was a big fat lie.

I was hurt.

And it was so stupid! I had ran out of there first. And besides, I couldn't be with Foster. I could count a million reasons why acting on my feelings for him was a terrible idea. Number one, I was leaving Oklahoma in a week. Number two, he could lose his job. Number three, my sister hated him, and he'd put her/me on administrative probation. Number four, Alison liked him, and even though we weren't close, she still trusted me. And number five, the real kicker, he didn't know who I actually was. And that was it, really. That was the main reason why I needed to cut him loose.

After I finished the matinee, I attempted to scrub him from my mind by swimming about a bazillion laps at the gym pool, taking myself out to dinner at a lively cantina and overindulging in one too many street tacos, then returning to Soph's house for a bottle of red wine and Netflix. As the night grew late, I let Sophie's cat curl up in my lap and forced myself to relax instead of wonder what was happening at the homecoming dance. It was… complete and utter torture.

Two low thuds knocked on the door.

I bolted awake to the stab of cat paws against my stomach as the little devil darted away. I sat up, my heart thundering and my eyes bleary. I must have fallen asleep on the couch. I was sweaty from the thick throw blanket and hazy from the wine. My white sleep T-shirt clung to my body as I stumbled to the front door and cracked it open.

"Hello?" My voice was husky from sleep. Also from the dream I'd just been having involving a car chase and a certain off-limits principal.

"I'm sorry I left you like that." Beck was there, hands buried into his black pants pockets. The neighbor's porch light was on next door, brightening the planes of his face. He looked haggard. I mean, he also looked amazing and all dressed up from chaperoning the homecoming dance. But the pain awash in his expression was unmistakable. It was the look of regret.

Was it regret for coming here? Regret for the attraction between us?

"It's okay." I opened the door and stepped outside, wrapping my arms around myself. I was suddenly all too aware that I wasn't wearing pants or a bra under my long white shirt and Foster was, too. His eyes traveled down to my bare toes and back up again like a caress.

"How was the dance?" I asked, swallowing down my emotions.

"Pretty good." He stilled, thinking for a long minute. "But I kept looking for you."

I smirked. "I did my homecoming duty last night, thank you very much."

"Will you dance with me?"

I was so surprised that my mouth popped open. I wasn't expecting this. "There's no music."

"We don't need it." His voice was brazen confidence as he slid his hands around my waist and tugged me close. We began to slow dance, swaying side to side, bodies flush together, moving like we'd done this a million times before.

But we hadn't.

In fact, I couldn't remember the last time I danced like this with a man. But here we were, slow dancing under the moonlight on Sophie's front porch, clinging to each other like teenagers. I could feel every muscle of him, and it made my heart skid. The humid September heat had released to the night, and I shivered despite myself.

"Are you cold?" he whispered.

I shook my head because I wasn't actually cold. I was hot all over. Here we were; me, in nothing but a thin T-shirt and panties, and him, sexy as sin in a perfectly pressed black tux.

"What are we doing?" I asked breathily.

He answered with his hands. They slid up my arms, round my shoulders, and cupped my face. His eyes were dark pools of desire—unleashed in a way I'd never seen from him before now. I inhaled just as his lips claimed mine.

There was kissing and then there was *kissing.* Beck made every sexy silver-screen kiss look insignificant as he scooped his hands under my thighs and wrapped my legs around his middle. I could worry about the neighbors, but why? It was about time they saw Sophie get some sexy time.

"Are you sure about this?" I asked huskily, pulling back for half a second before launching back in without giving him a chance to answer.

Beck pushed the front door closed behind us as he carried me inside and mumbled a hungry *"mmhmm"* against my lips.

When he laid me down on the couch I used my free hand to shove Sophie's Kindle under the cushion. No way was I going to get caught with *The Hunter's Conquest* open to the getting down and dirty in the dungeon scene while I was attempting to get down and dirty myself.

Beck tore his lips from mine and looked into my eyes. "I'm *not* sure about this."

It was like a big glass of frigid cold water. Why,

Beck? Why! I raised up onto my elbows and prepared to redraw the boundaries we had just so clearly crossed, but Beck rested his palm on my cheek, and I melted back into the cushions.

"I'm not sure, but I don't care."

Music to my ears. "Agreed," I whispered and pressed my lips and body against him, losing all sense of thought after that. There was only feeling. And I felt it all.

The next morning, I woke before Beck, watching him sleep with a satisfied smile on my lips as I replayed all the things that happened after his sexy confession of "but I don't care." They were excellent, wonderful, late-into-the-night things that were well worthy of a new crush post on Instagram. Ordinarily, I would share an artsy shot of his back standing near an open window with some form of a carb in one hand and coffee in the other, but I didn't want real Sophie to fly back early and murder me, so instead I snapped a picture of his adorable, sleep-rumbled face instead and saved it to my "just for me" gallery.

For once, I was shooting something I really liked, not something designed specifically to make other people envious. Although, with his cute five o'clock shadow and tousled bed hair, there was quite a bit to covet.

My phone buzzed, and I snuck out of the bedroom to answer.

"How's my favorite sister?"

"Tired," I answered truthfully. She didn't have to know the very good reason I was so tired.

"Well, wake up! It's Sunday, a great day for experiencing wonderful things in beautiful Halo, Oklahoma. Just kidding, nothing is open. Get yourself a Starbucks and binge watch some more *New Girl*."

"Wait, where's the Starbucks?"

"Also kidding!"

"You're evil."

She just laughed.

"Hey," I grumbled at a barely audible level. "I'm not going to share my Hulu password anymore if you are going to use it to make fun of me."

"Why are you whispering?" snapped Sophie. That girl never missed anything.

"I'm not," I whispered back.

"Yes, you are," said Sophie. "Who don't you want to hear you? Oh... my... gosh." It was like I could see her reacting. She was totally twisting a lock of blonde hair around her pointer finger right now. Her lips pursed into an ugly line of judgement. "You hoe! Are you banging someone as me? Who are you banging? That is so against the rules!" She was shrieking so loud that Beck stirred in the other room.

"That's not what happened," I lied, sneaking out the kitchen door to the back patio.

"So, he knows you aren't Sophie Sparks then?"

"Well, no, but that is for your benefit."

Sophie growled, and I prepared for the big screaming tantrum that would come next, only lucky for me, her mysterious Mexican lover called after her in the background.

"I have to go," said Sophie with a growl. "But I want you to know, I am ready and able to hurt you if this blows up in my face."

"It's not going to," I promised before hanging up and pinching the bridge of my nose.

Well, I hoped it wasn't going to, anyway.

Technically, I wasn't lying. This wasn't going to blow up in her face; it was going to blow up behind her back and then just like, a little bit in front of her face. Who was I kidding? I just slept with her boss who thought I was her. There were like four hundred things that could go wrong, and one of them was that Foster Beck was *going* to get hurt.

Not a little bit hurt, majorly hurt. I needed to come clean about the swap but not before the musical was finished. Those kids had worked too hard for everything to be ruined because I couldn't keep it in my pants.

As soon as the last bars of *Oklahoma!* were finished, I would tell Beck the truth. I just had to cross my fingers that no one outed me to him first.

Chapter Twenty-Three

#RomanticComedyMontage

"Did you make this?" Beck grinned at Sophie's floral knitted hand towel while he dried his hands. He'd just loaded the last dish from our dinner into the dishwasher, and now he was asking what should be a harmless question. I stared at him like a deer caught in the headlights.

I tried not to grimace as my mind whirled. "It's homemade, yes." Technically, not a lie. Ugh, who was I kidding?

He kissed the top of my head and pulled me into a hug. "I want to show you something."

"Does it mean we have to leave our happy little bubble?" We'd spent all day in the house, and normally I liked to get out and about, but I most definitely liked this Foster Beck bubble better.

"Yes, but I promise it includes a sunset."

"How did you know sunsets are my favorite?" I pressed a simple kiss to his lips.

"Lucky guess." He chuckled. "Come on."

One thing about Oklahoma was that it was truly as flat as they say. There were loads of trees around Halo too, so it was hard to find a discernible horizon unless it had something to do with farming. Twenty minutes later and we were driving up the only legitimate hill I'd seen so far in this town.

"Are you taking me to the local make out spot?" I teased.

Beck tightened his fingers over the steering wheel and smirked. "Maybe."

"Wait, for real?" The last thing we needed were high school students seeing us together. But then again, it was a pretty cute gesture.

"Well, some people park here for that, but you'll see why I brought you here when we get up there."

He pulled off to park on the side of the old country road, which actually only went about half way up the hill. We got out of the car and started hiking toward the top. My calves and glutes burned with each steep step but in a good way. I laced my hand through Beck's, and he squeezed back. After a few minutes of climbing, we reached the top and sat down in the soft grass.

The countryside stretched out on all sides. As promised, the sun was setting, and the sky was that perfect glow of orange and red. The clouds dotting the horizon were blazing pink.

"Wow." I sighed, breathing in the country fresh air and leaning into him. "It's beautiful."

"Yeah, I like to come here to think. I've lived in Halo all my life, you know?"

I couldn't imagine living in one place all my life, especially not in such a small town, but I kept that thought to myself.

"Some people might call that small minded," he said, as if knowing my exact feelings, "but I think it shows commitment." He pointed to the distance. "See those wheat fields over there?"

I looked toward what was obviously a farm field but didn't see any wheat. "That one?"

"Yeah, well, they will be wheat fields come spring. Right now, it's planting season. Anyway, that was my grandparent's farm. I spent every Sunday dinner there as a kid. My uncle runs it now, but I still go around once a month to help out with this or that and enjoy my aunt's cooking. The farm has been in the Beck family for generations."

"Wow." I bit my lip, remembering something from American history. "Let me guess, your ancestors were Sooners?" I was talking about the settlers who'd come to Oklahoma to claim land before it was legal. There had been a lot of that in OK.

"Well, it's not something I'll ever admit to," he teased and poked me in the side. "Actually, I'm not sure. We're told no, but I have my doubts." He moved on, "And see over there?" He pointed to a cluster of little sparkling ponds with a slow river winding through them. "That was my favorite spot as a kid. I'd swim and fish there every chance I could get."

"Hey, I could see myself doing that now. Well, more like hanging by the shore with a beach towel, a book, and a margarita."

He laughed.

"It's all pretty great, Foster."

"It is."

"Oh, and see those horses?" He nodded animatedly toward a barn style, white farmhouse with a real barn next to it. A fenced-in pasture was filled with what had to be at least twenty horses. I rarely saw anything like that back in California. I did always have a soft spot for horses though, ever since I got to ride Old Bessie at Y-Camp as a kid.

"Let me guess," I teased. "You rode them?"

"No, but cleaning their stalls was my first real job."

When I wrinkled my nose, he kissed it.

The sun continued to descend beneath the horizon, the red sky bleeding to darkness. I wasn't ready to leave. I could have stayed wrapped up in his arms all night, talking about anything and everything, be it big or small. He must've felt the same way because we did just that for several hours, until the sky was ink and the air was crisp and the stars winked down on us as if to whisper, "You're never going to forget this moment."

Beck and I agreed that our budding relationship had to stay top secret. We were new, and neither of us knew where this was going. What was the point of declaring anything to the school board now when we weren't even sure we were compatible?

No, we had to keep things on the downlow, which was actually perfect. It meant I didn't have to have an awkward talk with Alison, and there was very little chance that Beck would behave inappropriately toward Sophie for those few days at the end of the week when she would be teaching classes and I would be directing the musical.

I thought we were doing a pretty good job keeping things covert, but then Jeanine barged into my room just before rehearsal, closed the door behind her and howled, "Are you insane?"

At first, I thought she was referencing life skills. I hadn't veered away from the curriculum by any means, but I did take a slight detour to the TurboTax website. "Well, it is a life skill to know where to get help. It's called delegation, Jeanine."

She threw her hands up in the air and dropped the bomb. "You cannot date Principal Beck!"

Oh, that…

I wanted to reply that what we were doing probably wasn't considered dating in most places, but now was not the time for snappy jokes. Jeanine, who was always tossing out gems of optimism, stood with her arms folded across her chest and a disappointed look in her eye.

"Maybe this is just fun for you, but Sophie is going to have to deal with the consequences. And Foster, have you even considered how foolish he is going to feel when this is all over?"

I lowered my eyes and stared at the granular wood pattern on my desk. I hadn't planned to hurt anyone, but the closer we got to Sophie's return, the more it began to sink in that there was no happy ending. I would have to quit Halo the same way I had quit on getting my teaching license and becoming a Hollywood actress.

There was no point in lying to Jeanine about what was going on between Beck and I. She was the only one who knew I wasn't Sophie, and therefore the only one who would be extra sensitive to a change in his attitude toward me.

"I'll make it right before I go," I swore.

"How?" cried a frustrated Jeanine. "How are you going to make it right? Foster is head in-the-clouds infatuated with you."

I felt a little tug on my heart. "He's not…"

"Yes! Yes, he is Dani. This morning in the break room, he went on and on about how great the production was going to be, how you'd really motivated the kids to step outside their comfort zones, and how even the kids that he thought would cause problems were making a marked improvement."

"Those are nice things to say, but it doesn't mean—"

Jeanine shook her full head of disastrous curls. "Don't treat me like a fool, Dani. I may seem decrepit to you, but a woman knows."

I threw my hands up in defeat. "Okay, so something is happening, but I don't know what it is yet. I need time to figure it out."

Jeanine nodded sadly. "Time is a thing you don't have."

"You know," I replied, "it's not like we're the only ones on this campus with a secret love affair."

Jeanine's cheeks went flaming red, and she lowered her voice. "Yes, well. Fred and I's relationship isn't against school policy. It's just *no one's* business but ours."

The way she said *no one* made me want to tuck my tail between my legs and sprint for the auditorium. Maybe she was right, maybe I was doing more damage in Halo than I thought. Did Sophie even know about Jeanine and Fred?

"I have to get to the auditorium," I said, slowly backing toward the door.

"You need to tell him the truth," she countered.

"You're right, and I will. I promise. Just let me figure it out, okay?"

She let out an exasperated sigh. "He's one of the good ones, you know. He deserves to be treated right."

Tears burned my eyes as I left her standing in the classroom, but what could I say? She was spot on, and I was an idiot. Except, this love affair was more than a starved libido for me—I had real emotions invested. I was falling hard for Foster Beck. And maybe, for once in my life, I deserved to be with one of the good ones, too.

"You're back," I fake-squealed, smiling at Mrs. Sanchez. "We've missed you."

I was such a bad liar, but she didn't seem to catch

on. She was resting on the piano bench, a little pale and tired around the edges, but apparently ready to return to work. This meant Beck wouldn't be needed today, I noted with a long sigh.

"I'm back," she confirmed. "That flu was awful."

"The devil's work." I nodded. "Are you feeling better?"

"Oh, heaps. Plus, I lost ten pounds." She grimaced. "Silver lining?"

"Ew, sorry."

"I will be haunted by my toilet for the rest of my life."

I laughed for real this time because I never pegged Mrs. Sanchez to be one for poop jokes, especially since she was older and her generation didn't usually talk about stuff like that.

"Well, I'm glad you're back."

We started the rehearsal, but I was extra distracted. The only person in the world I wanted to see today was Beck. I kept thinking about our chemistry together, about how we complimented each other so well in bed and out of it.

As far as Sundays go, I'd just had the best one in my entire life.

We'd had a great time lazing about the house and cooking meals and watching movies and, of course, engaging in loads of amazing sex. And we'd talked, too. About everything. I'd only ever talked with Sophie like that in the past, but since our drifting apart three years ago, I hadn't had anyone to have deep conversations with in ages. It felt good to chat about stuff that wasn't all about money and sponsors and parties like I was used to back in California. There wasn't an ounce of gossip or a superficial compliment to be had between Beck and I the entire day. I knew him on a deeper level now. I knew about his family, his politics, spirituality, about what he thought of the world and how he wanted it to be and where his place was in it.

Foster Beck was perfect.

And I was terrified of losing him.

"That's a wrap," I called out to the kids. "Tomorrow is tech. Wednesday and Thursday are dress, and then it's opening night! Who's excited?"

They cheered, genuine happiness exuding off each and every one of them. A swell of pride rose up in my chest for being a contributing factor in their joy. Even Tyler looked enthusiastic.

As I walked to my car, I couldn't help myself from stopping by Beck's office.

"Knock, knock," I said shyly, finding his door open.

"Hey, you." Even the way he said "you" was sexy, as if I was the only person on his mind, too. He was sitting at his desk, papers strewn everywhere, but he dropped work immediately and came to pull me inside the little room, closing the door behind him and pressing me flush against it.

"Well, hello to you, too." I giggled.

"Hi." His lip twitched, and his blue eyes darkened. "You're trouble."

I ran my hands up his broad back to tug at his hair. "You have no idea." He kissed me, deep and long, our bodies responding just as they had over the weekend.

Part of me wanted to throw caution to the wind and continue down this path, but a bigger part of me knew we couldn't. Not here.

I broke away, panting. "Come over tonight?"

"You come to mine," he responded, his hands still roaming all over me. "I'm going to cook you dinner."

"Oh, and what's on the menu?"

"Shrimp scampi." He smirked. "Your favorite."

I opened and closed my mouth, reality sinking in. Shrimp scampi was, in fact, not my favorite meal. It was Sophie's favorite. My twin loved seafood, but I detested it. Go figure, since I was the one who lived on the coast.

"Is that all right?" His face faltered. "I remembered from the ice breaker activity we did during teacher training last summer."

He remembered… my heart squeezed. He didn't remember me because he didn't know the real me. He remembered Sophie. And why would he remember something like that if he wasn't carrying a torch for my sister? All this time, I'd thought they'd been enemies, thought he'd hated her but had warmed up to me. What if I was wrong?

"Sophie?"

I wanted to tell him. I needed to. Had to. But I couldn't bring myself to do it. I was a selfish person, wasn't I? I was feeling things I hadn't felt for anyone, and I didn't want to ruin it, not until I was sure about how to go about it so that he didn't dump me right on the spot. Not to mention, I had my sister's job to consider.

I pushed the painful thoughts away and refocused on the here and now. "Shrimp scampi sounds wonderful," I lied. I'd just have to eat dinner before I went over and then pick at the food he made for me, maybe distract him with my cleavage or something. My web of lies was growing bigger by the moment, but damn he was just too cute to resist.

He kissed me again, and he felt so good. He also felt off-limits—forbidden—and my body loved that, taking over my good conscious like the bad-girl she was. I snuck my hands under his shirt, running my fingers over his flexing abs, hot skin, and the hard line where his suit pants cut me off. I wanted to throw professionalism out the window, and I could tell he did, too.

But he was Beck. He was professional to a fault. And he peeled me off of him with a soft chuckle. "You're so impatient."

I raised an eyebrow. "Is that such a bad thing?"

"No." He let out a labored breath. "I'll see you tonight, okay? I'll text you my address. How's seven?"

That was barely two hours away. I could handle two hours.

I grinned. "Okay, seven it is. But I'm not staying the night." I was teasing. I was actually planning on bringing an overnight bag.

"Hmm, I'll have to see if I can get you to change your mind."

"And how are you going to do that?"

"Dessert." He arched a wolffish eyebrow, and my whole body lit up. This man was doing things to me. I had to go before I jumped on him and pushed him past his breaking point. I waved a coy goodbye and opened the door, letting myself out before shutting it behind me.

My face was probably beet red and my hair a mess from his hands in it, but I didn't care. The office ladies had all gone, and my heart was busy doing cartwheels across the room.

"Were you—was that—" Alison's voice startled me.

I turned to find her staring, mouth agape, eyes bulging with realization.

Chapter Twenty-Four

#MamaDidntRaiseNoFool

"But you wouldn't." Her voice shook.

I swallowed hard. I didn't even know what to say. Guilt ate me alive the moment her face fell and those pretty doe eyes welled with angry tears. "I thought you were my friend. I thought you were putting in a good word for me." She shook her head. "I'm so stupid."

"We didn't mean—"

"Save it," she spat, folding her arms over her chest. She had pale blue scrubs on today with little red apples sewn into the design. It was such a sweet look. She was such a sweet person. And here I was, breaking her heart. Well, not me, Beck, but I certainly had something to do with it. Except, Beck had never liked her romantically. He had no interest. I was going to break it to her after the game but hadn't found the right time, and now I couldn't say anything without hurting her more. The knife was already in her back. I wasn't going to twist it.

"I'm sorry," I whispered.

"No, you're not." Her lip trembled.

She was right. I wasn't sorry, not for being with him, and not for being happy. But I was sorry for lying, for the mess I was in, and for hurting her. Suddenly, a new thought struck me. "You're not going to turn him in are you? It could ruin his career."

She laughed bitterly. "I wouldn't do anything to hurt Foster."

"Thank you." I relaxed.

"Keeping my mouth shut is not for you, Sophie. It's for him." And then, she turned and stormed from the building.

I dragged my feet as I left, feeling like a college kid doing the walk of shame all over again. I never should have stopped by his office. If Jeanine could tell we were hooking up, of course someone else would notice.

I wanted to get excited about seeing his place for the first time, but I was haunted by Alison's mopey face and the way she said, "you wouldn't." It wasn't that she had some claim on him that made me feel bad, it was that I could have talked to her. I could have told her that he didn't see her that way without her having to witness me leaving his office looking like I'd just stopped in for a quicky.

And then, there was the fact that she was obviously way better for him because she didn't hesitate for even a second before putting him and his career over her feelings.

By the time I arrived at his house for a meal I was going to have to choke down, I was pretty sure that I was Satan's first born. I did not deserve a hot guy to be cooking me dinner, but I couldn't back out now.

Beck, as it turned out, lived in a kitschy old farmhouse. There wasn't a neighbor in sight when I pulled up the long gravel driveway and parked in front of his picture-perfect wraparound porch.

Any minute now, I expected a golden retriever to pounce out the front door and welcome me with a flashy tail wag.

Instead, music floated from the open kitchen window, and Beck grinned out at me, a dish towel hanging over one shoulder as he yelled for me to let myself in. I pulled open the screen door, and it screeched and moaned with the effort.

What was a principal's salary such that he had his own farmhouse on what looked to be a few acres of property? Beck scooped me up the moment I entered the kitchen and set me on the counter beside where he worked.

If I liked shrimp, it probably would have been a little sexier watching him quarter lemons and deglaze the pan with white wine. As it was, I was just trying not to wrinkle up my nose when the scent of seafood assaulted my nostrils. One would think, having shared the same womb, that Sophie and I would have more in common, but the only thing that had ever matched on us was our faces.

"You look delicious," he said suddenly, eyes zeroing in on the little red dress that I'd found in the back of Soph's closet. Two thin straps held it loose around my neck, showing off the girls.

I flipped a lock of blonde hair over my shoulder. "You don't look so bad yourself."

I couldn't drool over the food, but I could certainly drool over the man. At work he was all buttoned up, fancy shirt, leather belt, slick shoes—the works—but here in his home, he wore well-fitted jeans with a dark green cotton T-shirt. I couldn't help but notice how well sculpted his chest was behind material that didn't have to be starched and ironed each morning.

"Look at me like that at school, and neither of us are going to have a job anymore," warned Foster, catching my eyes on their quest to drink him in from top to bottom.

"About that," I replied, hating to ruin the mood but not wanting to miss the opportunity. "I ran into Alison on my way out of your office today."

Foster went white as a ghost. "You don't think she—"

"Oh, she absolutely did."

Foster covered his face with his hands, rubbing the worried lines that formed across his brows.

"She did promise not to tell," I added. "For your benefit."

Foster looked both relieved and pained.

"We're lucky it was her and not someone who thinks less of me."

I could think of a few people who would be

delighted to see Foster fail, and it occurred to me just how different this conversation would be if someone like Mr. Vance had been outside that door and not Alison.

"We can't push it like that at school anymore. Until we know what this is… this has to stay between us."

I nodded, wanting to add that *this* was about to expire in a week, but I didn't because if there really only was one week, then I wanted it to be the best week in a long time. We both deserved that right? A chance to be happy, even if it was short lived?

I looked around the spotless white kitchen and attached living room, noting the masculine touches like the brown leather sofa and rolling metal bar hosting a line of expensive looking whiskey bottles. On one wall, he had a black and white framed photo of himself with his parents and siblings. On another, was an old world map. A small wood fire crackled in the fireplace despite it still being warm outside.

Wow, Beck had really gone all out to make the evening special.

"Right this way, m'lady," he said, directing me to the tiny farmhouse table. It was covered in a lace tablecloth and bright red chargers beneath our entree plates. I took a conservative helping of the scampi and a not so conservative pour of red wine when the two of us sat down to eat.

"This looks wonderful, Foster." I smiled. "Thank you."

He smiled back. "You're welcome. And I don't know, I kind of like it when you call me Beck."

"Oh, do you now? What about Principal Beck? Mr. Beck?" *Daddy Beck*, okay, I didn't say that last one out loud.

"No, just Beck."

"Then, you can call me Sparks." I met him with a wink, but actually, I only said what I did because I was tired of hearing my sister's name on his lips.

I chewed the shrimp and chased each bite with wine, but a few mouthfuls in and I realized the cleavage tactic was a better option. I raised a hand to cover my mouth in an exaggerated yawn.

"I'm so very tired," I teased, batting my eyelashes.

"Really?" Foster raised one eyebrow as he set down his fork.

"And I don't think I have it in me to drive all the way home." I threw my hand across my forehead in true southern lady fashion. "While this exhausted."

Foster stood and pushed in his chair. "Someone will have to put you to bed."

"Someone indeed." I smirked as he picked me up from my chair and carried me into the bedroom.

Chapter Twenty-Five

#TheCalmBeforeTheStorm

The next two days were movie montage perfect. If a bluebird landed on my finger and music started playing every time Beck walked in the room, it wouldn't have surprised me the least. Everything felt right. Teaching was good, fun even. And despite rehearsals being a mad dash to fit everything in and perfect each and every moment, I felt exhilarated instead of stressed. And those were just the days. There were also *nights*.

Nights that had me remembering what it was like when you were falling for someone and everything they did made you want to spend more time with them. It was perfect, but it couldn't last.

I rolled over in Beck's bed Thursday morning, snuggling into his warm side, when reality sank in like the knife in Sophie's back. Speaking of which, I checked my phone, and sure enough, there were two missed calls and three missed texts from her.

She would've gotten in late last night to an empty house.

Where are you?

You're with that man, aren't you? Who is it?

Dani!!! Pick up your phone.

I was going to have to face her and deal with all of this. My happiness was slowly being squashed by an anvil of guilt.

And fear.

Chill! We'll talk about it later. You're teaching today right? Leave immediately after school, and I'll pop in to take care of dress rehearsal, I texted back furiously.

You bet your ass we're talking later. Her reply came in an instant.

I groaned.

"Mmm." Beck rolled over and kissed my bare shoulder. "Everything okay?"

"Great." My voice was strained.

"What is it?" He sat up, sleepiness draining from his face. His eyes were full of concern and, could it be, love?

This was my chance. I could come clean about everything, and peering into those baby blues right now, it was all I wanted. But I couldn't do that to Sophie. I needed to talk to her first. And I needed to make sure the musical went off without a hitch before I pulled the rug out from under everyone.

"I'm just stressed out about opening night," I lied. Well, not exactly a lie.

His lips twitched, like there was something he wanted to say about that, but instead I got a, "It's going to be fine." He pulled me into a hug and kissed the top of my head. I no longer felt good in his arms. I felt like the liar that I was. I couldn't do this anymore. I just couldn't.

"Listen, Beck." I sighed and gathered my strength. "We need to talk."

He froze. "That doesn't sound good."

I pulled away from his hug and took in his troubled expression. The dreaded "we need to talk" was never what anyone wanted to hear. My heart was already breaking. I wasn't strong enough for this. "Maybe we should cool it until after the performances are over. We've just both got a lot on our plates right now, you know?"

His face transformed into an unreadable mask. "Okay, sure."

"Can we meet up after curtain on Saturday?" I tried to keep my voice light, but even I could hear the tremble. There were only three performances. One Friday night, a matinee on Saturday, and then an evening show. "And we can talk about everything going on here," I pointed between us, "without all the *Oklahoma!* stuff in the way."

He nodded once. "I'm going to go take a shower. I'll see you at school." But he didn't wait for my reply, and he didn't invite me to join him either. He left me there in his bed, and the anvil of guilt pressing down didn't lighten up like I'd hoped it would.

"I can't believe I forgot about the car thing," I squealed to myself. It was three-ten, and Sophie still wasn't home. Which, fine, she lived like eight minutes from the school and would have to deal with the parking lot traffic. I had to be at rehearsal in five minutes and there was no doubt I'd be late.

I pulled open the taxi app. There wasn't a car close enough, so I dialed Sophie's phone and prayed she picked up.

"Hold your horses," she ground out the second she answered. "I'm pulling onto Daisy Lane now."

"Oh, thank goodness!" I hung up and ran for the door, prepared to meet her in the driveway and trade places. There wasn't time to put on her clothes, but hopefully nobody would notice that while we both had on the same style of black dress pants, my button up top was a different cut and shade than whatever she'd worn today.

She stopped at the curb and climbed from the car, tossing me the keys. Her eyes were angry slits, and suddenly, they were all I could see. "Are you going to explain to me why the nurse gave me a scathing glare at lunch today, or why my work-wife, Jeanine, avoided me all day?"

My stomach dropped. "Later, I promise!"

She growled, throwing her hands into the air, and strode toward her house.

"Crap," I moaned. There was so much I was dreading, starting with "I'm sleeping with your boss" and ending with "who put you on administrative probation."

I jumped into the car and raced off to rehearsal. After all the times I'd lectured those kids on being on time to our practices, here I was, a total hypocrite, turning up late to our most important rehearsal of all.

I ran into the auditorium a good ten minutes late, but luckily, Mrs. Sanchez had gotten things started by warming up the kids' vocals. That didn't stop everyone on stage from quieting mid "*fa-la-la*" and staring at me.

"I thought you cut your hair again," Benjamin jeered, appearing beside me like a little he-demon. My whole body prickled as I realized my dumb mistake. Oh, no.

I cleared my throat. "Um, it's always been short. I use extensions."

He smirked. "Pretty good extensions if you ask me."

"Yeah, and removable ones at that," I choked out. Now I knew why the twins cut their hair to match in *The Parent Trap*.

"And you changed your shirt?" He raised an eyebrow. "That's not odd."

I swallowed hard. Why did this kid have to be so observant? Um, hello, he was the odd one here. "I spilled something on it and ran home to change. That's, uhh, also when I put my extensions back on and why I was late." I waved him off. "Anyway," my voice rose so everyone could hear me, "you lot look amazing!" And they really did, all dressed up in their folksy farmer costumes. Yesterday, we'd worked out the last of the kinks, and I was more than ready to see the result of all our hard work. "Today, we're going to run it through without stopping."

They erupted in nervous conversation, their attention finally off of me and my magical hair extensions. I turned away and rubbed my hands over my face. That could have gone better.

"Get to your places," Mrs. Sanchez chimed in, beginning to play the overture notes. They bled seamlessly into *Oh, What A Beautiful Morning*, and my eyes filled with frustrated tears.

If only it *was* a beautiful morning and a beautiful day and everything was going my way.

I hadn't talked to Beck since he left me for his shower. Or at least, I didn't think I had. There was a high likelihood that Sophie and he had at least one interaction throughout the school day. If I wasn't lying to both of them, I could just ask her how it went. Instead, I had to be cagey. I had definitely asked to cool things off with Beck this morning, but I didn't know that would mean radio silence. No text, no popping into rehearsal, nothing.

I suddenly realized just how much contact the two of us had had since I started at Halo. Now, going a day without seeing him felt wrong. How was I supposed to go back home and live like this everyday?

Benjamin snapped his fingers in front of my face. "You're zoning out. Do you want me to take over?" The evil glimmer behind his eyes was at an all-time high. I so couldn't have him take over and terrify the cast at the final dress rehearsal.

"Thank you, but I got this." And I did. I worked with the props crew to make sure that all the key sets were on and off the stage before the lights came up on each new scene.

Mrs. Sanchez had whipped the orchestra into amazing shape. They ran their parts alongside my theatre kids without a hitch, even with the first chair flutist calling in sick and being replaced by a sophomore who didn't have the best attendance record.

Nobody ran on stage in the wrong costume. That was not something I could say with confidence yesterday.

Mostly, I was proud of Kayla because when Tyler went in for the kiss, she almost looked like she *wasn't* going to throw up. I mean, she didn't look like she was attracted to him by any means, but it was a marked improvement.

This silly mistake was turning out to be one of the best decisions I had ever made. If it weren't for the musical, I don't think I would have ever considered teaching again, but now it felt like, maybe I could do it? Not life skills, and definitely not economics, but drama maybe?

I was almost done being Sophie. Maybe it was time I figured out who Dani was supposed to be.

Chapter Twenty-Six

#ANightToRemember

"Who is the man?" Sophie asked the second I stepped in the front door. The dress rehearsal had run well past eight, and having hardly gotten any sleep the night before, I was bone-weary.

"You won't know him," I lied, kicking my shoes off and dropping onto the couch with a thud.

Sophie's hazel eyes narrowed, and her brows furrowed. "This is Halo, Oklahoma. There is no one I don't know."

"Who's your man?" I deflected. "Who's Marco?"

Sophie inhaled deeply, "It doesn't matter. It's not a thing anymore."

"Not a thing because you left Mexico, or not a thing because you broke up?"

"I don't want to talk about my guy anymore!" cried

Sophie, her voice shrill and eyes practically bulging out of her head. "I'm asking about yours."

"And I don't want to talk about mine," I barked. "Obviously, it doesn't get to be anything after this week anyway."

Sophie's face fell, and I was struck by what it would look like if I was sad and also had a bad haircut. Which reminded me…

"You cannot teach class tomorrow."

"What?"

"Because at rehearsal, this snot-nosed stage manager kid—"

"Name please."

"Benjamin Bailey."

"Gah," gasped Sophie. "Pure evil. Pure fashionable, very organized evil."

"Exactly. Well, he noticed my *hair extensions*." I held my fingers up in little air quotes. "And it is going to get a little silly if I keep claiming that I take them out for classes and put them back in for after school."

"Oh, well that would explain why Principal Beck was giving me funny looks. And others, actually."

I kept my face flat as paper.

Sophie cocked an eyebrow. "Does Dani need a sensible bob?"

I picked up the one remaining couch cushion to survive the day I starved her cat and chucked it at her head.

"I have done *things* for this twin swap, but I am not cutting my hair."

Sophie shook her head. "Compromise. I'll wear it in a bun tomorrow."

I grimaced. It was possible but certainly not long enough to make that look even remotely cute.

"Would you rather I have a bad hair day tomorrow or you have a bad hair day for a very long time?"

I conceded. "Fine, but I've been teaching as you this whole time. I don't see how one more day could cause a problem." The truth was I wanted an excuse to see Foster, but I couldn't exactly tell her that.

"Yeah," said Sophie, rising with a yawn. "I enjoyed reading my revised syllabus for both classes, but I think it is probably best if you stick to the theatre."

I wanted to argue that my course changes were actually very useful and probably would leave a lasting impact, but I kept my mouth shut because so far, Sophie had dropped the man thing and I wasn't sure how long I could brush off her questions if we stayed up talking all night the way we used to. Also, because I still needed to tell her about the administrative probation thing, but I was scared and sort of leaving that one for the last minute.

"Which you're good at that theatre stuff, by the way. Principal Beck stopped by my room today, and he was very excited to tell me how many tickets had pre-sold."

"He stopped by for that?" My heart warmed. I desperately wanted to ask more questions but knew if I did I would be showing my hand.

"Yeah, it was weird."

"Weird?"

Sophie laughed. "Weird in a good way. It felt like before he got the principal job and we actually could be civil with each other."

Now, my heart felt like it had just taken the elevator down down down to the cold land of sad and lonely people. When she said "weird," I'd hoped she had meant different. Familiar was awful. Familiar, I wasn't sure I could handle.

"Anyway, I guess I have you to thank for that. I'm not sure if I would have found a way to get him over that hump." Sophie stretched her hands up over her head and squinted at me with one tired eye. I was still stuck on the word "hump" because, uhh, I'd definitely done that.

"We can catch up tomorrow, right?" She yawned. "I'm still on west coast time."

"Absolutely," I answered with a forced smile and then waited for her to pad off to bed before visiting the refrigerator to pour myself a glass of her box wine. I could have upgraded two weeks ago when the first box ran out, but I was becoming oddly accustomed to this Halo lifestyle.

At my feet, her cat, now slimmer, hissed at me before returning to the tuna fish dinner Sophie had promptly provided him. Spoiled cat.

"Don't get sassy with me," I whispered. "You lasted longer than the plants."

"This is your chance to prove you trust me." Benjamin pointed from where we stood backstage to my reserved seat in the auditorium. "You can go give your little 'turn off' your phones' spiel, but after that you must sit your butt down in that chair and let me do my job." We were five minutes from showtime, and I'd just announced that we'd sold out. Everyone was abuzz with excitement. Even my limbs felt like jello, and I wasn't in the show!

I smiled and placed both hands on my stage manager's shoulders, peering deeply into his authoritarian-dictator eyes. "I trust you, Benjamin."

"Thanks." He smirked. "You should."

"And you know what? You're just as much of a lead in this show as anyone. We couldn't have done this without you, Mr. Bailey."

He shook me off. "Oh shut up, *Ms. Sparks*, you're making it hard for me to keep hating you."

I laughed and turned away, surveying the fresh set pieces and bright lights in front of the navy curtain, as well as all the actors quietly preparing themselves behind it. I smiled from ear to ear.

Nerves bounced around inside my chest as I strode out onto the stage. The crowd quieted, anticipation swelling into every nook and cranny of the auditorium. "Welcome," I said into the microphone propped stage left. "Thank you for joining us tonight. I'm Ms. Sparks, and I had the great privilege of directing tonight's performance of *Oklahoma!*"

Some of the crowd clapped, others seemed unsure.

"Yes," I encouraged them, clapping myself, until everyone joined in on the fun. Once that quieted down, I asked them to please silence their cell phones and keep food and drinks in the lobby. Okay, it wasn't a real lobby, it was the school hallway, but we'd be selling overpriced concessions at a table out there during the fifteen-minute intermission, so same difference.

I handed the mic off to a crew member and bounded off the side of the stage, taking my seat near where Mrs. Sanchez and her orchestra were ready to go. Shooting them a little thumbs up, I welled with pride when they began to play, the lights brightened on the stage, and the first two characters appeared.

The reserved seat next to mine was empty, and just when I was about to feel bad about that, Beck sank down into it. I exhaled a deep sigh of relief.

"Hi," I whispered. "You're here."

He nodded once but didn't look at me. In fact, his energy was all wrong. It was as if he was trying to avoid me, like sitting next to me was a burden. I folded my arms over my chest and sank back, trying to be mesmerized by the show and not distracted by Beck's sour mood. He continued to ignore me, not even looking at me when Tyler took the stage and blew the audience away with his amazing voice and natural charisma. The second Tyler finished his last note, Beck burst into applause, his face alight with joy. He was truly happy for the sophomore, as was I, as was *everyone*.

But what was going on?

"Amazing, huh?" I whispered to Beck, trying to get his exterior to crack and let me in.

Again, nothing.

A few minutes later, I attempted to sneak my hand into his, but he snapped it away. Was he mad at me for asking us to cool things off? Was he trying to be professional? Or did he *know*?

At that last thought, I grew hot all over. My throat constricted. My ears echoed, drowning everything else out. It made sense. Why else would he be so mad at me? We'd been having such a great time together, and yeah, he'd been upset about our conversation yesterday morning, but this was a different level of freeze-out. Then again, if he knew, surely Sophie would've tipped me off by ripping my head off. If he knew, he would have had it out with Sophie by now, and no way she'd not have said anything.

It was all so confusing.

Intermission came quick, and Beck was gone the second the house lights flipped on. Trying not to be too worried or give into my hurt feelings, I rushed over to Mrs. Sanchez to congratulate her.

"Congratulations to you too, Sophie." She patted me on the back. "This is a big win for the arts department. Have you heard the rumors lately? If they're true, we're going to need all the wins we can get and fast. Goodness, I'm so tired of the politics. You know, I've been thinking it's time for me to retire."

I stared at her. "What?" I was still stuck on the bit about needing all the help we can get.

"Mrs. Sanchez." A student tapped her on the shoulder. "I broke a string." The girl held up a violin. "Can you help?"

"We'll talk later," Mrs. Sanchez promised.

I tucked the gossip away for later and hurried backstage to congratulate the students. Backstage, at this point, wasn't actually behind the curtain. It was out the side hallway and in the band room with a couple of sheeted-off dressing areas on each side. The students were talking animatedly over top of each other, clearly pleased with themselves.

When they saw me, they burst into applause.

I felt myself reddening and motioned for them to quiet down. "We're not done yet. We still have another half and two more shows. But I just wanted to say congratulations to you all; you're doing a marvelous job!"

They cheered again, and I left them to it.

When I returned, Beck had found another chair, switching places with one of the grumpy math teachers.

What was her name again? I'd known it the first day, but my mind was completely blank now. It didn't matter. She hardly said two words to me and only clapped politely the rest of the show. She was here because she supported her students, not because she actually enjoyed the theatre, it seemed.

I tried not to let it get me down that Beck had abandoned me. I tried to focus on the good things, but my heart was in two places at once. It was on the stage with my kids, singing and dancing, having the time of my life. And it was back with Beck, shattered into a million pieces because he clearly wanted nothing to do with me anymore.

The finale went off with all the theatrical fanfare we'd hoped for, and the crowd rose to a standing ovation. I clapped right along with them, and when it was over, I went backstage, offered my final congratulations, packed up my things, and went home.

Maybe I should let this thing go. Benjamin could handle managing the performances tomorrow without me. I'd done my job here, hadn't I? Beck was clearly finished with me. Sophie wanted her life back. I held back the tears as I realized that it was time to close the curtain on this thing and go home.

Chapter Twenty-Seven

#ShitMeetFan

"But you can't leave!" Sophie gasped, lowering the lid of my suitcase and pulling it away from me in a single motion. "You still have two more shows tomorrow."

I grabbed it back, flopped it open again, and continued to throw my stuff inside. I was in the guest room now, and my suitcase was propped open on the bed while I tried to locate all my crap. "Yeah, well, I think I've done enough here."

"What happened?"

"Nothing." But it wasn't nothing, and she knew it, and I knew it, and my stupid tear ducts knew it.

She tried to pull me into a hug, but I dodged her.

"Tell me."

I couldn't tell her. I just couldn't. She'd hate me, and I didn't want to lose her, too.

"Is this about the musical? Is this because you're sad you didn't get to have your dream of being a drama teacher?"

Well, that was part of it. I nodded wryly.

She sat me down on the bed and peered knowingly into my eyes. "Dani, you're a marvelous drama teacher. You have to be. I saw *Oklahoma!* tonight."

"You were there," I gasped.

She nodded sagely. "Don't worry, I wore a disguise and sat in the back." She clasped my hands between hers. "But I'm telling you, that was the best show they've had at Halo High."

I snorted. "How would you know? You've only been there for three years."

"Um, hello! There's a reason why the theatre department got shut down. Trust me, you're a star."

I smiled. "Thanks."

"I think you should take the Praxis test," she added matter-of-factly in that Sophie way of hers. "Now, I know you're a terrible test taker, but I promise, it's not that bad. You'll pass, and then you can do your student teaching and get a real job."

"I have a real job."

Her face paled. "I know. Sorry, I didn't mean that. Your Instagram stuff is amazing. You should keep doing that. But you could stay in California and teach there. Or I don't know. Maybe you could try for the vacancy here? Maybe that guy—"

I cut her off. "He's gone."

She sighed, frowning.

I don't know what came over me, but before I could

stop myself from putting my foot in my mouth, I did it anyway. "So, you'll risk your job to help Nova get a tummy tuck, but you won't risk your job to help your own sister get her teacher's license?"

Silence spread between us, heavy and thick. She dropped my hands, and her face turned pink. "You really want to do this now?"

I raised a shoulder and an eyebrow, like the total brat I was, because I kind of did. I was being childish, taking my hurt out on her, but here we were.

"Okay, fine. I'm sorry, okay?" She threw her hands up in the air. "Twin-swaps are messy, and I shouldn't have asked you to do this one."

That wasn't what I expected. Her apology took the wind right out of my sails. We'd had years of a strained relationship and I was expecting an epic fight—the kind we used to have growing up like siblings often do—but maybe this time things were finally different. Maybe we were both ready to be adults about things. "It's fine." I deflated. "And I actually liked teaching. I think you're right. I'm going to study for the Praxis and take it myself."

"Really?"

"Really." My lips quirked at the side, hopeful.

She jumped on me, locking me in a painful hug. "I'm so excited for you! Oh, and you can't leave until after the shows tomorrow, okay? Promise me. You deserve to enjoy it; soak in the results of your hard work."

I peeled her off me and zipped up my suitcase,

setting it next to the dresser. "Okay, fine, but then I'm going back to California."

The doorbell rang. "Were you expecting someone?"

"No." Maybe it was a package or something.

"Hmm, I'll go get it," she offered.

I gathered up my dirty clothes to throw in the wash when I heard the screen door squeak open and Soph's hollow voice filter through the house.

"Oh, hello, Principal Beck. How can I help you?"

I froze for a millisecond, knowing exactly what was going to happen before my feet made a mad dash for the living room.

He hugged her, then turned her around so that his back was to me. His hands cupped her face and his lips crashed against hers. Sophie's eyes about bugged out of her head, and her arms remained frigid at her side. What was I supposed to do? Step out from hiding and explain the whole thing? I wanted to, but my heart was a bongo drum. I stayed out of view and watched as my two worlds collided. If there were dinosaurs on the happy planet I'd lived on this week, they were dead now. The asteroid, aka this kiss, just killed them. Total annihilation.

Beck pulled back, looking lovingly into the wrong set of hazel eyes. "I'm sorry for how I've treated you these last few days. I know we are supposed to be cooling it until after the show. I thought I could turn off my emotions, but I can't. I don't want to wait that long to tell you how I feel about you."

Horrible. This was horrible, but my feet were glued to the tile.

Sophie balled up her fists and wedged them into her hips. "Go for it. Tell me how you feel about *me*."

There was enough malice behind that "me" to make me want to grab my suitcase and never look back, but I couldn't, not till I heard what Foster had to say.

Foster winced a little, and I felt for the guy. I mean, he had been exceptionally cold tonight at the show, but it was obvious he came to apologize, and "I" was being pretty rude about it. Sophie took a deep breath and relaxed a microscopic amount.

"I guess what I came to say is that I don't really care how early this is. Alison already knows about us."

An audible huff escaped Sophie's nose, and I sincerely hoped Foster didn't pick up on it.

"If we don't work out, we don't work out. But we can't if we don't give things a real shot." Beck straightened his spine and looked directly into Sophie's hardened expression. "I want to declare our relationship to the school board."

I dropped the basket of laundry I didn't even realize was in my hands. It crashed to the floor with a thud no one was going to believe was the cat.

"Is there someone else here?" whispered Beck.

I held my breath.

"Yes," declared Sophie. "My sister." And I was sure she would follow that up with *get your butt out here,* but instead she finished with. "I haven't told her about you yet, and she won't be happy that I'm risking my job for a guy. You have to go."

Foster looked hurt. My heart didn't like that.

"Now," she said with a gentle shove. "We can talk later." Then, begrudgingly, "I promise."

I stepped back into the bedroom and prepared for the inevitable. The door hadn't been shut longer than three seconds before she shrieked my name like a banshee.

Dramatically, I grabbed the handle of my suitcase and wheeled it into the living room.

"Oh, no you don't!" she cried, jerking it out of my hand. "You don't get to run away from this one."

"I was going to tell you," I lied.

"Really? Before or after you got back to California? Before or after Foster declared your *relationship* to the school board? Are you insane? This is one hundred times worse than the time you lost my virginity!"

In my defense, she sent me on a blind date she didn't want to go on. It wasn't like I made sweet love to her boyfriend or anything. I just, you know, found myself connecting on a higher level than I could have anticipated. And it was *college*!

Sophie tore her hands through her hair. "I knew I shouldn't have trusted you with this."

"Shouldn't have trusted me…" The words felt like a dull dagger to an already infected wound.

"You know why I didn't take the Praxis for you?"

I didn't want to hear the answer.

"Because it was selfish for you to even ask. I could have lost my chance at a career because you were scared and unwilling to risk failure, but you're willing to risk screwing up my life, aren't you?"

"No," I cried. "It wasn't like that."

"Tell me this, Dani, when were you going to tell me I was on administrative probation? Was that gonna be a text, too?"

Damn, I should have known that wasn't going to stay a secret.

"I didn't bring it up because I didn't want you to feel bad," she pressed on. "I *thought* you were really trying."

"I was." Tears stung my eyes for the second time this evening.

Sophie shook her head. "The sad part is you probably were."

Ouch—I stepped back.

"It's late, and I don't want to talk to you anymore, so here's what you're going to do."

I bit my lip to keep the tears from falling, and she gave her orders.

"You're going to finish the play because you managed not to screw that up yet, and when it's over, you are going to clear things up with Foster Beck and go home."

What I hated the most wasn't that I had messed everything up, or that Sophie was angry with me, again. It was that when she said "home," I felt like I was already standing in it. Somewhere along the way, Halo had become my comfort zone. Going back to my overpriced apartment wasn't going to feel right, but neither was staying where I wasn't welcome.

When I didn't respond, she sucked in her bottom lip and waited, her tired expression tinged with anger and frustration.

"Yeah," I mumbled. "I can do that."

What I couldn't do was go to sleep until I had a plan to talk to Foster. I texted him an apology for my irrational behavior and asked him to meet me back at his office after the final performance tomorrow. I hadn't got to explain myself to Sophie, but I was going to tell Foster the truth. I just had to make it through the next two performances first.

Chapter Twenty-Eight

#LoveYourSelfie

The moment my eyes fluttered open the next morning, I squeezed them shut again. I wanted to go back to the yummy dream I'd just been having about Beck and not the reality that I was going to have to tell him the truth tonight. If he really had feelings for me, feelings that were as strong as my own, then surely he'd say, "I totally understand you were doing a favor for your sister. It wasn't your fault. I forgive you. In fact, I'm madly in love with you and want us to have lots of sex and babies."

I snorted and sat up. Fat chance of that happening. Deep in my gut, I knew it was more likely he was going to send me packing. Or at the very least, we'd start a long distance relationship on shaky ground, making our future together unlikely to succeed.

The pain of inevitable heartbreak deepened.

I plopped back down on the pillows and retrieved my phone—as one does early in the morning—to check my Instagram. Live Love Laugh had paid me a mere fraction of what they normally did, so when I saw the unread DM waiting from Annie, I almost didn't want to click on it.

"Rip the bandaid off." I winced, doing it anyway.

Hi, Dani. Unfortunately, we can't employ you as a brand ambassador for Live Love Laugh moving forward. It's no secret that your last unboxing had lackluster results and your account has suffered lately. Your numbers are down across the board, and your aesthetic has become muddled with amateur photos. Most recently, you posted a picture wearing a sunhat exclusive to one of our biggest competitors. Despite past successes, these discrepancies cannot be overlooked, and it's time for our partnership to end. We wish you luck in all of your endeavors and hope you'll always consider us at Live Love Laugh as friends. Take care, Annie.

"Friends? Yeah, right!" I growled and threw my phone across the room. It clattered against the hardwood. I jumped up, retrieving it to make sure I hadn't just cracked the screen. I hadn't. But seriously, could this day get any worse? I sat down and scrolled back to my Instagram account, trying to see it through Annie's eyes.

She was right.

My images were too bad-Photoshop looking.

Sophie had tried, but she didn't know how to model, and even though we looked alike, we were two different people. She wasn't me. How could I have expected her to be me? I should have just taken pictures of myself here in Oklahoma and used those. Pretending to be her being me in Mexico? It was inauthentic. And even though nobody called me out on it because nobody knew, it still came across as fake. No wonder my numbers had suffered.

Not to mention, I should have told Annie from the beginning that I didn't have the box and needed to skip this month's unboxing video. I should have been honest with her. And I definitely shouldn't have posted a picture of my sister wearing a competitor's sunhat, not that I knew. But I could have done my research.

I was normally so much better at this. Professional. The top of my game. But I'd let it all slide to help my sister. But that wasn't exactly true either, was it? Because helping Sophie was only part of it. I'd been the one to get wrapped up in the rehearsals and Beck. I'd been the one to avoid my real job. This was on me.

I lay back on the white sheets, held the phone above me until I found a good angle, and took the shot. My hair was a mess of sleepy waves, my hazel eyes were a little red from crying, and I didn't have a stitch of makeup on. But this? This was real. And I was ready to start being real.

Before I could talk myself out of it, I posted it with the caption, "*Time for truth, vulnerability, and authenticity. I'm not perfect and that's okay. #NoFilter #NoMakeup #LoveYourSelfie.*"

I might lose followers over this, or I might gain even more—I didn't care so much anymore. I'd find another way to pay my bills if I had to, there were plenty of service jobs in Dana Point, and anyway, I was finally going to get my teaching license. If my sponsors dropped me because my page wasn't a perfect magazine spread all the time, then so be it. Perfect was overrated.

The matinee went off without a hitch—not a missed line, a late entrance, or a note off key. Once again, we were sold out, but this time with more children in the crowd. And once again, we ended in a standing ovation. As I left the building to grab some dinner and take a break before returning for the closing performance, my eyes brimmed with tears. I was going to miss this whole thing far more than I'd ever expected. But I needed to be strong. Sophie needed me to be strong. Beck did. The kids did. And most of all, I did.

When I approached Soph's car—most people had left the parking lot by now—I was stopped short by raised voices. Not just any voices either, familiar ones.

I turned to find the booster club president Jim Vance, the PTA president Carli Joe Jenson, and the superintendent Tom Wainwright, all standing around what I guessed was Jim's sports car by the MRVANCE on the license plate. Not to mention, only a guy like that would have such an overly flashy "look at me" type of ride. The three were clearly in the middle of a heated argument. Carli Joe's hands were flailing, Jim was pointing at her, and Tom's face was beet red. I couldn't quite make out everything they were saying, but phrases like "narcissistic pig" and "blatant favoritism" were being swung by Carli Joe while Jim hurled back "jealous hag" and "nobody cares." Meanwhile, Wainwright looked about ready to blow.

I wanted to jump into my car and race away. This wasn't my business. But then my mind filtered back to something I'd forgotten about, something that now seemed important. Last night, Mrs. Sanchez had mentioned there were rumors surrounding the arts department and that we needed the musical to be a success. That must be related to whatever was going on between these three, right? My eyes narrowed, and before I could stop myself, I marched over to them.

"Um, excuse me," I said boldly. "But you're being quite loud over here, and we still have students and members of the public leaving the parking lot."

"She's right." Mr. Vance raised a knowing eyebrow at Carli Joe. "You're being unprofessional."

She threw her hands in the air. "Are you kidding me?"

"Ms. Jenson," Tom added in a condescending tone. "There's no need for hysterics."

"Do you know about this?" Carli Joe turned on me, her eyes wide and crazed. "Do you know what they're doing to the auditorium?"

"That's on a need-to-know basis only," Tom jumped in. "The bond—"

"I don't care about the damn bond," Carli Joe interjected. She glared at him and then returned to me.

"They're tearing down the auditorium to make room for a new gymnasium."

I froze. "What?" My voice squeaked out, sounding hollow and far away.

"The bond's already passed and is getting signed on Monday," she continued. "They fed me some bullshit story about how they'd wait to see how the musical went to keep me from taking this public, but clearly none of that even mattered. It's already a done deal."

If the ground was quicksand, I would have been sucked right under. I blinked at them, disbelieving. "But—but—we sold out."

"The auditorium is old and failing." Mr. Wainwright shrugged. "Surely, even you can see that it needs to go."

My ears were buzzing.

"The money from the bond was supposed to go toward improving the school," Carli Joe went on. "This should include renovations."

"A new gymnasium is improving the school," Vance scoffed. "There are more athletes than arty kids anyway. And all the numbers say—"

He prattled on and on, but my mind had tuned him out. All I could think was that if this was happening, if the auditorium was going, then Beck must have known all about it. He'd said we needed to rush the rehearsals because the school had a lot they needed to do in the auditorium, but I never imagined it was because they were demolishing it. I remembered that day when he'd hidden away architectural plans as I'd gone into his office—the man had avoided telling me at all costs.

My mouth hardened into a thin line. I glared at the men in front of me, but I didn't say a word as I turned and stormed back to my car. Sure, I'd lied to Beck, but I'd done it to protect my sister. He'd lied to me—omitting this truth was a lie as far as I was concerned—and he'd done it to protect what? His good standing with the superintendent? His budding romance with me? The athletes? Himself?

All this time, I was beating myself up and feeling like a complete jerk for my secrets. And yet, here Beck was, pulling the wool over my eyes, keeping secrets of his own. Too bad I turned out to be the twitterpated-idiot who fell for them all.

Chapter Twenty-Nine

#TheShowMustGoOn

Maybe Beck was okay sitting back and letting these kids lose out on the opportunity to do something they love so that Mr. Vance and the rest of the money-hungry athletic fans could score another chunk of budget pie, but I wasn't.

Kids like Tyler, Kayla, and even that tyrant Benjamin Bailey deserved an opportunity to shine just as much as the football team, maybe even more because whereas athletic scholarships were offered left and right, theatre was poorly funded. Kids who wanted financial assistance to pursue acting had to shine twice as bright, and without an auditorium, Halo High kids didn't have a chance.

It was kind of Ms. Jenson to keep things quiet, but the ink wasn't dry on that contract, and Dani Sparks was about to blow this covert operation out of the water. It was the one thing I could do before leaving Oklahoma, and I wasn't backing down.

Forget food, I needed a high-powered makeover and claws. With my mind on the mission and the mission alone, I pulled into Sophie's driveway, stomped into the house, and flung open my suitcase. Down at the bottom, in the "haven't used it once since I arrived here" section, laid my power pants.

Pin striped and tailored to every curve, these pants were incapable of failure. Pair them with a white silk blouse and sky high stilettos and no one stood a chance. Especially not that pandering pansy Mr. Wainwright.

I shot him a glare that would wilt roses as I marched onto the stage for the director's closing comments. This was supposed to be the part where my students would bring me flowers, and I'd act all surprised, and then I'd ask the audience to give the performers an extra round of applause and thank them for their hard work during rehearsals. No one was getting that speech tonight.

"I hope you enjoyed the final performance of Halo High School's *Oklahoma!*" The crowd roared, even though they had just spent the better part of five minutes clapping as each actor and actress took their final bow.

"Raise your hand if you have enjoyed watching the cast and crew bring this musical to life."

Hands rose all around the building. I spotted Tyler's housekeeper sitting next to a fine looking couple absolutely dripping in wealth and a couple of teachers from trivia night sitting toward the back with Alison.

"Raise your hand if you came here tonight because your child is in the orchestra," I continued, and more hands rose.

"Now," I said, wiping the smile from my face and replacing it with a hardened glare pointed directly at Mr. Wainwright. "Raise your hand if you can't wait to see this place demolished and replaced by a second practice facility for Halo High athletics."

Confused expressions littered the crowd as one by one hands dropped to their laps.

"I didn't think so. I could be mistaken, but there is already a gym in this school. Is there not?" Snickers emitted around the room.

"And baseball and football, those are outdoor sports, yeah?"

These were meant to be rhetorical questions, but given we were in a room full of theatre kids, someone did yell, "Sportsball can definitely be played outside!"

"Thank you," I replied with a smirk. "Sportsball can definitely be played outside. So well put. You know what doesn't work as well outside? Or in a gym? Large scale musicals. One might say you need an auditorium for that. And shucks," I held my arms out to my sides and bugged my eyes with shock and awe, "we totally have one of those!"

In the front row, Jeanine beamed. Whatever hostility she had been holding onto this past week dissipated when the two of us made eye contact. Next to her, however, Foster Beck did not look so pleased. In fact, Foster looked a lot like he wanted to pull me off the stage with one of those over sized canes.

"So, let me ask you guys to raise your hands again. Only, this time, raise your hand if you think Halo High theatre kids *deserve* a place to rehearse. And furthermore, that Halo High orchestra kids *deserve* a place to perform."

Every hand in the room was extended in the air, except for that of Superintendent Wainwright and Principal Foster Beck. I had a feeling I was about to experience one hell of a "What were you thinking?" conversation, but at the moment, I absolutely did not care.

"Superintendent Wainwright, could you stand please."

The man's face turned beet red, and I watched as he tugged to loosen the tie at his neck. I cocked one eyebrow and tapped my foot expectantly. The man stood reluctantly.

"If you could face the crowd please."

Mr. Wainwright did as he was told, but he did it with clenched fists and his mouth pursed in a firm line.

"If you think the auditorium should stay an auditorium and continue to be a place where kids can hone their skills in the performing arts, show Superintendent Wainwright your support by clapping for tonight's cast and crew."

The applause was thundering and so was the look on Beck's face when he motioned for me to meet him in his office before briskly marching out of the auditorium. My plan had been to tell him about Sophie and

I, but now I was too fired up that he would rather let the auditorium be demolished than stand up to the superintendent.

The relationship babble could wait, and besides, I was pretty pissed off at him, too. The moment I walked in his office door he spun around, hands on hips, and gaped at me. "Have you lost it? You don't make a fool of the superintendent in front of a house full of people!"

"Make a fool of the super?" I laughed. "I'm not the one making a fool of the superintendent. He's doing that all on his own."

Beck shook his head. "Sophie, it's not that simple. This conversation has been going on longer than you've been involved in the theatre department. Where were you last year when this first came up? Where were you when the booster club pitched the idea of a new practice center? These things don't happen in a vacuum. You can't just make a rousing speech at the last minute and expect to get your way."

"You should have told me what was going on," I retorted. Because I mean, hello, he can sleep with me, but he can't tell me that my musical is going to be the last one? It was complete and utter crap, and he knew it.

Beck threw his hands up. "When? When should I have told you? I didn't know what was going to happen between us, and you've spent the last three days telling me to keep my distance. You change daily. Even your hair is unreliable."

I gasped. How dare he? Except, then I remembered

why he was saying it, and it became significantly more difficult to argue that *he* shouldn't have kept anything from *me*. There was no time for arguing about us anyway because a line was forming outside of his open office door that included half the cast of *Oklahoma!*, an absolutely elated Ms. Jepsen, and a much less elated superintendent.

Beck's eyes were wide with terror.

"That was some stunt," barked Mr. Wainwright. "Foster, I'm really put off. If you objected to the project, you should have voiced your concerns earlier."

Ms. Jepsen let out a bitter laugh. "And what exactly would you do with those concerns? Pat him on the shoulder and then show him the number of scholarship dollars the booster club puts out? The only opinion you've heard in the last four months is your own."

Admittedly, I did not have a good understanding of how the PTA, booster club, high school administration, and superintendent were supposed to work together, but the energy in the room was beyond toxic, and Foster was right at the center of it.

Mr. Wainwright shook his head and disregarded everything that came out of Ms. Jenson's mouth, choosing instead to turn his wrath on me.

"And you, you're already on probation." His shiny potato head turned red, and his eyes narrowed into accusatory slits. "What made you think you could get up there and rile the crowd up like that?"

I swallowed hard and shoved my hands into the pockets of my power pants. "I thought people deserved to have a say in whether or not you tear down the auditorium. I thought these kids deserved to have a say," I replied, looking around the room, where Kayla, Tyler, and Benjamin stood waiting to see if all I had said on stage was true.

Ben and Kayla would go on to college next year. They didn't need the Halo theatre program anymore, but what about Tyler and all the kids that would come after him?

Mr. Wainwright pinched the bridge of his nose between two fingers. "It's my job to think about all of the students, not just a small grouping of kids who enjoy performing on an old stage."

"If it were about the students, you'd have asked us," said Benjamin, stepping forward for the first time since the argument began. "This is about money. Same as it always is."

"It's not appropriate for students to be a part of this conversation," declared Mr. Wainwright. "You all need to go home and let the adults discuss the outcome of the auditorium."

Benjamin's skin turned fiery as he pointed at us. "You sure you can handle that? It's been over a month since school started, and you two haven't noticed that Ms. Sparks has been hijacked by Beverly Hills Barbie."

And that—right there—was the moment when shit officially hit the fan.

Mr. Wainwright scowled, Ms. Jenson looked confused, and Principal Foster Beck looked like he'd just been handed the final piece of a puzzle he'd been struggling with for far too long.

Ben shoved his phone in Mr. Wainwright's hand.

"Dani Sparks, California girl through and through, or so her profile says. Identical twin sister to a Ms. Sophie Sparks."

Mr. Wainwright's mouth formed a little O shape as he rectified the image on the phone with the woman standing in front of him.

"Do you still think we better leave you grown ups to the big decisions? It seems like if you can't tell a teacher from an Instagram Influencer you might need a little assistance."

Mr Wainwright passed the phone back to Benjamin and pulled the keys from his pocket. "I'll handle this Monday morning."

"What about the auditorium?" asked Benjamin.

"Quite frankly, kiddo, it's none of your business."

If Benjamin Bailey hadn't already been at the losing end of one fight this year, I think he would have hauled off and punched the superintendent right then and there. As it was, the kid clenched his jaw and puffed little bursts of angry air out of his nostrils.

Mr. Wainwright, paused at the door to Foster's office "As for you, I'll expect you to meet with me and the rest of the school board at the crack of dawn next week."

Foster opened his mouth ready to plead his case, but it was too late. Mr. Wainwright was already hustling down the hallway and out the front door, his noisy, shiny shoes click clacking the whole way out.

Foster ushered the kids out of his office, and Ms. Jenson followed suit. I turned to face him, ready to explain the whole messed up situation, but when I looked into his eyes and saw the hurt and anger colliding in a pit of swirling blue confusion, I lost my nerve. Not that it mattered.

"You too," said Foster coldly. He held the door to his office open and gestured for me to leave.

"I promise I…"

"Sophie… or Dani," he corrected, "You've made a mess of my *job*, and I'd like you to leave so I can start cleaning it up."

But this wasn't all my fault…

I could feel my chin beginning to quiver, but I sucked it up and turned to leave. Suddenly, my power pants and stilettos felt less like weapons of mass destruction and more like chains dragging behind me as I turned my back on the best thing to happen to me in a long time.

Chapter Thirty

#FaceTheMusic

I should have gone straight to the airport and purchased my flight home the night of the final production. My sister was furious with me, Foster didn't want to talk to me, and it was a student that blew up the twin-swap and left me standing with my mouth open in the principal's office.

I had basically failed at everything I came here to do, so why stay? Maybe because I was glutton for punishment and wanted to be there when Sophie came home bawling her eyes out because she'd been fired. I knew it was going to happen. She knew it. Everyone knew it. But that didn't make it any easier.

She returned to the house Monday morning, right about the time she should have been teeing up her economics class. Black mascara streaks stained her cheeks. Her hazel eyes were red, puffy, and shallow. She quietly hung her leather shoulder bag on the entryway hook, walked right past me to the kitchen, and poured herself a tall glass of water. Not once did she meet my eyes. Not once did she speak.

"I'm so sorry," I whispered.

Silence—except for the sound of her gulping down the water in one go.

"I shouldn't have gotten carried away like that," I pressed on. "This is my fault, and I'm going to find a way to make it up to you."

"How?" She turned, slamming the glass down on the counter, her body ridged. "Actually, I don't even want to know. Just go home, Dani. We're done here."

"I'm sorry, okay?" A hot tear splashed down my cheek. I took a step forward, but she held up a hand.

"I'm sorry, too," she countered. "I never should have trusted you. But it's not all your fault Dani, it's mine. Wainwright made a good point this morning."

I didn't dare ask her to elaborate, but she did anyway.

"The twin-swap was on me. I'm accountable for everything because I broke my contract and lied to my bosses. Whatever choices you made while pretending to be me are choices I now have to own."

"That's not—"

"I got myself fired," she snapped. "That's that."

I released a shaky breath. "So, what are you going to do?"

She shrugged. "Sell the house. Find another job in a new town. I don't know, Dani. But whatever it is, I'm doing it alone." She pulled a folded envelope from her pants pocket and handed it to me. "Please leave."

She slipped past me as I tore open the envelope to find a one way ticket back to California.

The taxi picked me up that evening, with Sophie still locked in her bedroom. She refused to talk to me all day or even say goodbye, which I got, but that didn't mean I wasn't hurt by it. I knew I'd made mistakes, but we were blood—we'd shared a womb—shouldn't that count for something?

"Airport, please," I grumbled as I slid into the stuffy backseat. The driver nodded and took off, silence settling over the cab. I was glad he wasn't chatty, which normally never bothered me, but I didn't have it in me today to fake cheeriness to a stranger.

As we drove out onto the two lane highway, I said a mental goodbye to Halo, Oklahoma. A month ago, I'd hated this place, and now, I saw it for what it was: not perfect but a town where the people lived a wholesome, simple, unassuming life. It wasn't the sophisticated beach town of Dana Point, but it wasn't better or worse. It was just different—a good different.

As the car approached the tree-lined road that led to Foster's house, my stomach hardened and my throat went dry. I didn't want to do it, I couldn't face him, but I forced myself to take action anyway.

"Excuse me," I said to the driver. "Can we please make a quick stop? I promise to double your tip."

The man shrugged. "Sure, there's not a lot of business out here anyway. Where would you like to go?"

I pointed him to the correct turn off and tried not to die of nerves as we wound our way to Beck's little white farmhouse. When we pulled up the dirt drive, I was overcome with a flood of good memories from the last week. I wished I could go back and redo some of them, but life didn't work that way.

Beck's car was parked out front. He was home.

"Give me five minutes," I said to the driver. "Ten tops."

"No problem."

I jumped out of the car and strode to the navy blue door, knocking hard before I could talk myself out of it.

Sure enough, Beck opened it after a few seconds of me standing there about ready to spontaneously combust.

He wore black gym clothes and was either getting ready to leave or having just come back, and I tried not to ogle his perfectly sculpted biceps or the way his dark hair curled at the ends. Even the return of that citrusy spice smell made my heart twist.

"What do you want?" His disgusted tone indicated the man was anything but happy to see me.

"To explain." I swallowed.

"Your sister already did." He moved to close the door, but I stopped it with my foot.

"I need you to listen to me, please," I pressed. "It was only supposed to be for a few days, and it was only because her friend had nobody else to help her. But obviously things changed, and it turned into a month, again that wasn't her fault, and—"

"I already know all this," he ground out, his eyes hard. They were two blue storms that refused to break, and I'd give anything to see them look at me the way they once had.

"Okay, but what about you and me?" I continued. My knees were starting to shake. "You have to know that I never meant for things to go this far,"—his jaw tightened—"but I don't regret that they did. I really care about you, and I'm sorry for hurting you."

He released a bitter laugh. "If you care about me, then why on earth would you call out my boss in front of an auditorium full of my students and their parents?"

"Because someone had to stand up for them." I was trying not to match his tone, but suddenly, all I could think was that he wasn't completely innocent here either. "That's why Sophie didn't want you to be principal, by the way. It wasn't because you'd be bad at it. It was because you're so good with these kids, and she knew you'd end up pandering to the school board."

"Well, then I guess she was right." He glared. "Did you ever stop to think that I care about these kids just as much as anyone? Or that maybe I was trying to save the auditorium, too?"

"Then, why didn't you?"

"Because I'm the principal, not the superintendent or the school board, or the booster club that had already raised most of the funds they needed," he growled. "And I can't just make money appear out of thin air to remodel the auditorium, which you know it needs."

He had me there. I knew as well as anyone that it smelled like dust, the curtains were probably as old as my grandmother, the chairs were hard and squeaky, and half the stage lights didn't work. But still, if there was a bond with money allocated to the school, then some of it should've been earmarked for the auditorium.

I shook my head at him. "So what? It still doesn't make it right."

He ran his hands over his face. "I can't believe I'm arguing with an Instagram Influencer over school politics."

The belittling way he said my career title was enough to bring the old Dani raging back to the surface. "Fine. I don't know what I'm talking about because I'm just some silly girl with a silly social media account with half a million silly followers. Whatever, right? Don't listen to me." I glared. "I'm leaving anyway, and you'll never have to see my face again."

"Good."

I thought my heart was broken, but it pretty much shredded into a million bloody pieces in that moment. I held back the tears and tried to push the anger back down, too. "You're really going to let Sophie get fired over all this?" I scoffed, my hands flying into the air. "Most of it was my fault, not hers."

"I'm glad that you recognize that," he deadpanned.

"Okay, so?"

He stared at me until the storm of his eyes finally

parted enough for me to see what he was hiding back there. I was expecting heartbreak and anger.

I wasn't expecting defeat.

"It's over, Dani," he said, closing the door in my face.

Chapter Thirty-One

#FlightOfShame

"Would you like something, Miss?"

I turned from gazing out the airplane window to blink, blurry-eyed, at the friendly airline attendant. "Um, just water please."

"What about a snack?" she asked cheerily as she retrieved the little bottle of water and handed it to me with a cup of ice. "We have peanuts, cheese crackers, granola bars, or cookies. Or if you'd rather purchase something off the menu, we have—"

She prattled on about their array of "westbound meals and snacks," but it was almost like I was underwater. I couldn't really hear her or internalize anything she was saying.

"No thanks," I croaked out, turning back to sulk as

the sun sank into puffy white clouds below us, washing everything in bright orange light.

Maybe I should have tried harder to convince Foster to give Sophie her job back, or maybe I should have kept pushing for him to hear me out, but the cold tone of his voice and the way he was so anxious to shut me out, left me feeling like nothing I had to say mattered anyway.

I had all of these great arguments about how it was all a misunderstanding—I wasn't trying to hurt anyone, things spiraled out of my control, etc. But when I was alone with my thoughts, say on a three-hour plane ride from Oklahoma to California, it was fairly easy to refute each and every one of those points.

If I had been an Alison instead of a Dani, I never would have gone rogue on the closing speech. Foster was one hundred percent right when he said I didn't think about him or his job when I made the decision to call out the superintendent in public. I acted out of passion. I acted because I thought it would make a difference to the students, and in the end, it felt like all I did was smash any chance of Foster and I into a billion pieces. Superintendent Wainwright certainly wasn't going to go running to the school board to plead that they save the auditorium now.

Why hadn't I thought about that then? A sickening thought planted itself in my head. I hadn't thought it through because per usual I was too busy thinking about me and how great it was going to feel to stand in front of everyone and make the bad guys feel bad.

I didn't know how to fix this. Running away always seemed to work, but did I really want to run away from Foster and Sophie? The whole reason I had agreed to the twin-swap was to make things better with my sister.

By the time the plane landed, the sky was black and the sparkling skyline outside of LAX reminded me of home. It also made my heart hurt even more.

I took a cab home from the airport, even though it was a good hour. I would much rather spend the money than have to rehash the last month of my life to any of my friends. I keyed into my apartment and took it all in, the white and tan furniture I'd so meticulously picked out last year after receiving a particularly large paycheck. The pale blue curtains closed tight over the windows that had been here when I'd moved in—I'd liked them well enough to keep them. The bohemian rug I'd bought from a vendor near Venice Beach. The guy had sworn on his mother's grave that it was authentic Turkish, but I'd had my doubts and still did. What used to feel quaint and self-made now meant nothing to me. It was just stuff. Just lonely and artificial stuff. There was nothing truly personal to me in here, no pictures on the walls of friends and family, nothing real. Everything was clean and organized, photo ready, but none of it meant anything to me.

It was almost laughable that Live Love Laugh had dumped me for not being professional or authentic enough when really, Sophie's horrible pictures and unboxing video were the realest of any I'd posted. I mean seriously, when she opened the candle and her face went *eh* instead of *ooh*, that was real. That was what most people opening that box were going to feel.

If I didn't have bills to pay, I might say screw it and be done with it. It would come as a relief. But what was I supposed to do? I was twenty-six, and no way would I be going home to mom and dad. As it was, I had some work to do to get back in the influencer game. Luckily, the no-makeup selfie had resulted in a hoard of new followers. It turned out people wanted to see that my life wasn't all beaches and cocktails, and fortunately for them, I had a lot to work with when it came to living the not so glamorous life lately.

I dragged a chair into my closet and climbed up to reach the very top shelf where I shoved things better left un-remembered. My fingers grazed a framed photo of an ex-douchebag before I felt the thick paper spine of my Praxis study guide. It had been a few years, and there were probably newer and better editions out there, but it was a start, and I needed a start.

With my suitcase open and articles of clothing displayed artfully spewing out the sides, I laid the Praxis book in the center and snapped the shot.

A short caption was all I needed because this time I was selling a feeling not a product.

Vacation's over. Time to face an old failure with new energy. And then, even though she was being a big hoochie mama hater right now, I added #sistergoals #makeitright #youinspireme because the truth was, without being Sophie for a month, I wouldn't have realized what a mistake it was to give up on teaching.

Live Love Laugh had already unfollowed me, but

Babe Book Club would eat this inspirational hoopla right up. And who knew? Maybe others would follow. I crawled into bed, sighing because even though life sucked right now, it was nice to be in my own bed again. I had high hopes that morning would bring a truckload of likes and some much needed positive feedback as I clicked post and tucked my phone away for the night.

I dreamed that a giant hashtag dressed like Foster Beck was chasing me around Halo, shouting, "Strip her of her verification. She's a liar!"

I woke up drenched in sweat, terrified that my little blue checkmark would be ripped from my undeserving profile forever.

Still out of breath, I grabbed the tablet off my nightstand and urgently tapped the Instagram app just to be sure some menace hadn't reported me for letting Sophie masquerade as me over the past month. Everything was fine of course, but I wouldn't put it past Benjamin Bailey to take one last sucker punch and wipe out my real career as well as my fake one.

Relief washed over me when I saw that the number next to followers was still ticking upward, and plenty of people had liked and commented on last night's post with messages of affirmation.

I clicked over to my DMs and found several messages of encouragement, as well as a party invitation from one of my closest influencer friends. Talia's brand was all about natural, organic, vegan life, her sexy Italian boyfriend, and their blonde teddy bear looking goldendoodle.

Are you back, yet? Dani!! I need someone cool to come to this lame product party with me. Please say that someone is you? I'll drive and everything.

I sent her a quick message back, agreeing to go with her tonight because why not? I need to get my mind off Foster and Sophie.

Which, by the way, there weren't any texts or calls from either of them. Those were the two people I most wanted to hear from, not all these randoms online. What was the point of having a life-changing revelation to only share it with internet strangers?

I had managed to put off any reflection while distracted in Halo, but now that I was home, it was sinking in more and more every minute that I wasn't proud of my life and I didn't like it as much as I had been trying to convince myself I did.

Now that I knew I wanted to do something more than hock products I didn't care about, it would have been really nice to have a sister, or say, a boyfriend, to guide me through the transition.

Instead, I had to go it alone. For someone with half a million followers, it was a scary concept.

But I was ready to start… tomorrow.

Hello, I just went through a traumatic breakup! Today, I was allowed to sulk around the apartment, binge watch TV, day drink, maybe drag myself to the gym, and then accompany Talia to whatever this lame party was she'd lined up for us. Maybe I'd even get glammed up just in case a certain someone back in Oklahoma decided to stalk my Instagram account. I'd show him what he was missing.

Chapter Thirty-Two

#Truth

Circus-themed parties were never a good idea. Sure, circus performers had gotten a sexy new makeover since Cirque du Soleil came into the picture, but the off-brand version prancing around me right now? Terrifying. I stood next to Talia and shivered when a clown on stilts careened past us. I half expected a red balloon to come trailing behind him.

"What's this party for?" I asked.

She pointed to the vodka brand logo hanging on the far wall of the warehouse type event space. "Not really my typical sponsor, I know," she slipped her arm through mine, "but the money was too good to pass up."

"A few more weeks, and they could've made this a

halloween party," I mused. "At least then the decor wouldn't be so freaky." I nodded toward the gaudy display of fun house mirrors installed along the edge of the party. This was so not the California scene I was used to. True, the parties here always had a sense of everyone and everything trying too hard, but they also had a level of sophistication that any girl could appreciate.

A waiter passed by with a tray of shot glasses, and Talia plucked two off and handed me one. "Drink up," she commanded, her cat-like dark eyes filling with anticipation. "Let's get some good photos and have some fun. You need it."

I hadn't actually done any day drinking today, so maybe she was right. I sniffed the drink, and my eyes immediately watered. Whatever this new brand of vodka had going on, it was certainly going to be strong. "Getting drunk with a bunch of clowns around sounds like a terrible idea," I deadpanned. That only made her laugh, and together we clanged our glasses together and downed the liquid fire.

An hour later, the clowns and I were old friends.

In fact, the same could be said for a bunch of people at the party. I was outgoing and extraverted by nature, so circling a large crowded room came natural to me. I danced with a few guys, met a bunch of new people, and drank a few more shots.

I was in the middle of dancing to a particularly thumpy techno song when Talia pulled me to the side and introduced me to the brand manager for the vodka. The guy looked like a club promoter, all suave and icky at the same time with his pressed black suit and two-hundred-dollar haircut.

"This is Cain," she said, and I wondered if that was his real name because honestly, who named their child after a biblical villain? "Cain, this is my friend Dani. Have you seen her Insta? She's got like five hundred thousand followers."

"Six hundred," I corrected, winking at Talia. "It's gone up."

Cain did that little smirky smiling thing that guys do when they're trying not to look too impressed but they totally are. "Very cool. Would you be interested in working with us, too? We're looking to add a few more female influencers to the roster."

I paused, his offer sinking in deeper than the buzz of alcohol or the thrill of the party. A month ago, I'd have jumped at the offer. No doubt these people had money if even Talia, with her bohemian vibe, had taken the deal. But now? Things had changed. I was different. And I was only going to work with sponsors who had products and causes I actually believed in. Vodka simply didn't make the cut.

"No, thank you," I said politely. "Good luck with your launch though."

"You're loss." He shrugged as if he didn't care one way or the other, and Talia widened her eyes at me like I'd gone and lost my mind. But I knew what I was doing, and I knew I wasn't losing anything. I left her to finish her conversation and melted back into the throng of dancers, hoping to have the kind of fun like I kept telling myself I could have now that I was back in California.

That Sunday, Talia and I sat at a table in our favorite brunch spot, both of us glued to our phones after having finished off too much food. I'd always liked that my Cali friends didn't give me crap for being on my phone a lot—they understood how my job worked. And I *was* working and definitely *wasn't* stalking Foster or Halo High School. That would be super weird. I was merely following the school's social media in an effort to keep in touch with the few good connections I had made there. I mean, keeping up with friends and followers *was* part of my job, right?

Jeanine, for example, had been kind enough to not banish me from existence and still sent me super hippie-fied messages of encouragement. And believe it or not, Benjamin Bailey had taken to following me and now liked just about every post I put up. Did I suspect he had come to his senses about his chances of making it big on Broadway and wanted to pick my brain about Hollywood living? Definitely, but I was going to make him work for it. That boy had to drop the first DM if he expected forgiveness.

It was totally normal for me to click on the Halo High profile and scroll through the recent updates. Less normal was when I shrieked at the top of my lungs and knocked Talia's mimosa into her lap.

She grabbed the butter yellow cloth napkin off our table and quickly mopped up the mess.

"Channing Tatum better have just followed you, or you owe me dry cleaning."

I eyed her knit sundress, now soaked with orange juice and champagne. "I'm so, so sorry."

"No Channing then?" she asked, her scowl quickly turning to a look of concern.

I passed my phone across the table.

"What am I looking at here?"

"That," I pointed out, "is Sophie's school auditorium, or it used to be anyway, and that is the turd I told you about from the booster club, proudly standing in front of it as the wrecking crew gets ready to tear the whole thing down in a few days."

Talia shook her head angrily. "How is it this type of guy always wins?"

"Because no one ever fights this type of guy," I grumbled, remembering the way Foster kept his mouth shut during each and every one of the conversations centered around turning the auditorium into a practice facility.

Talia grinned and swiped my Mimosa from across the table. "Well…"

"Well, what?" I asked, preparing myself for one of Talia's terrible ideas. This was a girl who kept a poster board in her closet just in case an emergency protest opportunity rendered her unable to resist resisting. I freely and shamefully admitted to having picketed Whole Foods with her when they stopped selling vegan breakfast burritos.

"Why don't you fight him?" she asked.

I laughed. "You put the morning booze down right meow."

Talia rolled her eyes. "I'm being completely serious here. Why don't you fight Mr. Vance for the auditorium? What do you have to lose? Sophie already lost her job, and Foster isn't returning your calls."

"Thanks for the fun reminder," I groaned.

"Think about it. Half a million people care what you have to say. You post a picture of yourself in a bikini and a quarter of them take the time to tell you your tan looks nice. What if you actually asked them to do something meaningful? This is exactly what you need."

"I don't know," I started, but Talia was already extracting herself from the table.

She dropped a fifty dollar bill in the center to pay for brunch and pulled me up from my seat. "You care about those kids, right?"

"Of course," I answered. "But you're forgetting the part where I'm not a real teacher and lied to them all. I hardly think anyone is going to want me to be the one fighting their battles."

Talia waved her Uber driver down with one hand while she tugged me along with the other. "Don't be silly. Those kids don't give a lick that you don't have your teacher's license. They connected with *you*, and you can't abandon them now."

As we climbed into the back of the sedan, I spotted a group of male twenty-somethings walking down the sidewalk. They were openly checking us out, and even the Uber driver was giving Talia the up-and-down. A chief perk of being friends with Talia was her ability to turn any head. With her sleek black ponytail, flawless olive complexion, and megawatt smile, people were drawn to her. It was why she never seemed to struggle to gain or keep a sponsor and why it was nearly impossible to say no to her. I used to relish this kind of attention myself because it meant I could hook up with any hottie I wanted, but now it all just felt… hollow. Maybe Talia was right. Maybe I needed to do something *more* with my online presence?

Once inside the cab, I pulled up the picture of Mr. Vance and the auditorium again. He had that "king of the mountain" look on his pudgy little face. He was used to getting whatever he wanted and stomping over whomever got in his way. In this case? It was my theatre kids. Even though I was gone, they'd taken up permanent residency in my heart, and I hated that I'd let them down.

"Okay, I get where you're coming from, but even if I wanted to fight him, how would I make a difference? The booster club has earmarked that bond money for a new gym, and there has got to be twice as many athletes at that school than there are theatre kids."

Talia smiled. "Maybe in Halo, Oklahoma, but who says we have to stop there. If you want to beat Mr. Vance, you have to do what you do best."

Turning a favor into a tragedy didn't seem like the best solution to this problem. After a moment of clueless silence, Talia shook her head. "You're a flipping influencer, Dani, own it!"

"Somehow, I don't think an unboxing video is gonna help,"

Talia looked like she was going to pull her perfectly arranged hair directly out of her head. "Think bigger. If you can get thousands of people to buy scented candles and fancy magnetic bookmarks, you can talk people into throwing ten bucks at saving an auditorium for some poor unfortunate children."

Talia's idea was finally starting to click. "You think I should raise the money for the auditorium myself." Now, my mind was whirling. What if Halo had enough money to renovate the old auditorium *and* build a new gym?

"Bingo." She smiled triumphant.

I chewed on my bottom lip. "You really think that would work? That's not the sort of thing my followers signed up for."

Talia instructed the driver to pull over in front of her second-story apartment and unbuckled.

"Give them a chance to prove you wrong. The worst thing that can happen is you don't raise enough money to finish the project and end up donating it to be used by the theatre program for something else."

No, I thought as I watched Talia climb the steps to her unit, the worst thing that could happen was I publicly failed for the second time and proved that Foster and Sophie were right to turn their backs on me.

I tried to push her idea out of my head, but it kept creeping back in, and by dinner time, I was brainstorming ways to get a massive amount of attention in the shortest amount of time. I took a deep breath, sat down at my computer, and rolled up my sleeves. Metaphorically, of course, considering I was wearing a strappy tank top.

Chapter Thirty-Three

\#TheRealDani

Talia was right when she said I needed to give my followers a chance. They knew me on a very surface level—my favorite beverage, celebrity crushes, top ten snack choices, that sort of thing—but they didn't know what drove me and or how far I was willing to go when I really wanted something.

So, I was starting at the beginning with an introduction post, a *real* one.

I grabbed a snapshot of Sophie and I graduating high school off the mirror in my bedroom and posted the picture.

Bet you didn't know I was a twin. Maybe, that's because my sister and I haven't been so close these last few years. I'm trying to change that, and I could really use your help. So if you'll bear with me, these next few posts will be all about Sophie, and how I screwed things up but am ready to make it right. #LoveMySister #OnceATwin #AlwaysATwin #ImSorry

Pretty much the moment I hit post, my phone began exploding with notifications. It was tempting to read the comments and respond to each one, but I had a plan and part of it was to tell the whole story bit by bit, ensuring people stayed glued to their phones and my plea for help didn't get buried beneath another shot of a pretty girl on a beach or friends saying cheers over cocktails.

Plus, I needed time to set up a donation page, and to do that I needed to know exactly how much money we were shooting for. If I was anyone but me, I would just call Foster and ask, but seeing as how he had been radio silent since I climbed back into that cab, calling for the details was out of the question.

Instead, I wrangled Jeanine into hooking me up with Carli Joe Jenson's phone number. The woman about came unglued when I told her who I was and why I was calling.

"I can't believe you left! You can't just mic drop like that. The whole school is talking about the new practice facility. Yesterday at lunch, my son crushed a pudding cup over the head of the captain of the soccer team to establish 'performing arts dominance'."

I tried to remember if any of the kids in the chorus had the last name Jenson, but I was coming up empty.

"Your son was in the play?"

"No," laughed Carli Joe. "He's a terrible actor, but he's a state champion jazz choir soloist who now has no auditorium to perform in."

I could just picture Carli Joe sitting in her home office, an 8 x 10 portrait of her son in choir robes framed at her desk while she drafted one scathing letter to the editor after another.

"Well, maybe we can still change that."

"Just one second," murmured Carli Joe, then in what was clearly an attempt to muffle the sound by placing a hand over the speaker Carli Joe hollered, "Make your own damn grilled cheese sandwich, Mommy's busy!"

"If now is a bad time," I started.

"No!" cried Carli Joe. "Now is the only time. You may not know this, but Mr. Vance and I went to Halo High together."

I did not know that of course, but boy did I love a juicy backstory.

"And he was every bit the jackass then that he is now. I'm tired of watching him get his way in this town just because he threw a football well in the nineties."

I strongly suspected there was more to the story, something like an unrequited crush or Mr. Vance beating her husband out for quarterback, but I didn't push it.

"Here is the thing Carli Joe." I steeled my voice. "I want to fix what I screwed up in Halo, and that means two things. Putting pressure on Mr. Wainwright to rethink his decision to fire Sophie and raising enough money to give those kids an auditorium."

There was a pause on the other end of the line.

"It's an awful lot of money, Dani."

I had suspected as much, but I wasn't turning away from the challenge just because it was going to be hard.

"How much?"

I heard some shuffling of papers and tapping that could have been a calculator before she sighed deeply into the phone.

"The last time the school board discussed the auditorium project, it was determined that it was cheaper to tear the thing down than to renovate it."

My heart burst like a balloon loved too hard by a toddler.

"So, it's a no go? There is no chance the board would consider saving the auditorium?"

"Saving it, no," said Carli Joe. "But… " Her voice trailed off.

"But what?" At this point, I was desperate for any crumb I could get. Talia's off the cuff idea had quickly morphed into purpose for me, and I wasn't ready to give up before we had even started.

"This school gets attention for its sports programs, but it neglects to acknowledge the accomplishments of the rest of the students. Why not go balls to the wall and build a new performing arts center?"

I *so* wanted to get caught up on the whole "balls to the wall" comment, but she was totally right. I had taught at Halo High School for a month, and I didn't know who her son was, let alone that he had won an award for jazz choir, heck I didn't know there *was* a jazz choir.

"I need a number," I reminded her.

When Carli Joe first said three million dollars, I

about wet my pants, but then I did the math. If every follower I had donated three bucks, we were halfway there. Throw in a few sponsors and enlist some serious talent like Talia and we could do it.

Okay, maybe it was a long shot, maybe it was impossible, but a lot of people donating a little money could go a long way. I'd seen Go Fund Mes go viral before and go "balls to the wall," as Carli Joe put it.

By the time I hung up with her, I was ready to put the full weight of my career behind building this damn performing arts center.

"So, as I just explained, I made some mistakes. I tried to help my sister but got her fired from a job she's truly amazing at. Standing up for the theatre kids only made things worse for the school by inciting a rivalry between the athletes and the artists. And to top all it off, I lied to someone I love and broke his trust. Please, help me make it right by donating to build a brand new, state-of-the-art auditorium for Halo High by clicking the link below. Thanks, guys!"

I rewatched the clip back for what felt like the thousandth time.

"Post it." Talia raised her eyebrows. "It's perfect."

We were sitting on my couch after having spent the day filming, editing, and setting up the donation website. But now that it was all ready, my nerves had turned from a small ember into a raging fire.

"What's the problem?" Talia pressed. "Out with it."

I released a slow breath. "I'm not scared to admit

the truth, but I am scared of what Sophie and Foster will think. What if Sophie hates me for telling the whole world what we did? And what if Foster…"

"Doesn't love you back?" Talia slid across the couch and pulled me into a hug. "From everything you've told me, I'd bet he does. But either way, you're going to feel so much better getting the truth out there and taking steps to make this right."

Why did vulnerability have to feel so scary? Before I could talk myself out of it, I swallowed hard and pushed "post" on the video.

Immediately, I put my phone away and did a little scream while kicking my legs. My whole body felt like I'd just dropped down the hill on a rollercoaster and the ride was barely getting started. "I seriously can't look, Talia. You're going to have to watch this for me and tell me what happens."

"I got you, boo." She blew me a kiss and got up to pour us some wine. "Let's catch up on last season's *Bachelorette*, and I'll stalk your account for you."

"Deal."

Three episodes and a lot of man-tears later, and I couldn't take it anymore. Talia sat with her phone lighting her face, a little grin on her lips. She wasn't even paying attention to the show anymore. I paused it, and she looked up.

"Okay, is it good news or bad news?"

There was a chance it was bad news, that people were making fun of me or commenting nasty things, that nobody wanted to donate, or that Sophie and Foster had seen it and were now denouncing my name.

"It's good news!" She shoved her phone in my face. The donation page was lit up with the number $300,640 and was counting upwards every second.

I catapulted off the couch, screaming. "What? It's working?"

"Oh girl, it's working. Everyone is sharing this. If you can raise three hundred grand in a few hours, I have no doubt you'll be able to get to your three million or at least pretty dang close."

My heart thundered in my chest and for the first time in I don't even know how long, my smile was one hundred percent authentic when I snapped a quick teary-eyed selfie and posted it with with the hashtags #Unbelievable #YouGuysRock #ThankYouForever #KeepItGoing.

Now *this* was the kind of influence that mattered.

Chapter Thirty-Four

#GetThatMoney

I was sunbathing beside my gym's pool a week later, Talia at my side, scrolling through my phone and trying to answer the million and one emails in my inbox, when I clicked on one that sent my heart racing. I bolted upright, my sunhat nearly falling off my head.

"What?" Talia turned to me and tipped her sunglasses down.

"It's from Sophie."

It simply read "Maybe they can help" and included a link. I was hoping for more, but this was better than the silent treatment I'd been getting. I saw it as an olive branch and clicked the link with a hopeful smile on my face. The link redirected to a nonprofit's website called The Coalition for the Betterment of Arts Education. I clicked open the "About" section and read.

"Oh my gosh," I whispered. "This is perfect."

"What's perfect?" Talia snatched the phone away from me and nodded. "Oh, yes, this *is* perfect."

"They have loads of grant money," I squealed. "If I apply and explain where we're at with the funds and the momentum behind this movement, they might give us what we need, don't you think?"

The last week had been a blur of activity, and all the while the amount of funds raised was ticking up. We were sitting at just over two million in donations now, but things were cooling off, and we were still a million dollars away from our goal. Talia was convinced she could get me onto *The Ellen Show* and that would make the difference, but I wasn't so sure this had enough pull for daytime television. Plus, they'd probably want Sophie to go on too and my sister wasn't the TV type. In any event, the old auditorium was already being dismantled, so that was done, and I needed to reach my goal before I could approach the school board with my offer and hopefully give my theatre kids a home.

"Oh, I'm sure they'll want to help you," Talia agreed. "Actually, I'm surprised they haven't already contacted you about this. You've gone viral, after all." Her eyes narrowed. "You know what? Maybe they have. You've got so many emails in here you could have missed them. Let's do a search."

Her hands flew over the phone and seconds later she let out a "whoop," jumped up from the lounge chair, and did a little happy dance in her tiny black bikini that had half the people out here staring at her.

"What?"

"See for yourself." She thrust the phone at me.

Ms. Danielle Sparks,

I'm writing to inform you that we here at CBAE are impressed with your fundraising efforts and would like to invite you to apply for one of our grants—

I joined Talia in the happy dance, my towel and sunhat flying by the wayside, with my phone held high in the air like a trophy. "Holy crap! I can't wait to tell the kids!"

And that was the other thing. All the theatre students were following my account now and pitching in their own ways, many doing live streams to showcase their talents or to state their case. Tyler and Kayla had even performed their song and done the kissing scene, which if you asked me, looked about a hundred times more real than the first time they'd kissed. If I didn't know better, I'd think that they were secretly hooking up. Maybe they were—I was pretty sure I saw tongue! Though all this, we'd become our own little family, everyone committed to making this new auditorium happen. They were totally going to go bananas when I secured that grant and announced the good news.

Chapter Thirty-Five

#BackToOZ

I was so incredibly close to victory I could taste it. Well, that and the iced chai latte I was currently holding in one hand while I walked back from my corner Starbucks. In my other hand, I pressed my phone to my ear, telling Jeanine all about the fundraising campaign and how I'd just secured the grant money.

"We are going to pack the house with musicals, one acts, orchestra performances, and whatever jazz choir is! And when that happens, Mr. Vance is going to have a hard time arguing that sports are the only thing that bring money into Halo High!"

I'd been rambling about performing arts as the dominant extracurricular for a good five minutes before Jeanine interrupted my monologue.

"Do you really mean we?"

A lump formed in my throat. "I'll be there in spirit."

I had been doing everything in my power to make this project happen. The kids were talking to me again, even if it was only on social media, and so many people were telling me how great it was that I was doing this for Halo High School, but that wasn't what she meant. I was here in California, and I was going to make sure the auditorium got built, but I wouldn't be there to see it in use or the look on Mr. Vance's face when the first show sold out.

Which, by the way, wanna know who hadn't been making any videos or giving any interviews to the press? Mr. Vance. Probably because we were going to build a performing arts center that would steal all of the attention from his precious practice facility. Who really cared about indoor practice when there was a big sexy auditorium on the way?

There was a long pause on the other end of the phone, of which I could only imagine Jeanine was preparing to really let me have it. She had been more than kind since I left Halo, but I hadn't forgotten her reaction to discovering that Foster and I were hooking up.

"Dani Sparks, grow up!" she hollered.

"Excuse me?" I stopped short, nearly tripping on my wedge sandals. That was not what I was expecting. Not when I was calling to tell her how incredibly close I was to having raised the full amount of money to finish the project.

"Money is great," sighed Jeanine. "The auditorium

will be great, but that doesn't fix the rift between you and Sophie, and if I have to see Foster mope around campus like his dog died for another second, I am going to lose my already fragile mind!"

I didn't like being lectured, but I didn't mind hearing that Foster hadn't rebounded overnight. He was still branded on my heart, so it only felt fair that he should be tortured by our month-long journey into forbidden love as well.

"I already apologized," I tried.

"If they didn't accept it, it doesn't count."

I rolled my eyes, Jeanine was ever the optimist, but sometimes she forgot that the rest of the world didn't operate on the same plane of love and light that she did.

"I don't know what else I can do. I've said I'm sorry in person. I've said I'm sorry on video for the whole world to see, and I've more than made it up to those kids."

I couldn't see Jeanine through the phone, but by the tone in her voice it was easy to picture her standing with her shoulders squared, one finger raised in hippie indignation as she replied, "You need to march your little booty back to Oklahoma and demand forgiveness."

There was nothing I wanted more than for her to be right. I would apologize a thousand times in a thousand ways if I thought it would make a difference, but the facts were still the facts. Foster hadn't talked to me at all since I had left, and aside from the one email exchange suggesting I look into the grant opportunity,

Sophie had all but written me out of her life. This conversation had started out as good news, but defeat was beginning to creep in and contaminate the vibe big time.

"I'm sorry, Jeanine. I just don't think either of them want that." I let myself into my apartment and threw my keys a little too forcefully on the kitchen counter.

Jeanine sighed through the phone. "Look, I wasn't going to tell you this because I wanted you to come on your own accord, but Foster hasn't been able to find a replacement for Sophie. Your campaign to raise money for the kids has also thrown what you two did and how Sophie got fired into the limelight."

My stomach twisted. This was exactly what I didn't want to happen. Sophie had suffered enough at my expense. Her cute little house was officially on the market because of me—I had checked—and now she was facing public scrutiny. "I really didn't mean to draw more attention to Sophie. I just knew that a story like that would be more compelling than outright asking for money."

"Oh, it was compelling all right," laughed Jeanine. "It was so compelling that some of the parents on the PTA feel like her being fired might be a mistake. There is quite a bit of pressure mounting to give her a second chance."

My chest tightened. Holy crap! If Sophie got her job back, maybe she wouldn't stay mad at me forever. Maybe we could look back on this and laugh—the same way we laughed about Michael Flanagan realizing he'd given his break up speech to the wrong twin in tenth grade.

"Clearly, a lot of good has come from this situation," continued Jeanine. "I think if you come back and address the school board directly, there is a really good chance that they may reinstate her."

I took a sharp breath. When I made the decision to post about Sophie and the twin-swap, I had hoped people would see that she was trying to do a good thing for Nova, and that even if she broke the code of ethics, her intentions were good. I'd hoped that, but I hadn't heard a peep to indicate it was actually working.

"You think they'll really give Sophie her job back?" It felt a little too cinematic to be true. I stood motionless in the center of my kitchen, waiting for what I hoped would be good news.

"I think it's not out of the realm of possibility," said Jeanine cautiously, to which I did a little happy dance. "But not if you just mail a check and call it good, Dani. You started this mess, come back and clean it up."

I listened a while longer as Jeanine did her best to convince me that my returning to Halo could help more than the performing arts department, but I was having trouble committing. I had been trying to *clean this mess up* for weeks, and nothing I did felt like it had a real impact with the people I wanted to help most.

Hanging up the phone I was 60/40. Sixty percent of me wanted to get the first flight to Oklahoma, stand in front of that school board in my power pants, and let them know what they were missing by letting Sophie go, but the other forty percent was terrified to see Foster in person again.

His rejection was clear, even if he was moping around Halo instead of moving on. Sophie was used to my screwing things up, but Foster had taken a risk when he showed up on Sophie's doorstep the night of the homecoming dance. He risked his career to find out if what was between us was real, only to find out he didn't know *anything* about the woman he was falling for. He didn't owe me forgiveness, but maybe I owed him something.

In the few weeks I had been back in California, it had become obvious that this place wasn't where I belonged anymore, and part of what made it obvious was knowing that no party, product, promise of money, or even going to the beach, felt as good as spending the evening doing nothing in the middle of nowhere with Foster Beck.

He might not have known my name or what I did for a living, but he knew *me*. He fell for me. Why else hadn't he and Sophie connected in the past? The more I thought about it, the more apparent it was that, for the first time, I knew for certain that a guy liked me for who I was and not just what I looked like.

I didn't know exactly how I was going to do it, but I was going to make Foster understand that I regretted lying to him, but I didn't regret falling for him.

Come tomorrow morning, I was hopping on a flight to Halo, Oklahoma. I was getting my sister her job back, and I was getting my man.

Before I could talk myself out of it, I strode to my

room, retrieved my suitcase from the closet, located the pinstriped pants, and folded them neatly inside. Last time I wore them, I got dumped, outed by a student, and set the wheels in motion to end Sophie's career, but I was a big believer in second chances.

Chapter Thirty-Six

#OhHeyAgain

My palms were gross-sweaty, my heart was doing the polka dance in my chest, and as for the butterflies in my stomach? Forget it. They were more like a swarm of angry bees. I was a complete mess as I walked into that school board meeting a few days later, but I kept thinking of what Sophie's face would look like if I succeeded, so I pressed on.

There were nine members in all, five women and four men, some elected and some appointed. I'd studied their names and faces on the flight over, hoping it would make me feel prepared. Spoiler alert: it didn't.

They sat around a conference room table when I entered the room and motioned for me to join them. This was a closed meeting. Just the ten of us.

Nothing to worry about, right?

If it weren't for the three million big ones waiting for a new home, I probably would've thrown up by now. As it was, I had the upper hand, and I needed to remember that. They wanted this money—they had to. Even if small-town politics prevented some of them from taking it, the community knew all about it by now, and there was no way the people of Halo would stand by and let their school board screw them over.

I slid into the padded chair and smiled at the lot, channeling my own inner politician. "Thank you for agreeing to see me."

Silence.

A woman by the name of Teresa raised an eyebrow at me before waiving toward the door. In walked Mr. Wainwright, Sophie, and Foster Beck. I swallowed hard and did a little wave. Sophie waved back, albeit weakly. Mr. Wainwright's potato face turned bright red when he said, "Hello, Ms. Sparks. I wasn't expecting to see you here today."

And Foster didn't even make eye contact.

So, they hadn't been informed I was here? They'd probably just been told that the school board wanted to meet with them. Fantastic. I had to resist a well-timed eye roll.

I cleared my throat. "I'd like to say something if that's okay."

"By all means," Teresa replied. I really had no idea if any of these people were happy to see me. They wore the expressions of World Series Poker pros, but maybe it meant nothing. Maybe that's what it took to survive as a school board member.

"First, I want to say I'm sorry for the mess I created. I'm sorry for lying and causing a scene that embarrassed people or put a negative cloud over the school."

Mr. Wainwright folded his arms and leaned back in his chair, his eyes rolling toward the ceiling in a "so help me God" expression.

"We had fights break out, you know," another school board member interjected. "You pitted the athletes against the performers."

"I know," I steeled my voice, my eyes shooting over to Mr. Wainwright and back to that school board member, "but I wasn't the only one. Maybe you all should have been more transparent with the public about what was going on from the beginning."

Everyone stiffened. Well, there I went, only two minutes in and I'd already stuck my foot in my mouth. But it was the truth, wasn't it?

"There are things you can't begin to understand—" Superintendent Wainwright spoke up, but Teresa cut him off.

"You're right, Danielle." Her voice was the perfect balance of soothing and stern, and everyone turned to listen. I wanted to be her when I grew up! "We all made mistakes. The floor is yours, please continue."

I took a deep breath and nodded, trying to ignore the fact that Beck still wasn't looking at me. "By now, you all know who I am and have seen the fundraising campaign I've been working on the last few weeks," I continued. Their greedy little eyes lit up—they knew I was getting to the money part now, which lets face it, was the only reason why they'd agreed to meet with me in the first place. "I am happy to announce that with a generous grant from The Coalition for the Betterment of Arts Education, as well as thousands of donors, we have reached our three-million-dollar goal." I smiled from ear to ear, sort of feeling like Santa Clause, or at least I would when they accepted this money and I got to deliver the happy news to my theatre kids. "And I would love to donate that sum to Halo High so that you can build a brand new auditorium."

Again, silence. I could practically hear the drumroll.

"We'd love to accept," Teresa announced, and the entire school board dropped their poker-face act and smiled gleefully.

"There is one condition," I jumped in before anyone got too excited. I caught Sophie's hopeful eye and nodded once. "You need to reinstate my sister."

They exchanged knowing glances. They must have already discussed this at length. What were they going to do, turn down three million to prove a point? Maybe. But they'd be crazy, and the public would probably riot.

"Of course," Teresa added. "We'd love to have Sophie come back."

I jumped up, clapping—couldn't help myself—and ran over to bury Sophie in a hug. She returned it, and I knew that even if it took time, she was on her way to forgiving me for everything that had happened these last few months. It was all I wanted.

Well, that and—

I looked over to Foster, but the man still wouldn't meet my gaze. However, a satisfied smile rested on his lips. It was a start, right?

"There's one condition on our end to all of this," Teresa said, her commanding voice settling the room back to order. I returned to my seat, suddenly a little nervous. What could they possibly want?

"Your sister told us that you have a degree in education and are studying for the Praxis test. Is that true?"

I nodded. My hands started shaking so bad that I had to sit on them.

"And that you are owed all the credit for the success of the *Oklahoma!* production?"

"Well, Principal Beck and Mrs. Sanchez helped, too," I admitted. "And of course, I had great talent to work with."

She smiled at that. "We'd like you to take over Halo High's theatre department. You'll have to get your teaching license, of course, and complete your student teaching hours, but once that's done, the job is yours."

My mouth popped open in surprise.

I'd hoped for this. I'd wanted it. But now that it was mine for the taking, I was overcome with more joy than I'd ever thought possible. Tears gathered in my eyes as I nodded vigorously. "Yes, you've got a deal!"

Sophie and a few others erupted in happy cheers. I seriously wasn't expecting this outcome and *wow, wow, wow*! Screw California. I'd give that life up in a heartbeat to get to oversee the theatre department here in a brand new facility. It was a dream come true. My real dream, not the one I'd settled for when I'd given up on myself back in college.

"Oh, and one more thing." Mr. Wainwright turned toward me and Sophie, his eyebrows knitting together. "No more twin-swaps, you two, got it?"

"Got it," we said in unison and true twin fashion.

After the excitement wore off and a few details were ironed out, I left the building with my arm slung through Sophie's. It felt amazing to have her on my side again. I was just about to ask her if I could be her roommate for a while when I spotted Foster. "One sec." I let her go and caught up to where he was sliding into his car.

"Hey, can we talk for a second?" I was nervous but still riding on the high from the meeting. Now felt like the perfect time to make up with the man. And how could I not want to? He looked amazing. Part of me wondered if seeing him and having all the truth out in the open would mean that the chemistry would be gone.

It wasn't the case because I suddenly wanted him more than ever.

He stopped short and turned on me, his tone clipped. "Congratulations on all your accomplishments, Ms. Sparks."

My heart dropped to my stomach. "Um, thanks. But, like, I was hoping we could talk about *us*… "

"I'm a professional," he jumped in, "and I'd like to keep it that way in all of my professional relationships, including this one."

I blinked at him. "Why are you being so weird?"

He growled. "Look, Dani, I have nothing to say about what happened between you and I. It happened. It's over. Okay? I'll be your boss soon. Just let it go."

My bottom lip wobbled, and dare I say it, pity crossed his face. Stupid traitorous bottom lip! If he wanted to be a coldhearted jerk and pretend that what we had wasn't worth fighting for, then fine, two could play at that game.

"You're absolutely right." I straightened my spine. "I was actually going to suggest the same thing."

Hurt flashed in his pretty blue eyes, and I immediately regretted my words. All I wanted to do was kiss him. Not this. But clearly, he didn't want me anymore. A brick wall was stacking up around my broken heart, and I stepped back.

"So, we're on the same page." And then, he climbed into his car and drove away as if he hadn't just left me standing there with hot tears rolling down my cheeks.

Chapter Thirty-Seven

#DrinkingMakesItBetter

Probably, Sophie would have preferred to hold off on fully forgiving me for a day or two. You know, really make me suffer for my sins, but when she found me in the school parking lot bawling my eyes out as Foster sped off into the Oklahoma sunset, her reserve crumbled.

"There could be alcohol," she said, slinging one arm around my shoulder and guiding me to my car. "Would alcohol make you feel better?"

I nodded my head like a baby child and followed my sister back to her adorable, no longer for sale home. I parked my rental behind her and watched as she yanked the for sale sign from the front lawn and tossed it in the big green trash can at the curb.

"I was considering becoming a lady of the night to

keep the mortgage reapers at bay," she said with a sigh. "It's probably a good thing you came back before the full-scale downhill slide began."

"Full scale?" I asked.

"Oh, yes," laughed Sophie. She pulled the screen door open and ushered me inside. "I've been steadily declining for roughly one month now. Please withhold your judgement."

When I stepped inside the kitchen my jaw dropped. *Oh no no no no no no, not again.* When we were little and something bad happened, Sophie didn't cry. Sophie crafted.

When she didn't get picked for the school play and I did, Sophie gave all of her Barbies pixie cuts. When our grandpa died, she weaved an area rug. And when her college boyfriend left her for *his* college boyfriend, Sophie took up knitting and made blanket after blanket for the old folks home next door to our dorm. Sophie had a crafting problem and judging by her current surroundings, not much had changed.

The girl had gone and sewn a quilted cover for every damn appliance in the place. I stared at the pale blue fabric shapes lining her countertops. It was like looking at Tetris pieces, only none of them fit together.

"So, when you need to use the toaster…."

Sophie smirked and waggled her eyebrows. "It's like a super fun game of memory. Lift the cover, oops not the toaster! Try another!"

Wow, I mouthed.

"Hey, you're lucky you got here when you did. Yesterday, I got a pattern for a couch cover on Etsy, and the designer said there was a good chance she could whip something up for my recliner as well."

I tried to imagine Sophie's home had Jeanine never called me. Would it all be one big quilted cover up? Or would she start knitting herself curtains to match? I had really fallen flat on my face with Foster, but at least Sophie was happy now.

"Tell me more about the alcohol," I inquired.

"Well, after the meeting today, a couple of teachers and PTA members suggested we go out for a celebratory cocktail. So, how about taking them up on that?"

"Who is they?"

Sophie grabbed my suitcase by the handle and wheeled it into the spare room.

"If you're worried about seeing Foster," she called back, "don't be. He never comes to anything fun anymore."

"Did he before?" I asked, genuinely curious. I'd seen Foster at the movies by himself and at the homecoming game to crown the king and queen, but when I thought about it, I'd never actually seen him interact with other people outside of work.

"Mmhmm," buzzed Sophie. "Before he became principal, he was a regular at everything. Trivia night, cocktails on Friday's, he was actually fun before the job swallowed him."

It wasn't the first time I had wondered why Foster gave up teaching to take the principal job. I'm sure the money was better, but if he was miserable, was it really worth it? Didn't he miss being able to throw one back and joke with the staff?

My first day in Halo, I'd judged the rest of the teachers to be complete snores, but over time, I'd come to like most of them, and I strongly suspected that Foster did too.

I agreed to meet up with the rest of the staff at the same bar Alison had taken me too earlier last month on the condition that Sophie let me style her hair and pick her outfit. Whoever this Marco dude was, I wanted him to squirm when he saw the pictures I posted tonight of the two of us having a Marco-free evening.

"Are you sure sequins are necessary?" asked Sophie. I'd lent her a red halter top that did delightful things for her cleavage and dark denim jeans to keep it classy on top and casual on the bottom. Basically, it was the perfect girl next door, out on the town look. I knew it would be perfect because I rocked it non-stop in Dana Point, and we were carbon copies of each other.

"Sequins are always necessary," I said, pushing her out the door. This day had been a rollercoaster of emotions, and I was ready to mellow everything out with a few brain-numbing shots.

I hoisted myself up onto the barstool next to Sophie and nodded across the table to Carli Joe, who I was pretty sure was going to be my Halo bestie once I moved here permanently.

We hadn't been seated more than two minutes when Alison walked in the door and took the chair directly across from us. Why hadn't I assumed she would be here? I needed to gulp down some conversation starter and fast, so I flagged over our server and ordered a round of shots for the table.

I had tried to apologize to Alison, just like I had tried to apologize to Foster. Apparently, if you live in this town long enough, you get really good at ignoring people because Alison hadn't responded to any of the half dozen "I'm so so so sorry" messages I had sent her.

Now that she was sitting in front of me, I could try again in person, but damn if my ego wasn't on its last leg tonight. I wasn't sure if I could take another person reminding me I'd hurt them.

Sophie nudged me underneath the table, and I knew she was expecting me to give it a go anyway. I was just about to lead in with an additional, *k, but I'm so so sorry,* but Alison squealed and hopped up off her stool to wrap her arms around the beefy bartender we'd both been ogling the night we came for trivia.

I raised a questionable eyebrow at Sophie who winked back at me as he passed our shots around and headed back to the kitchen.

"We're cool," said Alison, who must have noted my mouth hanging open as I watched him leave. "I should probably actually thank you. If I hadn't come here bawling after our run in, I doubt Nick would have sat down to talk to me, and then who knows how long it would have taken for him to ask me out."

I smiled sadly, I was glad she was happy and had found someone, but I definitely didn't want her to thank me.

"I'm glad it ended well, but I'm sorry for the way it started."

Sophie squeezed my hand under the table, and for

once I actually felt like I had said the right thing. If only I could figure out the right thing to say to Foster.

I knew he was mad at me, and I knew he was choosing his profession over the possibility of us, but something in his expression today told me it wasn't as easy as he was pretending it was.

It didn't take long for the group of us to get things started, and despite our suspiciously short tab at the end of the evening, it felt like the drinks just kept arriving. By midnight, I was feeling it hardcore, and Sophie had to shove my phone in her purse to keep me from sending Foster *another* text. Considering I didn't remember the first one I had sent, it was probably a good decision.

Before the night was over, Carli Joe, Alison, and I had forged a bathroom friendship so strong that I doubted I would ever meet such true and dedicated companions again, or so I told them as they helped to hoist me out of the handicap stall at closing time.

I apologized to Alison another hundred and four times for good measure before promptly passing out in the passenger seat of Sophie's car.

When I woke up on her couch with my shoes still on and my phone clutched tight to my chest, I groaned in anguish. Thank the lord Carli Joe was the only member of the PTA to actually show up. They really didn't need to see their future drama teacher lit like a candle, singing *Total Eclipse of the Heart* to the bottom of her empty shot glass.

In the kitchen, Sophie searched in vain for her

butter dish before giving up and bringing me a plate of dry toast with a banana on the side.

"Are we done mourning Foster Beck?"

I reached my hand up to shield my eyes from the sunlight creeping in through her closed blinds.

"His memory has been officially drowned in alcohol."

"Good," said Sophie, tossing a brand new copy of the Praxis test book on the couch beside me. "You don't have time to worry about him anyway."

I nodded and crunched into my dry toast, but it wasn't going to be that easy. Foster and I hadn't been officially together very long, but all of my memories of Halo were tied up in him. From my first staff meeting to the night he showed up on Sophie's doorstep, Foster had been Halo for me. The rest was just window dressing. How was I ever going to work beside him and not want to be with him? I couldn't think about it anymore. Sophie was right, I didn't have time. I forced down the last bite of toast, chugged an eight-ounce glass of water and cracked open the book.

Chapter Thirty-Eight

#DaniQuitsQuitting

Things are harder when you are older. That is just a fact. If I had taken the Praxis at twenty-three like I was supposed to, I wouldn't have to relearn everything I learned in undergrad. As it was, I was riding front and center on the struggle bus. The good news was I had a cheerleader.

Sophie wasn't starting back at Halo High until the end of the first trimester, which meant she had plenty of time on her hands to stare over my shoulder and shake her head no every time I started to fill in the wrong tiny bubble on the answer grid.

It would be annoying, except I was so happy to have her back in my life that I was willing to put up with anything and everything she threw at me. Her idea of helping was talking non-stop Praxis, all day, every day. It was like she had absolutely nothing better to do. Whenever I allowed myself to think negative Nancy things like that, I reminded myself that she still had the pattern to that sofa cover saved on her desktop. Besides, aside from being annoying, she knew what she was talking about.

It was Sophie who pointed out that studying was important, but if I really wanted to pass, I had to start by conquering my fear of testing.

So, with the help of Sophie and Alison, I began practicing high-pressure activities. Example, I bet fifty bucks on a Halo basketball game with only three minutes and a short list of stats to help me pick my team. I lost my money and had to suffer through an hour and a half of listening to Mr. Vance shout, "That's my boy!" But it was still a worthy endeavor because I accomplished what I set out to do. I made a choice, committed to it, and entered my final selection before my time was up.

It sounds like a small thing, but it made my palms sweaty just thinking about it. Alison's job was to pretend to proctor me. Every day at one PM, I would drive over to Halo High School and knock on the door to her office. She'd pretend to be a stranger, check my ID, crack a joke about violating dress code, and then set me up to take one of the online practice tests I'd subscribed to. By the time I finished, she'd have had any number of students in and out of her office, but the distraction helped make taking the test feel natural. If only I could get a few students to bop in and out during my actual test, then I would be right in my comfort zone.

The only downside to practicing with Alison was the possibility of bumping into Foster in the hallway. It had only happened twice, but both times his face went to stone and his cold "excuse me" sent me to the ladies room for ten minutes of feeling sorry for myself.

I had accepted that what I'd done was unforgivable in Foster's eyes, but that didn't mean I was glutton for punishment. I hated the way I felt after seeing him as much as I hated not seeing him.

If this was a guy who had broken my heart in California, I could block him from my socials and count on never seeing him in person again. Break ups in small towns didn't work that way. I'd seen him in the produce aisle, at the gym, and even in line for a movie. At least I had been with Sophie at the movie. Had I been there by myself again, seeing him would have resulted in at least three boxes of candy being consumed in solitude. He never really said hello, but outside of work, when he didn't have to be Principal Beck, he wasn't as cold. Mostly he just looked sad.

That made two of us.

On the day of the test, I awoke to heart palpitations and thought about making a run for the emergency room. Okay, not really, but my heart was racing, and any excuse to skip the test was a good one. But that was something the old Dani would've done. I had too much riding on it this time to give up prematurely.

The test was being administered at the community college two towns over. Sophie offered to drive me, but

I graciously declined. I needed alone time to settle my nerves, so I borrowed her car instead and drove in silence. Also, I didn't want to end up begging Sophie to fill in for me and have her all up in arms about it. Old habits die hard, what can I say?

I pulled up to the testing building a half hour early and stared at the red brick building with its shiny blue windows until ten minutes before go time.

"You can do this," I coached myself. "This is your destiny."

And with that final mantra, I strolled into the building, shoulders back, head tall, determined to rectify the colossal mistake of my past.

By the time I was finished two hours later, I was a sweaty mess and my brain was complete mush, but I was pretty sure I'd passed. There was no penalty for getting an answer wrong, so I focused on answering everything I was confident about first, then going through a second time to take a stab at the things that made me pause. At least I hadn't frozen up, so even though it was hard, at least I'd conquered test anxiety. Sophie was going to be so proud. Heck, I was proud!

"You'll receive your results in ten to sixteen days," the proctor announced, and me and the other future mind-shapers of America scurried toward the exit.

I walked out into the October sun with a huge smile tugging up my cheeks. I mean, worst case scenario, I failed. If that happened, I would study and retake it in January. Giving up was no longer on the table.

As I approached Soph's little black sedan, something rectangular and white stuck under the windshield wiper caught my eye. A flyer? No, an envelope. I got this crap a lot in California—usually a handwritten diatribe that was copied in mass and then distributed to every car in sight. My favorites were the ones about chemtrails and cell phones poisoning your brain. I'd never received one in Oklahoma though, and I was curious. What message warrants a good rant here? But then I saw the pointy scrawl of his perfect handwriting, and my name in black ink. I froze. My heart bounced around like a pinball in my chest.

Dani,
  Meet me at sunset?
  -Foster

It was cryptic, but it was *something,* more than I deserved, and I knew exactly what to do about it.

Chapter Thirty-Nine

#TheBigFinish

I'd taken extra time to perfect my appearance, curling my hair in long beachy waves, applying expert smokey-eye makeup, slipping into my tight black cable knit sweater dress, and pairing the look with the cutest cowboy boots Sophie and I could find at the local ranching store. I was painfully aware that my shopping habits had changed drastically since moving to Halo, Oklahoma. If someone would have told me two months ago that I'd be buying shoes in the aisle between the pitchforks and the fertilizer, I'd have told them they were crazy.

But the truth was, I really didn't mind it here as much as I thought I would. Actually, I liked it. I liked being around Sophie every day after spending the last three and a half years apart. I liked that we knew the neighbors—the Perez family on one side, with their lively brood of eight gorgeous and noisy children, and Mrs. Tollman on the other, the little old lady who loved to deliver fresh baked cookies to Sophie's doorstep because she always made too much, but also because she liked to chat with "us young women." I liked that I was making friends at the gym, people who actually invited me to get-togethers and genuinely took an interest in me. I'd officially been added to Sophie's romance book club, which was loads of fun and good for a few laughs. And I so kicked butt at the local trivia nights; Alison wouldn't let me miss a single one. And that was the people, but there was also the land that went on forever, the mature trees, clean air, and space to breath.

There was only one thing missing from my life here.

One person, actually.

And as I trudged up the hill toward Foster Beck's favorite thinking spot, my heart pounding and my palms in nervous fists, I prayed he had found it in his heart to forgive me. But I also prayed for more than that. I wanted him back.

As I neared the top, he was already waiting for me, his tall silhouette a black form against the orange sky. His hands were tucked into the pockets of his jeans, hair a little curlier than normal, and when he turned to me, his expression made me speed up.

He was smiling.

"How did the test go?"

"Good." My voice shook. "I think I passed."

"I'm sure you did." He nodded, and I braved a

closer step. I could smell him now, that spicy citrus scent mixing with the crisp fall night. I wanted him so bad it hurt. But what if this meeting wasn't what I hoped it was? What if this was just his way to rebuild a friendship between us and nothing more?

I didn't think I could do it. As much as I wanted to be theatre director at Halo, it would be absolute torture to work side by side with a man I was in love with, but who didn't see me the same way.

Because I was in love with him. I hadn't been able to admit it before, but now, standing here with him in this sacred space, overlooking the bleeding sunset and the town he cherished, there was no denying the truth.

"I have a confession to make," he went on, squaring his shoulders. His blue eyes were hooded and unreadable in the darkening light. What if his confession was love for me? What if he wanted to say the words that were now on the tip of my tongue?

"I'm stepping down as principal."

My mouth popped open. That was not at all what I'd expected. "Why?"

"I don't like the job," he continued. "It's not the right fit for me."

"I'm sorry." I didn't know what else to say.

"Don't be. It was a road I needed to take or else I'd have never known that it was the wrong one. Sometimes you have to take a chance to see if something is right, you know?"

My heart perked up at that. "I do know."

We fell into silence. A car sped past on the highway,

and a horse whinnied in the distance. My mouth was suddenly dry.

"So, what will you do now?" I asked.

"Go back to teaching," he went on. "Not this year, we don't have any vacancies, but Mrs. Sanchez is retiring, so I'll be taking over as the new choir director next year."

I couldn't help but smile. He used to be a history teacher, and I'm sure he was good at inspiring minds to care about the distant past, but he'd be an excellent choir director, one who'd get kids to dream about their future. I told him as much.

"Thanks." He reached out and took my hand. "But there's more." Mine was cold, his was warm, and it was perfect.

"I told the school board about what happened between us."

"Oh, snap." I stepped back, genuinely shocked. If he was giving up the principal job he didn't need to out our relationship. Teachers could date one another without scrutiny. No one balked when Jeanine and the janitor turned out to be in the throws of a dramatic and passionate affair, and I was pretty sure it wasn't the first interoffice romance to take place at Halo High School.

I was probably supposed to keep my mouth shut and let him finish his story, but there were too many thoughts swirling around in my head. Thoughts like did that mean he wanted to do this thing for real?

"Why?" I asked, unable to wait any longer.

Foster's eyes went wide, like he couldn't believe

what I was asking. He tugged me closer. "Isn't it obvious?"

Okay, so maybe it was a little obvious, but we were standing in front of a sunset at a super romantic location, after he summoned me here by windshield love letter. Still, I deserved to hear the words out loud.

He squeezed my hand in his. "Dani, I don't want to spend any more time without you."

The giant anvil that had been sitting on my chest since the night of the final *Oklahoma!* performance dissipated under the weight of his words. It was so much emotion at once I had to look away.

"I want to love my job again, and going back to teaching is going to make that easier, but since I met you—er got to know you." He paused for a second and grinned. "You know telling the how we met story is going to be weird for us, right?"

I laughed, but I wasn't letting him off that easy. There was more to this confession, and I wanted all of it, every last dreamy word.

"On with it," I probed, turning back to face him so I could take in all of that glorious orangey sunset as it lit up the contours of his face.

His fingers crept out of mine and came to rest on either side of my waist. It should be awkward, this moment of excessive eye contact, but after weeks of avoiding one another, I was hungry for the weight of his eyes on mine.

"What I'm trying to say is I want more than my job now. You gave me something to look forward to at the end of the day and something to think about when I start it." He winked, and I blushed thinking of a particularly hot morning, waking up to the only thing better than coffee.

I knew exactly what he meant. Teaching felt great. Teaching felt more than great; it made me feel like I had a purpose and was doing something real with my influence, but it wasn't enough to be fulfilled by a job. I wanted a whole life in all the ways it was supposed to be. Rough edges I could handle, so long as there weren't any missing pieces.

"I want you *and* the job, Dani." His eyes studied my face, his mouth worrying into a thin line where his smile belonged. "If you still want that, of course."

I paused for dramatic tension, watching the tortured look on his face grow more strained with each second that passed. He'd put me on administrative probation, closed his door in my face, and had given me the cold shoulder for a prolonged period of time. The dude deserved at least a moment of self-doubt to make up for the pain and anguish I'd suffered at the hands of his heartbreaking skills.

When his grip on my waist began to loosen and he looked appropriately terrified that he had messed up the best damn thing he was ever going to find, I let the smile I'd been stifling slip across my face.

"Okay, I'll take you back on one condition," I teased.

His eyes flashed with hope. "And what's that?"

"Never cook shrimp scampi for me again."

Epilogue

FOURTEEN MONTHS LATER

#HappilyEverAfter

Backstage was alive with a flurry of activity as my students prepared to perform *How The Grinch Stole Christmas*. It was opening night, our first opening night in our shiny new auditorium, and the buzz of excitement was so palpable that I could practically taste it. A gaggle of girls dressed in eccentric Whoville outfits hurried into the girls' dressing room to touch up their already perfect makeup and silly hairstyles. Tyler hopped about the hallway in his ridiculous green Grinch costume, making everyone laugh, his girlfriend, Kayla, the loudest. She was visiting from college but the two were still going strong. They'd started dating last spring which had been huge high school gossip at the time. I stood off to the side, observing everything play out with a satisfied smile on my face.

"Hey, you." Foster slipped an arm around my waist for a brief second and squeezed before letting go. I would've kissed him right then and there, but the man was big on no PDA at school. "Are you ready for this?"

"I was born ready." I nodded toward the kids, specifically the freshman who played the dog Max. The boy was fully in character, dressed up like a cute brown dog with antlers. He crawled around on all fours, barking at the other students.

"Question is, are they ready?"

Ruff! Ruff!

Beck and I burst out laughing.

Maybe it was being here with the man I loved, maybe it was opening night after a year of anticipation, or maybe it was the general holiday cheer, but I didn't think I'd ever been happier in my entire life.

And life was good.

So good.

I'd moved in with Beck months ago, and our relationship was stronger than ever. It helped that he was the new choir director and I was teaching drama. We both loved our jobs, and we got to work together on the shows, which turned out to come naturally for us, proving our "power couple" status.

I, Dani Sparks, was one half of a power couple. Heck yes, I was! I have to admit that being part of a power couple was a real upgrade from just owning power pants, especially since they had split right down the middle three months ago when I officially received the drama teacher position and tried to relive my cheerleader days with a celebratory toe touch.

I loved my students like they were my own kids, both the current ones and last year's graduating class. The old seniors kept me up to date on their new lives. Benjamin had taken my advice and followed his talents to California. He was going to school part time at USC, studying film while working part time as a bottom-feeder assistant to the assistant on a television sitcom. I had no doubt he'd one day be climbing that Hollywood ladder all the way to the top and would either be dazzling the world in front of the camera or running the whole damn show behind it.

My influencer account was still going strong. I was more choosy about who I partnered with and what I promoted. Most notably, I'd been invited to join the board for The Coalition for the Betterment of Arts Education, which was turning out to be incredibly rewarding. We were in the process of building an arts-based charter school in the poorest county in Mississippi. Beck and I had even driven down there when we'd broken ground at the build sight. I had a soft spot in my heart for the cause, and my social media followers loved it, too.

And perhaps most importantly, Sophie and I were close again. We were the twin sisters we once were, sans the messy swaps. She'd gone through her own boy-drama in the last year, but luckily she'd told me all about it and I'd been able to be there for her. Now, she was dating the most perfect guy *ever*, and I couldn't be happier for them. It had been touch and go there for a minute, but all's well that ends well, right?

Oh, just thinking that gave me the idea. "Do you

think we should produce a Shakespeare comedy this spring?" Shakespeare of any kind was intimidating and took a lot of work, especially because those lines couldn't be memorized quickly, but the challenge sounded fun.

Beck nodded. "That's a great idea. *Midsummers?*"

"Nah, I'm thinking *All's Well.*"

"Hmm, good choice," he mused.

"All right, guys." I stepped forward. "Are you ready for this?"

They cheered in response. We'd been rehearsing for over six weeks, so they had this thing down. After hyping everyone up, Foster and I left to take care of things at the front of the house. There were a few musical numbers, and he had his orchestra kids ready to go. I'd be sitting close by in the first row. At show-time, I ascended the stage to introduce the show. My heart thundered but mostly from excitement and gratitude.

"Thank you all for coming out tonight to our inaugural performance in our brand new facility. Isn't it gorgeous?" The audience erupted in hoots and hollers. The whole town was pretty stoked about this building, but nobody more so than me. I'd gotten to help design it, from the padded blue chairs to the state-of-the-art fly system to the beautiful new lights to the backstage set up.

And it was perfect. It truly was.

"We're so excited to be here and are incredibly grateful to everyone who helped make this happen. We especially want to thank The Coalition for the Betterment of Arts Education for their generous million dollar grant, as well as each and every individual who donated to the fundraising campaign. Thank you all so much!" My smile was so big my cheeks hurt, but I didn't even care. "Now, please silence your cell phones and enjoy the show!"

Just as I turned to go, my stage manager caught me and shoved a dozen white roses into my face. She squealed into the microphone. "And thank you to Ms. Sparks. Without you, none of this would have ever happened!"

The audience rose into a standing ovation, and I felt my cheeks flame red. I smiled and waved, like this was all normal, and hurried to my seat. Tears gathered along my lashes, so much so that everything went blurry for a moment as the overture began and the curtain raised. The set started with Whoville and the pieces were designed to either turn, or raise and lower on a pulley system when it came time to reveal the grinch's lair.

Suddenly, the music changed, no longer the whimsical looping melody I had ingrained into my brain from weeks of practice. No, they'd changed over to the *Oklahoma!* song. The students came on stage, singing the lyrics "We know we belong to this land and this land we belong to is grand, Oklahoma, Ok!" with so much passion that I was momentarily transported back to last year and all the feelings that came with that time in my life.

What in the heck was going on?

I turned to catch Beck's attention, but he wasn't

sitting with the orchestra anymore. Double what in the heck?

The audience rustled in their seats behind me, whispers stirring beneath the loud music.

The students lined the stage, happily singing and dancing last year's musical number, despite their *Grinch* costumes. And then suddenly, the song changed again, fading into *Oh, What a Beautiful Morning*. It was my personal favorite song from the musical, and Beck knew it. And then there he was, right in the middle of the rows of singing teenagers. He sang right along with them, dressed in his pant suit, smiling down at me like I was the only person in the entire auditorium of three hundred seats.

I stood, my legs shaky, as he finished off the tune, belting the last notes on his own as the students quieted. His deep baritone radiated into the auditorium. "I've got a beautiful feeling, everything's going my way. Oh, what a beautiful day!"

He finished, and if I thought the crowd was enthusiastic before, they were positively ecstatic now. But the sound of their cheering turned into nothing but buzzing background noise when Beck knelt down and held out a black velvet box. My eyes flicked from his ocean eyes to the little box and back again. I wanted nothing more than to run to him, to kiss him, to say yes.

He spoke, all mic'd up for everyone to hear.

"Danielle Georgina Sparks, I love you more than anything or anyone else on this earth, and I promise to always love you no matter what. Will you do me the honor of becoming my wife?" I was crying again. He cracked opened the box and even from here I could see the beautiful diamond engagement ring sparkling. "Will you marry me?"

I breathed in the moment, letting it settle over me, because even though I figured someone was filming this, that it all would be posted online, that I'd have more than enough video and photo evidence, nothing could possibly compare to the real thing. Nothing would ever replace this wonderful moment, here and now, me and him.

Smiling wide, I straightened my festive dress, squared my shoulders, and strode to the stage.

IVY LEAGUE
Liars
GRACE COSTELLO

Grace Costello is what happens when two author friends decide to write a book together—and boy, are we glad we did! Thank you so much for reading Twin-fluence. If you enjoyed it, please leave a written review on Amazon and Goodreads, and please tell your friends. This pen name is brand-spankin-new so we seriously can't make this a success and keep writing in this genre without your support. And don't forget to go check out our next book, Ivy League Liars.

Love,
Grace Costello

Acknowledgments

First of all, we have to thank each other. Grace is the pen name for Nina Walker and M.F. Lorson, a couple of friends who decided to give adult romcom a shot, and we couldn't have written this book without the other. It's been an amazing partnership! We also have to thank the community that rallied behind us, our editor Caitlin Haines, Amanda Steele at Book of Matches Media, our fabulous illustrator Viktoria at Yarets Art, and Melissa Craven for the paperback wrap. And of course we have to thank the readers for giving Twinfluence a chance. We hope you loved it and you'll continue the romcom journey with us.

About the Author

Grace Costello is the pen name for Nina Walker & M.F. Lorson. If Grace were a person, we'd take our best traits and make her a wacky librarian with soft spot of cats. Unfortunately, Nina isn't a cool enough to be a librarian and M.F. foolishly hates cats. We'll leave Grace up to your creation and hope she's fun enough to invite your girls' nights, sophisticated enough to trust for dating advice, and compassionate enough to for a late night pseudo-therapy sesh complete with a Godiva chocolate and a deck of tarot cards.